HALF
A
MIND

HALF
A
MIND

Wendy Hornsby

NAL BOOKS

Published simultaneously in Canada by Penguin Books Canada Limited.

 REGISTERED TRADEMARK—MARCA REGISTRADA
NAL BOOKS
Published by the Penguin Group
Penguin Books USA Inc., 375 Hudson Street,
New York, New York 10014, U.S.A.
Penguin Books Ltd, 27 Wrights Lane, London W8 5TZ, England
Penguin Books Australia Ltd, Ringwood, Victoria, Australia
Penguin Books Canada Ltd, 2801 John Street,
Markham, Ontario, Canada L3R 1B4
Penguin Books (N.Z.) Ltd, 182-190 Wairau Road, Auckland 10, New Zealand

Penguin Books Ltd, Registered Offices: Harmondsworth, Middlesex, England

LIBRARY OF CONGRESS CATALOGING-IN-PUBLICATION DATA
Hornsby, Wendy.
    Half a mind / Wendy Hornsby.
      p   cm.
    ISBN 0-453-00710-4
    I. Title.
PS3558.O689H3   1990
813'.54—dc20   89-13366
                                                     CIP

Designed by Julian Hamer

First Printing, March, 1990
    2 3 4 5 6 7 8 9
PRINTED IN THE UNITED STATES OF AMERICA

To Alex, Alyson, and Christopher

1

The November heat wave was a tease, a molecule-thick layer of warmth laid over the chill of fall. It wouldn't last, Roger Tejeda thought. In another few days the joggers would have the beach to themselves again; no more tourists lying on the damp sand—which had to be thirty degrees colder than the air temperature. Tejeda could feel the cold seeping up through the soles of his well-worn Reeboks. And there would be no more picnickers tempting death by playing chicken with the riptides around the base of Byrd Rock where it jutted into the surf like a giant thumb.

Tejeda watched the crowd around Byrd Rock grow to a frenzied swarm, but he held his running pace steady, kept his breathing slow and regular. Could be a sand shark in a bucket, the usual sort of draw on this stretch of beach, or a tourist caught in the drink. Tejeda reminded himself that no matter what had happened to reel in the curious, it wasn't his concern anymore. He raised his face to the wind and took a deep breath. The air smelled sweet, like May, because the onshore flow had blown the smog inland. He could see it trapped along the base of the San Gabriel Mountains like a load of dirty yellow fleece spilled over Pasadena. Tomorrow morning it would come back.

Carpe diem, Kate always told him. Seize the day. Tejeda wiped the sweat from his face with the tail of

7

his T-shirt. There was something else that she said when he thought things were too good to last, but he couldn't remember what. Something about picking flowers.

Two lifeguard Jeeps sped past him in the direction of Byrd Rock, forcing him into the frigid tail of an outgoing wave. He could hear the crowd now, the occasional high-pitched scream cutting through the general low murmur and defining whatever had happened as a gross tragedy. Then it flashed on him what else Kate said: "Gather ye rosebuds while ye may, Old Time is still a-flying." From the speed of the Jeeps as they bounced over crusted ruts in the sand, he knew some poor sucker must have gathered his last rosebud, or come close to it.

Tejeda held his pace the way a recovering drunk holds his breath when he passes his favorite gin mill. Whatever had happened in the treacherous currents around Byrd Rock had nothing to do with him, couldn't suck him along with the crowd. Not since he went on disability. But he clenched his jaw, remembering the jolt of adrenaline that could be more addictive than booze.

The fluorescent-orange lifeguard rescue boat powered into view around the far end of the rock. Tejeda shielded his eyes from the low sun to count the divers who bailed out over the side. Only two, but one he recognized as the sheriff's senior diver. He couldn't remember her name.

Then he turned and saw the coroner's Forensic Science Services' white Dodge Ram van winding down the bluff road toward the public parking lot. Tejeda unleashed his stride, running in the hard sand along the surf line, ignoring the cold water splashing around his ankles. Maybe just one more shot, he thought, straight from the bottle.

A lifeguard Jeep bounced across the sand to the parking lot. As it took on passengers from the coroner's van, Tejeda followed its trail with his eye, extending the line from the crowd at the rock, across the white beach and the black ribbon of asphalt parking lot, then up to the top of the overhanging bluffs, where Kate's estate stood out as an open gap in the nearly solid wall of condos, like a tooth missing in a kid's smile.

Everything up there seemed normal, the three massive California-mission-style mansions spaced along the bluff, the crisp white gazebo at the edge glowing pink in the late-afternoon sun, the beach stairs freshly rebuilt since the fire. Then, as he followed the spine of beach stairs down the face of the bluff, Tejeda touched the soft spot at his temple where the gun butt had obliterated a chunk of the skull underneath. Yeah, he thought, everything looked peaceful. But looks could be deceiving.

Impulsively he started to sprint, urgently needing to see Kate or his daughter, Theresa, or some sign of them. Just to make sure.

Then he slowed, fell back into his regular pace, forcing himself to fight the panic. No one knew the dangers of these waters better than Kate. And Theresa had told him she would be gone all afternoon. Whatever had happened this time, it couldn't concern any of them.

He took a deep breath, felt the pulse at his neck, and checked his watch: he had made four miles in thirty-one minutes, twenty-six seconds. Not his old time, he thought, but getting closer.

Tejeda wiped his face again and, standing at a fifteen-yard remove, tried to match names to the faces as the body squad arrived from the parking lot. Mild transitory aphasia, the doctor had told him. Why, he wondered, could he always remember that phrase when so many other labels had been swallowed by the black holes in his mind?

Tejeda dug out forensic investigator Vic Spago's name first—not from his bald head glistening in the sun or the porcine snort at the end of his laugh. It was the stench of Spago's thin black cigar carried by the breeze as the Jeep drove him past that jarred-loose twenty years' worth of memory clips. Vic Spago lit his Armenian cheroots only when he was working. The smoke, Tejeda always suspected, was some sort of Old World talisman against the deaths that were Spago's bread and butter. Or maybe it simply deadened his sense of smell.

Tejeda looked again at the fifty yards of open sand he would have to cross to reach Kate's stairway. No way he could do it unseen.

"What do you think it is?" An afternoon regular, one of the small legion who traded their Brooks Brothers and wing tips for shorts and running shoes after office hours, fell into place beside Tejeda, breathing hard.

"Don't know," Tejeda said. "Probably some tourist. Got himself caught in the riptide."

"Yeah," the man panted. "People should read the warning signs." But he seemed seduced by what he imagined he might find ahead, and sprinted on with new energy.

Walking now, Tejeda passed a once-pasty-white woman splayed on her back on the sand, apparently oblivious of both the incoming tide lapping closer to her feet and the brouhaha at the rock. She glowed red now from too much sun along the tops of her thighs and her round cheeks. Tejeda thought about how sore she would be tonight and how any local would have known better.

And would have known to stay away from Byrd Rock when the tide was coming in, he thought, as he noticed the brightly colored plastic toys scattered on the sand around her. There was no child in sight. As he thought about waking her, she opened her eyes and sat up.

She looked around, squinting. "Eric?" she called, scrambling to her feet. And then, with panic as she saw the lifeguards and the crowd, "Eric!"

As she ran past him, he wanted to tell her there was no need to hurry once Spago's services had been called for.

Spago looked up when he heard the woman's cry, and gazing past her, spotted Tejeda. He grinned and waved.

"Hey, Lieutenant," Spago yelled at him.

Tejeda waved back and thought again about escape, but Spago was already slogging out of the surf and heading for him. No way he could be avoided. It was just that this forgetting was so embarrassing.

The woman had plunged into the crowd.

Seeming unaware of her, Spago pulled a fresh cheroot from his pocket and lit it, grinning still at Tejeda through the smoke.

"Come on," Spago encouraged. "They won't take away your disability if you sneak a quick peek."

Vowing to himself that he would get no more involved than saying hello to everyone, Tejeda took a few deep breaths, then walked into the path that had cleared through the crowd.

"Hey, Lieutenant," Spago said again as he thrust his rubber-gloved paw toward Tejeda. "Couldn't stay away, could you?"

"Hey, yourself, Vic." Tejeda shook the clammy rubber. "What is this, department beach party?"

"Yeah." Spago gave Tejeda a cynical wink. "It's your backyard, you bring the wienies?"

"He is the wienie." What's-his-name, the gofer from the coroner's office, waited for a turn at Tejeda's hand. "Nice to see you out again, Lieutenant. Come take a look at today's blue-plate special."

Tejeda hesitated for a moment. Had to be something major to bring out this particular assortment of investigators. He was more than curious, but the lapses in his head held him back, chagrined: out of the nine officials here, Spago's was still the only name Tejeda could drag to the surface. Kate kept telling him to take it easy, that the pieces of his mind were slowly falling back into place. In the meantime, all he had to do was ask these people their names. Everyone knew what had happened to him, but he was sick to death of that pitiful stare people gave him when one of his pieces came up missing.

"He doesn't want to look." His former partner had waded out of the water to greet him, his smile reserved. "Doesn't want to come down out of his castle on the bluff."

"Right." Tejeda extended his hand to his partner, hoping the physical contact would jar the right name loose. But nothing happened. "How's it going?"

"Not bad. You're looking a hell of a lot better."

"Yeah." Without thinking, he touched his temple again, then dropped his hand when he saw his partner's smile collapse. Tejeda wanted to say something reassuring—hell, they'd survived worse during their years together in homicide. And he *would* say something, as soon as he could remember his partner's name. But for now he offered a smile, then kicked off his Reeboks and waded into the surf to see what they'd found.

Tejeda peered over Spago's bald head through a

pall of cigar smoke, fighting down the familiar surge that was equal parts revulsion and fascination—like a bullfrog hopping out of your birthday cake when you're six. He half-expected to see a small boy named Eric, though the woman had gone off down the beach, still calling. But there was only a hat-size box in the water.

"What is it?" he asked.

"Unidentified *cabeza*." Spago tapped his bald head. "Gift-wrapped and delivered right to your backyard, Lieutenant."

Tejeda knelt closer to the Christmas gift box decomposing in the wimpy high-tide swash."Who found it?"

"Couple of joggers." Spago aimed his thumb toward two men sitting up on the dry sand. Tejeda recognized them as regulars, though he'd never spoken to them.

"Gotta move Junior before the water gets higher." Spago slid a square of plywood under the box. Without thinking about whose job this might be, Tejeda took an end of the plank and helped Spago elbow through the crowd toward a dry spot beyond the surf line. The movement, and the weight of water and sand inside, made the sodden cardboard collapse.

"Jesus . . ." Tejeda's partner led a collective groan as the decapitated head inside the box, now exposed, rolled from side to side like a chipped marble.

As the crowd of onlookers fell away, a beach ball hit Tejeda in the back of the leg. He turned and saw a little boy, about four, standing with his mouth frozen open, staring at the latex-pale face on the plank.

"Where's your mother?" Tejeda asked, but the child didn't respond.

"Get the kid out of here," Spago snapped, making the head roll crazily as he stepped out of sync with Tejeda. Then he glared at the crowd. "The rest of you too. Scram."

Tejeda's partner shook off his own queasiness, lifted the boy up, and carried him up the beach to the sunburned tourist who was still walking along the surf line calling for "Eric."

"Damn people," Spago muttered as he and Tejeda waited for space to clear so they could set down the plank. "What do they want to see this for?"

Tejeda shrugged—there always seemed to be crowds, at least at the beginning—and knelt for a closer look at the head. While the situation was grim, the face itself wasn't much to see, a set of unremarkable features puffed up by salt water. Only the hair told him anything. He sat back on his heels, taking in a second-hand lungful of cheroot and thinking how good it felt to have his mind engage on a problem. Like muscle memory taking over.

"Sidewalls," he said, indicating how the hair was short over the ears but fairly long on top. "Could be Navy. But my guess is . . ." He appealed to his partner, "The Halls of Montezuma."

"Marines?"

"Right," Tejeda said. "Marines. Could be a Marine."

"Possibility." With forceps, Spago rolled the head until it sat on its crown, then probed the bloodless line just above the Adam's apple where the head had been severed. "Clean slice. Probably no knowledge past Biology I, but neat. Very neat."

The coroner's gofer wrote furiously in a spiral notebook. "How long's it been in the drink?"

"Overnight. No more than twenty-four hours." Spago looked up at Tejeda. "What do you say, Lieutenant?"

Tejeda shrugged. "You're the expert."

Spago turned to Tejeda's still-nameless partner. "Eddie?"

Eddie? Tejeda ran the name through his mind a few times, but it wouldn't register. He clenched his fists and fought off the frustration: at first, it had seemed as if the blow from the gun butt had rattled his head so hard that it had shaken loose all the labels and now they floated around inside like dust motes, visible in the right light but impossible to catch. And lately, names had been coming easier. All he usually needed was one prod and, as often as not, the name or label would stick. He called Kate "Kate" at least eighty percent of the time, Theresa "Theresa" nearly as often, consistently enough that Kate had quit worrying so much. But it was still frustrating as hell.

"Eddie." Tejeda tried the name out loud. It sounded wrong and Eddie looked at him strangely.

"What is it?" Eddie asked.

"Nothing." Tejeda turned back to Spago. "How long was he dead before he hit the water?"

"Can't say yet. But it wasn't long, unless he'd been in cold storage."

"Pinpoint his age?" Eddie asked.

Spago scraped the green-tinged cheek with the end of the forceps. "Dark-colored hair, light beard. I'd say between eighteen and twenty-something."

"Mark," Spago said, looking up at the coroner's gofer. "I think you better bag him before he dries out any more."

Mark. Tejeda had another name, this one suddenly very familiar. While Mark and Spago got the head and the remains of its box sealed in heavy plastic bags, Tejeda looked around the group, feeling the connections fall into place. There was Angelo from the harbor patrol, but in civvies; maybe his day off. And Rebecca Farmer, the sheriff's chief diver, peeling off her wetsuit as she came out of the water, her face tanned nearly black, even this late in the year, a startling contrast to her sun-bleached hair. He recognized two rookie homicide detectives trying to look useful. And Craig Hardy, from the local newspaper, quietly absorbing everything, as usual. And, thank God, someone whose name he knew for sure he had never known.

Eddie had busied himself with the business of protecting evidence. He signed the seals on the plastic bags, directed a search of the sand around the area where the box had been found, and kept the surging crowd from churning their feet through everything. But all this time, Tejeda noticed that Eddie was keeping an eye on him. The scrutiny made him uneasy, as if maybe Eddie was expecting something from him. And he seemed so depressed.

Spago and Mark loaded their gear and the remains onto a Jeep. Then Spago turned and looked past Eddie to speak to Tejeda. "We'll burn the midnight oil on this one, Lieutenant. When flesh has been in the water awhile it tends to deteriorate in a hurry. Anything special you want us to look for?"

"You're asking the wrong man." Tejeda put a hand on Eddie's shoulder. "This dance is on my partner's card."

Eddie looked down at his own hands and rubbed a puffed burn scar along the edge of his thumb; a mark just the length and shape of a french fry. Tejeda remembered the smell that night, when Eddie got burned while busting a preschool teacher who had buried one of his charges in the desert. The suspect had been cornered at home while he fried potatoes for his dinner. He had tried to escape by dumping a pan of half-cooked french fries on Eddie. Though covered with still-sizzling potatoes, Eddie had managed to collar the suspect. There had been a lot of press coverage, all of it with more about the french fries than the crime.

With great relief, Tejeda realized why "Eddie"

sounded all wrong. He grinned and tightened his grip on his partner's shoulder. "Okay, Fries, give the man your orders."

"Spud. You always call me Spud." Somewhat shyly, big Eddie Green looked up at Tejeda. "Welcome back, Roger."

"What?" Tejeda smiled. "I been away?"

"Seems like it," Eddie said as he turned to give his attention to Vic Spago.

Tejeda retrieved his Reeboks. He sat to put them back on as he listened to his former partner, aka Spud, give instructions. Under his bare thighs, the thin crust of warm sand quickly gave way to the cold lurking underneath.

"Do what you can," Eddie was saying. "I'd like a full dental workup, ASAP. We'll get on-line with LAPD's computer, try to locate the rest of this poor sucker. I go along with the lieutenant: we'll connect with Camp Pendleton and the Navy base in Long Beach, see if they're missing a grunt with a new haircut."

Tejeda listened. He was still out on disability, but Spud wouldn't mind if he tagged along, put in his two cents. Just thinking about being back on the scent was like taking a bit of the hair of the dog. He thought about all the things the doctor had warned him about, then glanced up at the bluffs again, saw the windows of Kate's house catch the last sun. He tied his shoes and stayed quiet. This time, there was too much at stake.

Eddie came and leaned over him. "Think of anything else?"

"You covered it, partner." He stood up, brushed the sand off his faded shorts, and extended his hand toward Eddie. "I have to go, Spud. Got a date with a beautiful woman."

"Good to see you." Eddie gripped his hand firmly. "Give Kate a kiss for me."

"Kate?" Tejeda feigned a blank look. "I don't remember a Kate."

2

"What are you up to this time, Carl?" Kate slid the insufficient-funds notice she had received from the bank across her ex-husband's desk.

"You look good, Kate," Carl said, smiling, ignoring the crumpled pink paper while he looked her over, leaning his head to one side and squinting through his reading glasses as if to bring her into focus. "Your scars are hardly noticeable anymore. How's your cop?"

"Fine," she said. The thin scar line that V'd from the corner of her mouth down to her chin and back up along her jawline itched furiously, but she resisted touching it. Instead, she stood, watching Carl closely, just in case he had something lethal hidden in the shiny snakeskin shoe propped against the edge of his polished granite desk. "Roger is just fine."

"Glad to hear it." He had finally picked up the bank notice and was smoothing it in front of him. "Roger," he said as he read. "Doesn't sound right, the way you say it. Let me hear you say 'Rigoberto.' "

"Cut the crap, Carl."

"That's his real name, isn't it? Rigoberto Eduardo Tejeda. Somehow it doesn't go with Katherine Margaret Byrd Teague."

"I haven't used 'Teague' since our divorce."

"Katherine Margaret Byrd," he said, as if testing its

rhythm. Then he put his foot down and rolled his leather chair closer to his desk, shrugging himself into a businesslike posture. "So you bounced a check. Why come to me? Need a loan?"

"Fred Elbridge at the bank tells me some judge has placed a hold on all of my funds," she said. "Mr. Elbridge suggested I ask you what you know about it."

He leaned back, quiet for a moment, apparently thinking. She watched his face, hoping it would give him away. He was a good actor, in fact his jury summations were often high theater, drawing a regular audience of press and lawyer fans. During their twelve years together she had learned how to read him, to find clues in a lift of his pale eyebrow, a twitch at the corner of his lips. But they hadn't been together now for over a year, and she found that the silent vocabulary between them was rusty from lack of use.

Carl let out a long breath and ran his fingers through his perfectly cut blond hair—lighter blond than she had remembered. She wondered if he had done something to it, a little Summer Blond spray every morning before jogging maybe. He read again the insufficient-funds notice, as if it might reveal something he had missed before. And then he looked at Kate. "*All* of your funds?"

"Every nickel. Savings, checking, trust funds. I can't make withdrawals, and every check I've written since the first of November has been returned."

"It's a mistake, a clerical fuckup," he said. "The bank was only supposed to hold up payments from your grandfather's trust."

"Oh, Carl." Kate sat down, hard, on the cold edge of a chair—leather to match his, but scaled smaller—and forced him to look her in the eye. "What *are* you up to?"

"I'll fix things with the bank, I'm sorry for the bother," Carl said. "But I think there should be a reevaluation of your grandfather's trust."

"I think you're nuts," she said, and started to rise. She needed a lawyer, fast. And one who wasn't a member of the family firm.

Carl's ancient secretary, Estelle Baumberg, slid noiselessly into the room. "Sorry to disturb, children. Mr. Teague, Mr. Evans is in court on break and needs some figures, could you speak with him? Line two."

"Kate, please," Carl pleaded as he reached for the receiver, "don't go."

She hesitated, then gave in, feeling suddenly exhausted, unprepared to slog through another of Carl's quests. When he saw she would stay, he picked up the telephone and swiveled his chair around so that she only saw some of his profile. Estelle seemed to be hovering beside her.

"How are you, Estelle," she asked.

"Fine. Busy." Estelle smiled. "You know how it is around here."

"Yes, Carl's a slave driver. I don't know how you can stand to work for him."

"Actually, he's easier than your grandfather was. At least, he doesn't chase me around the desk." Estelle touched her stiff silver froth of hair, glanced at Carl, and smiled. "Not that I'd mind in his case."

"Mind what?" Carl turned around and hung up the telephone.

Kate smiled. "Isn't it about time you took Estelle out for dinner?"

Carl looked at them both carefully, never sure when he was being teased. Then he smiled. "How about Friday night, Estelle, if you don't already have a date."

"Me? A date?" Estelle laughed as she walked toward the door. "I haven't had a date since Louie the

Mouth Caporello tried to weasel some information about one of Kate's grandfather's clients."

She stopped at the door. "That Louie was some dancer. Not much in bed, but boy could he tango." Smiling at the memory, she looked at Carl. "Thanks for asking me about Friday, but I'm going up to my daughter's for the holidays."

When the door closed behind Estelle, Kate turned to Carl. "As succinctly as you can, Carl, tell me exactly what it is you want."

"Fairness," he said. "Your grandfather's trust was to be equally divided among his grandchildren. Now that my paternity has been established, I want my share."

"Your paternity has not been established," she said slowly, as if instructing a slow learner, which Carl certainly was not. "Someone persuaded Uncle Miles that you were his long-lost bastard, so he left you his estate. But that proves nothing, and you know it. I have as much evidence to show that Uncle Miles was tricked and that you are not his son as you have to show otherwise."

"But you declined to challenge his will."

"Why bother?" she said.

"Heavy price to pay to avoid scandal."

"Scandal?" She leaned back on the squeaky leather and chuckled. "I've always thought our family owed this town a certain quota of scandal. Helps keep property values up and sells local papers. And beyond the local papers, well, who gives a damn?"

He tented his fingers and studied her over the tips until she felt uncomfortable. To avoid his eyes, she looked over his head at the wall behind him, at the row of framed credentials—Stanford, Harvard Law. Then she looked back at him, at the face that was beyond handsome, at the hair that was too well-cut,

the suit from London, tailored to his athletic body so
exquisitely that he stood out from the department-
store-clothed crowd at the courthouse. And anywhere
else he went, for that matter. But none of it meant
anything to him, she knew, because of an accident of
birth.

Then she shrugged, thinking that maybe Carl had
earned his inheritance by sharing the myth of the
long-lost bastard with her Uncle Miles. And if Miles
had been fooled, then so had Carl. She thought of
Miles with sadness, remembering his loneliness, wondering how different his life might have been if he had
had a child to love—not her, though she knew how
deeply he adored her—but a child of his own, a golden
child like Carl. The illusion that he had found his son
had given him happiness at the end of his life. And it
had nearly gotten Kate killed.

Kate broke the silence. "It wasn't my place to challenge Miles's will. And why should I? I'm sorry you
got his house only because it's so close to mine. But
for the rest, well, God knows I didn't need more
money. Managing what I have already, when I have
access to it, is a pain. Then there's the law firm. With
Miles's quarter share, you've done magnificently, given
the firm back the luster it had lost to old age."

She moved forward and stretched her arms across
the smooth desk toward him. "Can't that be enough?"

He remained rigid. "I got everything except his
name."

"Is that so important?"

"Maybe not to you." He looked at her over the rims
of his reading glasses. "Will you fight me if I pursue
this?"

"Of course," she said. "There has to be an end."

"I'm sorry about the bank." He reached out and

covered her fingers with his warm hand. "I didn't mean for you to be involved, or inconvenienced."

"I was. I am." Then she forced a smile; Carl always came around, unless he felt pushed. She took her hand out of his and picked up the insufficient-funds notice. "This check I bounced? It was the deposit on my Thanksgiving caterer."

"Let me cover it." He opened the desk drawer where she knew he kept his checkbook.

"You're too late. Henri was so offended he accepted another gig." She shook her head. "If we can't find someone else before Thursday, Roger and I will have to cook."

"Suppose I should be glad I'm not invited, then," he said. He was smiling, but she could see a wistfulness in his face. Maybe just nostalgia interruptus. Or loneliness. She had no idea what he was doing for Thanksgiving.

Kate picked up her shoulder bag and stood. "So now what?"

"I'll call Elbridge at the bank, straighten things out," he said. He ran his fingers through his hair again. "I just wish I knew what was best for both of us."

"For *all* of us," she said.

"Right." He rose from behind his desk and came around to open the door for her. He seemed chastened. But she couldn't be sure; he'd always been a good actor. He touched her shoulder as she passed him. "You never told me, actually: how is Roger?"

"He's fine," she said. "Getting restless. I think he'd like to go back to work, but the doctor says he still needs rest and quiet."

"I'm planning to start remodeling Miles's house. I'll try to keep the noise down."

"As in jackhammers from only nine to five?"

"No, Kate, believe me." He seemed very sincere. "I would never do anything to hurt you."

"I know," she said. She paused in the open doorway. "At least, not intentionally."

3

The cooling Rolls motor pinged as Tejeda passed it on his way to the house. Kate had left the car on the wooden turnabout at the end of the drive, but hadn't taken time to turn it. He pushed the button on the side of the garage and leaned against the wall to watch the car make its decorous 180-degree rotation into position to pull into the garage or to drive out again.

The turnabout, one of the indulgences Kate's grandfather had allowed himself when he built the estate in 1929, was fun, he thought. But the car—it was parade and picnic all by itself. A 1953 Rolls Royce Silver Dawn, with GM Hydramatic transmission, 4.6-liter-capacity engine, hydraulic-action front brakes, painted mauve over burgundy by some heretic. A Sunday-drive car, if you were Rose Kennedy.

Tejeda loved the car, and so did Kate. In fact, he found her attachment to it oddly out of character. She didn't give a damn about all her money. Though the three mansions that comprised her family's oceanfront estate could have served as the back lot for MGM, she lived as simply as circumstances allowed.

So maybe this was small excitement, he thought, watching the car complete its stately rotation. Small, at least, compared to the treasure hunt Spud faced. He looked down at the beach, where a few of the persistently curious still milled around the investigation scene. Then he walked over to the Rolls and flicked a bug speck off the hood ornament's butt. The way things were at the moment, he had excitement enough.

He heard salsa music and followed it across the back lawn and into the institution-size kitchen of Kate's house. The loud music covered any sound he made coming in, giving him the luxury of just watching Kate and Theresa together. Kate, with a Diet Coke in one hand and a pen in the other, was leaning over a heavy cookbook propped on the counter, making notes, while his fifteen-year-old daughter, Theresa, seemed to be taking inventory of the contents of the massive stainless-steel refrigerator. They were both laughing, singing, and moving to the music from the radio. Tejeda stood there quietly, watching them, wishing again that some accident of time had brought the three of them together before there was so much history to overcome.

Seeing them from the back, he could almost fantasize that Kate could have been Theresa's mother if he had connected with her at the right instant in history. Their dark hair was nearly the same shade; Kate's cut short, tailored, no fuss, like everything about her, Theresa's a long windblown tangle pulled up on one side with a yellow plastic clip. They were both slender, athletic, though the narrowing at Kate's waist hinted at a delicacy, however deceptive, that was missing in Theresa's ripe-peachlike robustness. The greatest difference he saw between them was that Kate seemed so much more comfortable inside her body than teenage Theresa did in hers.

He thought about the half-dozen times during his life when he had encountered Kate before—and here he touched the scar on his scalp, having no other label for the episode of terror that had brought them together. But among all the unassociated bits of memory scattered in his mind, his images of Kate were crystal-line: Kate at ten, with new braces on her teeth, cutting the ribbon dedicating the school named for her grand-father, the school where Tejeda's mother taught; Kate as a teenager, home from boarding school for Christ-mas, walking alone on the beach while he caroused with a pack of locals. They had all stopped to watch her, the princess of the richest family in Santa Angel-ica. He smarted now to think how their reverential silence as she passed must have isolated her.

He had touched her once, when he was a rookie cop already with a wife and baby son, while helping her onto a sheriff's bus during a mass arrest of war pro-testers. How easy it would have been for him to have taken her to the side to save her from all the grief the press had given her when they recognized her famous name.

His passivity then, and at every other encounter with her, he now saw as a regrettable lapse, a lost chance to have somehow merged their separate fates.

"Put down celery." Theresa held up a limp bunch of celery. "Did you put turkey on the list?"

"Yes," Kate said. "But how big?"

"I don't know." Theresa shrugged. "Just big. Get enough so Trinh can make us turkey balls for a while instead of fish balls to go with the rice."

"How many people are coming for Thanksgiving?" Tejeda asked as he moved farther into the room. He reached around Theresa and took a beer from the refrigerator. "Should be some sort of chart in the cookbook."

"The things you know," Kate said, raising her face for his kiss. "You want to be the designated cook Thursday?"

"Please, no," Theresa protested. "And don't let him carve, either. Get Grandpa to do it."

Tejeda had a sudden flash of the neat, pale slice line around the throat of the severed head, and he shuddered. Kate came into his arms and put a cool hand against his cheek.

"You okay?" she asked.

He looked at Theresa over Kate's head, saw the concern on her face. "I'm fine. Relax, you two."

Theresa turned to Kate for reassurance; then a smile spread across her face, lighting her huge brown eyes. "Do you think he's strong enough for the news?"

"Never." Kate snuggled against him. He couldn't see her face but he could feel her ribs moving as she stifled her laughter. "But go ahead. Tell him where we went today."

He put the beer bottle on the counter. "Yeah, go ahead."

Theresa blushed furiously. "Kate, you tell him."

"DMV," she said.

"Motor Vehicles?" Tejeda looked Theresa over again, searching for evidence of vehicular mayhem. "Any problem?"

"You forgot, didn't you?" Theresa reproved. "I'm fifteen and a half today."

"Theresa got one hundred percent on her Motor Vehicles test," Kate said proudly. "She has her learner's permit to drive now."

Tejeda took a moment to let this bombshell sink in. "Happy half-birthday."

Theresa suddenly smiled so broadly her full set of braces showed. "Kate let me drive home."

"Oh, yeah?" Tejeda tried to imagine the trip home from across town. Kate seemed unscathed. "How'd she do?"

"Okay." Kate hesitated. "For a first run, she did just fine."

"In a Rolls-Royce, Daddy," Theresa bubbled. "Can

you believe it? Kate's going to show me how to drive in her Rolls-Royce."

"No way," Tejeda protested.

"Why not?" Kate asked. "It's an easy car to drive, and nothing can hurt her—it's built like a tank."

"I can't afford to replace Rolls bumpers. I'd rather she used my Cutlass."

"Can't," Theresa said. "Richie has the Cutlass up at Santa Barbara."

"He does?" Tejeda looked to Kate for confirmation. Was this something else he should have remembered? "How long has Richie had it?"

"I told you. Richie was coming down from school every weekend to be with you while you were in the hospital," Kate said. "It was too expensive for him to fly back and forth, so he took the Cutlass back to school with him."

"So"—Theresa smiled—"I can't learn to drive in the Cutlass if it isn't here." She opened her hand and held the Rolls key out to Kate. "Where do you want this?"

"In the big Chinese vase on the table by the front door."

Theresa looked at the key possessively.

"I'd let you hang on to it," Kate said, "but the car washer comes tomorrow morning. He needs the key, and that's the only one I have."

Theresa shrugged and folded the key into her palm as she opened the door into the passageway.

Tejeda waited until the door had closed behind Theresa before he got serious about embracing Kate. She returned his long kiss, teasing him a little with her tongue. Then she pulled back and smiled up at him.

"I can tell you're getting better," she said.

"Why's that?"

"Your lips aren't numb anymore, are they?"

"Not when you kiss me like that." He traced her thin scar, wishing it, and all the full-color, wide-screen horror behind it, would go away. Then he gently kissed her chin beside the scar. "I appreciate what you're doing for Theresa."

"Teaching her to drive?" Kate shrugged. "She tries not to let it show, but the last couple of months have been damned hard on her. It's about time something terrific happened for her."

"I don't know if I want her driving," he said. "It's a sick world out there."

She looked up at him, acutely perceptive as usual. "What's happened?"

"I ran into Eddie Green and Vic Spago on the beach."

"Getting ready for the marathon?"

"No. Working," he said. "They found a head floating in the bay."

"A head?" Kate pulled away from him, both repulsed and intrigued. "A human head?"

"Yeah."

"Whose?"

"Don't know yet. A young man with a short haircut."

"Did you see it?"

"Yep."

"It doesn't belong here, though, right? It just floated in from somewhere else."

"Yeah. Trespasser. Doesn't belong to us. You can call Eddie for the details."

"No, thanks."

The back door clicked softly and Trinh, Kate's housekeeper, tiptoed into the kitchen.

"Hello," Kate said before Trinh could make a shy retreat. "How was your class?"

"Very nice," Trinh said. She hugged her books close to her chest and kept her eyes averted. Tejeda had found that her quietude was a cultural thing, that behind her sweet, passive exterior was one tough cookie. Kate had told him what she knew of Trinh's story, how because she had been a university student she had been locked in a reeducation center outside Saigon and taught how to plant rice. Trinh herself rarely said anything about her life before she was rescued from a leaky fishing boat by Australian sailors. Occasionally she would let something slip—that her parents had died in a Thai refugee camp, that she had had a child. He wanted to ask her more, but the deep sadness in her eyes always stopped him.

"What was your class today?" he asked Trinh instead. "English as a Second Language?"

"Today is Monday. I have cooking."

Kate and Tejeda exchanged smiles. Trinh received room, board, a decent salary, and help with her English homework in exchange for housekeeping and cooking one ghastly meal a day.

"What did you cook?" Kate asked her.

"We learn to make Thanks for Giving dinner," Trinh said proudly.

"Wonderful," Kate said. "Turkey, cranberries, the whole thing?"

"Teacher say 'from soap to knots.' "

Kate jabbed Tejeda before he could say anything. He shrugged; Trinh never got his jokes anyway.

Kate smiled at Trinh. "Would you like to try something for our Thanksgiving dinner?"

"I don't know about these foods," Trinh said, her brow furrowed in a worried line. "You put some kind berries on the meat and something else." She looked at Kate for help. "Gravelly on whipped-up potatoes."

"Giblet gravy," Kate said.

"Okay. I think it's not very good." Then Trinh smiled. "I can make pumpkins pie and Jello-O."

"Great," Tejeda said, knowing his mother always insisted on making the pies. "It isn't Thanksgiving without Jello-O and pumpkins pie."

"Write what you need on the shopping list," Kate told her.

"I learn one more item today." Trinh opened her little silk wallet and took out a letter-folded paper. "Maybe you like to see."

Kate took the proffered paper and opened it. "Trinh, this is wonderful. Look, Roger. Trinh has passed her English proficiency exam. She can start classes at the university in January."

"I can still do my work here," Trinh said.

"You won't have time to study and work full-time. We'll have to hire a new housekeeper," Kate said. When Trinh's chin started to quiver, Kate gave her a quick hug. "You can move in upstairs with the rest of the family."

"I can't pay."

"Sure you can. Your choice, once-a-week laundry or floor polishing?"

"Laundry." Trinh smiled.

Theresa pushed open the door from the dining room. "Phone, Dad," she said, looking first at Kate, then at her father. "It's Mom."

When he didn't move toward the telephone right away, Kate patted him on the arm. "Excuse me," she said, "I have a briefcase full of midterms to read. Trinh, I'm proud of you."

Roger always looked a bit shell-shocked to Kate when he talked to Cassie, his ex-wife. Where marriage and family were concerned, she knew, Tejeda was a traditionalist; people got married forever and raised their kids together. Even though his marriage had bombed with enough fury to set Mr. Richter's needles moving, he still felt uneasy about the breakup. Increasingly frequent long-distance conversations with Cassie only reminded him that beyond the gates of this refuge there was an earlier life that still straggled a number of untidy loose ends.

Kate paused in the door long enough to make sure Tejeda was going to pick up the kitchen extension. She heard him say "Hello, Cassie" before the kitchen door closed behind her.

Kate caught up with Theresa in the long passageway that led toward the front of the house.

"So, how's your mother?" Kate asked, hoping the question sounded more casual than its intent.

"Mom's okay." Theresa shrugged. "I called to tell her I got my learner's permit." Theresa watched the Rolls key dangle from her hand for a moment. When she looked up at Kate, her eyes were full of confusion. "She asked me if my birthday present got here yet."

"Your birthday was in May."

"I think she forgot she hadn't sent a present until I called her."

"Maybe not." Kate slipped her arm through Theresa's. "Living where she does, it might be difficult for her to get things out."

"There's a Hallmark store in Taos," Theresa said. "And a post office."

Kate gave Theresa's slender arm a squeeze. "This is not a perfect world."

"I know."

The tap-dance patter of their heels as they crossed the marble-tiled foyer filled the silence between them. Kate paused at the bottom of the long, curving stairway.

"We thought we'd go out for dinner tonight," Kate said. "Can you be ready by six-thirty?"

Theresa nodded, then looked up from under her eyelashes. "May I drive?"

"It'll be dark," Kate warned. "And your dad will be in the back seat."

A nervous smile flashed across Theresa's face. "I'm not ready for Dad to watch me yet."

"Maybe in a week or two we'll be ready to show off for him," Kate said. "Are you coming upstairs?"

"I have to put the key away."

But when she didn't move, Kate asked, "Something you want to talk about?"

"Are you driving the Rolls to work tomorrow?"

"No," Kate said. "Probably get stripped if I left it in the faculty lot. Why?"

"I thought we could go out driving, and maybe you could pick me up at school."

"In the Rolls?" Kate ran through her schedule for the next day: classes until two, then a curriculum meeting that could last a couple of hours. She understood that Theresa wanted her friends to see her in the luxurious old car, which meant driving home for the Rolls, then getting back across town to the high school around three, when Theresa finished her last class.

"Never mind," Theresa said. Kate watched her fold the key into her palm before she turned to cross the foyer to put the key into the Chinese vase.

"I'll meet you in front of the administration building at three-ten," Kate said.

"You mean it?"

"Yes," Kate assured her, smiling. "Given the opportunity, who wouldn't skip a dry old curriculum-committee meeting to tempt death with you?"

Theresa laughed. "No, really, I'll pay attention."

As Kate mounted the stairs, she heard a near-silent, jubilant "yesss" just before the car key hit the bottom of the Chinese vase. Then the sound of quick footsteps crossing the marble floor caught Kate off-guard. She found herself listening expectantly for the next sound

in a once-familiar sequence, the way an audience might
if a conductor suddenly stopped the orchestra in the
middle of a piece. But nothing followed—no ice cubes
dropped into crystal with a splash of Scotch. Kate
shook off the strong feeling of *déjà vu*. She had to go
back down a few steps, to look, just to make sure. But
her father wasn't there. Hadn't been for twenty-five
years.

She turned and continued up the stairs. She'd been
feeling her father close by all afternoon. Probably, she
thought, because of the car and Theresa's pleasure
with it. It was so right, Kate thought, that the car, a
relic from her father's brief passage here, should be
the instrument of such joy.

Kate had once heard her grandfather proudly de-
clare that Cornell, her father and his youngest son,
was like Falstaff, born for no reason other than to give
pleasure. That was his work, and he had done it magnificently. For everyone except maybe her mother,
Kate thought. But Kate had been too young then to
understand that being pleasant and holding his liquor
well were perhaps not enough for his marriage to
thrive on. And she didn't know which had come first,
her mother's bitterness or the escalation of her father's
drinking. She only knew how wonderful it was to be
with him. And how much she had missed him when he
wasn't here anymore.

Without turning on the lights, Kate crossed the room
she now shared with Tejeda and opened the bay window. The evening air was chilly, fresh with the fishy
smell of the ocean. Someone down on the beach was
setting up a portable floodlight, and she wondered
why until she remembered about the head. These were
either police or ghouls; she shuddered, trying to block
any image of that grim attraction. Then she realized
that the picture in her mind's eye was of her father's

handsome face; his body had turned up in the bay below the house, snagged on an outcropping of Byrd Rock. Even after three weeks in the water, his maroon necktie had still been fastened in a perfect four-in-hand knot.

A sudden gust off the ocean ruffled through the room like a sad whisper. Kate picked up a cardigan Tejeda had left on the window seat and pressed it against her face, breathing in his scent as she tried to hold back the surge of terror that more and more often threatened to break through the barriers she had erected.

She and Tejeda had been through so much together already, she thought. Then Tejeda was suddenly behind her, his arms folding around her, pulling her close. She turned her back to the spotlight on the beach and buried her face against his hard chest, putting aside everything except him and the safety of that moment.

4

"Nice, clean-cut kid," Eddie Green said. "Except he had semen in his mouth."

"Yeah?" Tejeda put down the plastic squeeze bottle of mustard. "Before or after?"

"Coroner says he blew some guy, type A positive. Got his throat severed before he could swallow all the spume."

"I thought this was a social call." Tejeda picked up a slab of sourdough and held it up to Trinh, who hovered by the door to the kitchen. Then he dropped the bread on top of his stack of cold cuts and cheese. "See, Trinh? You put everything inside the bread. Except rice. No rice in the sandwich."

"Not difficult." Trinh shrugged. She wiped her hands on a damp tea towel as if she'd touched something distasteful. "I can go back to kitchen now?"

"Sure. Lesson's over." Tejeda looked across the mahogany table at Eddie Green, not ready to buy what he was offering. He pushed the plate of cold cuts closer to his partner. "Try the salami, Spud. Homemade. Kate gets it from a little deli down by the marina. Costs more than filet."

Eddie leaned closer to Tejeda, the reflection of the underside of his face on the polished table exaggerating his heavy jaw. "Spago said to tell you he thinks you were right about the kid being military. Government-issue stainless-steel crowns on four molars."

"Great. Case is solved. Just go find a mother who never taught her boy how to brush his teeth."

"The head was in water twenty-four to thirty-six hours," Eddie said, eyeing Tejeda as if he had an ace in his pocket. "But not in salt water."

"Okay," Tejeda conceded, "that's weird. But don't let it distract you. I think you have a fairly ordinary sex killing. There are two possibilities. One, the kid died during rough sex and his lover panicked and dumped the body in pieces. Two, the killing itself was the thrill. Maybe the head was the object."

"Why the fresh water?"

"Get rid of the blood and keep the body cool." Tejeda shrugged. "Maybe the head was a trophy, kept in a goldfish bowl like a pet."

"Spago's in till four this afternoon," Eddie said. "Why don't you come talk to him?"

Tejeda picked up the salami knife and bisected his sandwich with more force than he'd intended. Damn Spud, he thought, checking to see if he'd cracked the plate. So persistent. Obsessive even. Made him a good detective, but not a lot of fun to be around when he had a bug under his collar. He saw his own reflection in the table, and found a lot of Spud in it.

"I can't remember a lot of things," Tejeda said, "but it seems to me we used to talk about sex and football during lunch, not this forensics shit."

"You're right," Eddie said, flipping the cap off his Corona beer with a church key. "You don't remember a lot."

Tejeda sighed. "Okay, Spud, what's the rest of it?"

"Arty Silver."

"Arty Silver?" Tejeda took a bite of his sandwich.

"Arthur Ronald Silver."

"Arthur Radley Silver," Tejeda corrected. "The Surfside Slasher."

"You do remember?"

"Who could forget?" Tejeda heard the defensiveness in his own voice.

"The similarities got to me. Silver would pick up a Marine, preferably very young and goofy-looking, who was hitching a ride up to L.A. from Pendleton on a weekend pass. Arty would give him some beers from a cooler he kept on the back seat. Then some pills. Then, when the kid was out of it, Arty would go to perform his rituals, taking pictures of his handiwork along the way. When he was finished, Arty would hack off the kid's head and take it home for a souvenir."

"Not hack off," Tejeda said. "Slice off. Very tidy. Worked in his uncle's butcher shop off and on."

"What did Spago say? Not a pro, maybe Biology I?"

"What's the point?" Tejeda said. "Arty Silver has been in jail for the last five years."

"Believe it or not, he finally comes to trial Monday morning," Eddie said. "And he still has friends."

"What was that kid's name?" Tejeda asked, feeling an old pain grip his stomach.

"William Tyler. Little Willie Tyler has a private cell on Death Row for the help he tried to give Arty."

"Shit." Tejeda pushed his plate away and stood up, putting a little distance between himself and Spud's intensity. Five years ago he had run Arthur Radley Silver to ground. Arty had enjoyed the chase, taunting Tejeda, manipulating the press. By the time he was caught, Arty Silver had dipped his corrupt finger into the peaceful waters of Tejeda's personal life and stirred until nothing could ever be the same for him or his family again. Cassie, Tejeda's wife then, had been the worst casualty, left feeling so scared and vulnerable that she had literally taken to the hills. Now she was teaching Hopis how to make pots or something and staying as far away from family involvements as she could.

What had made Arty so scary, and so hard to find, was that he seemed absolutely ordinary. Until he tripped himself up, there was no way to identify him. He displayed neither the cranked-up charm of a sociopath like Kenneth Bianchi nor the charismatic bizarreness of Charles Manson. During the eight years of his killing binge, Arty had led a quiet life with the same lover, gained professional respect as an industrial architect, bought and maintained a little beach cottage. An exemplary life, except that on holiday weekends he went cruising for well-muscled young men, drugged them, raped them, beheaded them, then threw their emasculated bodies from his moving car.

And still his friends loved him, believed in his innocence. Friends like William Tyler, who had tried to get Arty off by pulling a copycat murder. But not many people have the stomach it takes to mutilate human flesh in the pattern of Arty Silver. And now William Tyler, convicted by his own confession three years before his friend Arty Silver could be brought to trial, had about even odds to be the first man executed in California under the new death-penalty law.

Tejeda had the feeling there was something else, something he couldn't quite remember. It seemed to flash close to the surface, then slip away; one of those dust motes flitting through his memory bank.

"Arty still write to you?" Eddie asked.

"Occasionally."

Eddie picked at something between his teeth and grinned at Tejeda. "You two made the big time together—mass murderer taunts photogenic detective."

"Photogenic?"

"You looked great in *Time*."

"No." Tejeda smiled. "I looked boyish in *Time*. I looked great in *Newsweek*."

"Shit," Eddie said. "Seems to me that when Arty Silver had to compete with you for press coverage, he got awfully personal about where he left his heads."

"So?"

"That head yesterday?" Eddie said. "I think it was meant for you, dumped in your own backyard."

"My backyard is the Pacific Ocean."

"You jog that strip of beach every afternoon between four and four-fifteen." Eddie pointed a stubby finger at Tejeda accusingly. "Yesterday you were late."

Tejeda remembered yesterday, going up to put on his running shorts and finding Kate home early from her meeting with Carl. He leaned back and smiled to himself; matinee sex was one of the bonuses of being both in love and home on disability at the same time.

"Like, you're going to work, you leave the house every day at two-thirty," Eddie went on. "You warm up, run the four miles to Ollie's on the Beach for a beer and a bullshit session, then you run home, usually passing the spot in question between four and four-fifteen."

"You have me followed?"

"Didn't have to. Everyone on the beach knows your schedule," Eddie said. "But yesterday you were late, and at four-ten someone else found the head. In a gift box."

"Came in on the tide."

Eddie finished his beer, put the bottle on the table, then stood up. "Head was there before the tide."

Tejeda looked away, refusing to be sucked in.

"Silver still say he's innocent?" Eddie asked.

"If you ask *them*, there aren't many guilty men in county jail."

"Arty Silver's still one of the nicest guys I ever met."

"Tell it to the Marines."

Eddie pushed in his chair. "Wouldn't hurt if you gave Arty a call, found out who his friends are these days."

Eddie balanced the cap on his empty beer bottle, giving Tejeda time to respond. When nothing happened, he reached into his pocket, slid out a long folded paper, sharpened its creases, looked at it, then put it away again. "Wouldn't hurt to see what Arty has to say."

"So call him," Tejeda said with exasperation. "Spud, I don't want any part of this."

"Sorry." Eddie Green reached a hand back into his pocket, pulled out the folded paper again, and extended it toward Tejeda. "But you're in. I'll pick you up around eight-thirty, quarter to."

Tejeda looked at the document but didn't reach for it. "What is it, Spud?"

"Subpoena," Eddie said, dropping the document beside the mustard. "Coroner's preliminary inquest. Tomorrow morning at nine."

5

"What's this?" Kate asked, accepting the small white bag from Lydia Callahan, her office mate. "Women's volleyball team having a bake sale?"

"Hell, no. When I heard you were ditching the curriculum meeting to take the kid driving, I had these specially made for you." Lydia straightened the front of her linen blazer and looked around to see if anyone in the campus quad was within earshot. "Valium brownies."

"Sure." Kate looked into the bag. "Look like standard-issue cafeteria brownies to me."

"Trust me." Lydia grinned. "Soon as Theresa turns the key in the ignition, start eating. Halfway through, you won't care whether you survive or not."

"Very funny," Kate said, watching Lydia. "But not like you. What's up?"

"What do you mean, I'm not funny?"

"You're one of the funniest people I know," Kate said. "But spur-of-the-moment funny, not organized buy-a-brownie funny. Something's wrong, isn't it?"

"No," Lydia protested, but she shifted her briefcase from one hand to the other, then back again. "Okay, look, it's really nothing. I saw the late edition of the local paper at lunchtime and I thought you might need a yuck."

Kate paused. "Something about me?"

"It was about the . . ." Lydia drew one long finger across her throat.

"The head? Don't worry about it. Roger promised me, it's not *our* head."

"Roger?" Lydia repeated. "You say 'Roger' funny."

"Shut up, Lydia," Kate laughed. She thrust the white bag into Lydia's hand. "If you're going to the meeting, you'll need these more than I do."

"Yeah." Lydia looked suddenly serious. "Do me a favor?"

"Within reason."

"Don't read the paper today. You know the sort of junk they dredge up. Just go home and spend some time with that gorgeous hunk." Lydia made a pretense of looking down at her watch, but Kate saw the tears welling in her eyes. "God, I'm really late."

Lydia turned down a walkway that angled toward the administration building, her long athletic gait checked by her tailored skirt.

"Thanksgiving?" Kate called after her.

"All set." Lydia turned, taking a few backward steps as she talked. "Three o'clock, bring rolls. Reece need a tie?"

"No. Be comfortable."

"Call you later." Lydia waved and turned, then disappeared quickly into the shadows of the building's portico.

Kate took a deep breath; walking with Lydia was like jogging with anyone else. Lydia did everything on the run, Kate mused, even in the classroom. Her lectures seemed to be breathless dashes across the historical landscape, while Kate preferred to posthole, to dissect key issues before moving on. The amazing thing was how well they worked together, complemented each other. Three mornings a week they taught a huge freshman survey course, sharing the podium on the stage of the Humanities Lecture Hall. Lydia always started. After she had sketched in the skeletal framework of European history, Kate would hang flesh on the bare bones. It was fun. Some colleagues groused that the popular course was too much fun. But Kate rarely bothered to listen; the papers their students produced were well beyond the usual freshman level.

Kate shifted her briefcase to her other hand and walked on. The campus was quiet. A few sunbathers sprawled on the lawn, taking advantage of the waning heat wave, but this late in the day most students were either in class, or in the library, or at home.

"Hey, teach." Brent something-or-other from her ten o'clock class squinted up at her from the grass where he lay with his head cushioned on his backpack. There wasn't a textbook in sight. "Have a good one," he said, and closed his eyes.

She envied his insouciance. Her briefcase was heavy with ungraded midterms she should have finished over the weekend but could never find the time or, she admitted, the sustained interest to read. If she started reading papers immediately after Theresa's driving lesson, she thought, maybe she could finish before bedtime.

She checked her watch. She was running late. If no one else stopped her before she got to her car, and if traffic then cooperated, she figured she would just have time to change from her skirt into some shorts before picking up Theresa. She shifted her briefcase again and walked faster.

What Lydia had said bothered her. Was the local press somehow tying that grisly find on the beach to her or her family? After the press blitz that followed the death of her mother, she would rather avoid public notice, no matter what she had told Carl. She thought she had earned some privacy.

Do what Lydia said, she told herself, and don't read the papers.

The walkway to the faculty parking lot came up on her left. But without even thinking, Kate turned right instead and headed for the newspaper rack in front of the bookstore.

Theresa was a quick study, Kate found, with good reflexes and more common sense than she had expected. After an hour of jerky stops, jackrabbit starts, and near-panic when it came to lane changes, Theresa was actually driving the car. Kate wasn't exactly relaxed, but by four-thirty she no longer held the door handle in a death grip or pushed her right foot against the floorboard as if she had a brake pedal.

After cruising the high school one last time, Theresa essayed them home. "Not a scratch," Theresa said proudly as she waited for the iron gates across Kate's drive to open for them.

"Ready for parallel parking?" Kate asked.

"That's like really hard, isn't it?" Theresa said, drawing to a smooth stop on the turnabout.

"In this car, yes. We'll try it later in the Jaguar."

As she got out of the car, Kate looked across the courtyard shared by the three houses her grandfather had built. She was dismayed to see that the front of the house closest to her own had the beginning skeleton of a construction scaffold. Carl had warned her that he was ready to start work on the house he had inherited from Uncle Miles, but she hadn't expected it so soon.

Theresa caught up to her. "Was I okay?"

"You were great," Kate said. "Tomorrow, same time?"

"Mrs. Teague?"

Kate spun around, startled by hearing the married name she had dropped. A small muscular man with a full black beard and a regenerated-hippie sort of air loped across the brick courtyard toward them.

"Mike Rios," he said, thrusting a hand at her as he came to an abrupt stop in her path. "I'm construction foreman on this project."

His hand was dry and callused. "We'll do our best to stay out of your way," she said.

"Yeah. Good." His every movement was quick, charged with nervous energy and impatience, as if the rest of the world moved too slowly for him. Kate couldn't decide whether he antagonized her simply because he was working for Carl or because of some annoying quality all his own.

She side-stepped him. "Nice to meet you, Mr. Rios."

"Hang on a sec." He was in front of her again. "Listen, we ran into some problems in the dining room and we need to take a look at yours. Your husband said it would be okay."

"I don't have a husband." She quickly took back an idea she had almost persuaded herself was true: she and Tejeda hadn't found peace, only a few moments of relative quiet now and then. If Theresa hadn't been standing there, she would have told Mike Rios to tell his boss to go fuck himself. Instead, she took Theresa by the arm and walked away.

"Look, Mrs. . . ." Rios trotted up behind them. "I just need some idea what the original looked like. The old guy who had Mr. Teague's house before him didn't take very good care of the place. We want to do this project right. It'll only need a minute or two."

Kate sighed. Sometimes giving in was so much easier than continuing the struggle. "I get home from school at noon tomorrow. Come then."

"Now would be okay."

"Noon tomorrow," she said firmly. He acceded, but he let her know by his sarcastic bow that he didn't gracefully tolerate inconvenience.

Theresa had walked on ahead, and now she stood on the front steps, spotlighted by a long slash of sun streaming between two cypress trees. She was watching something so intensely that she didn't seem to hear Kate come up beside her.

"What do you see?" Kate expected to find workmen swinging from the scaffold or pelicans nesting on the chimney pots. Instead, there was Carl.

"Jesus," Kate groaned. She understood the effect Carl was having on Theresa; the same thing happened to nearly every woman who saw him. Including herself.

Carl's beige linen slacks were perfectly tailored to show off his rock-hard ass without seeming to intend to do so. Even his pose seemed artless as he came from the side of his house, spread a roll of blueprints across the hood of his shiny new Maserati, and leaned over them with one casually shod foot propped against the front bumper. He was too *GQ* to be real.

Kate recognized the man with him, Harry Jon Miller, an architect with a good, if only local, reputation. He was nice-enough-looking by himself. But next to Carl he might as well have been invisible.

"Who is he?" Theresa asked with unsettling urgency.

"That's Carl."

"*That's* Carl?" Theresa gave Kate a glance full of disbelief. "You divorced *him*?"

"Yes."

Theresa's eyes widened as Carl straightened up. It wouldn't help Theresa any, Kate thought, when she learned that Carl also had brains and money. Sometimes when she saw him like this, Kate had to remind herself what a world-class shit Carl could be.

From the way he now flexed his shoulder, Kate knew that he was aware that he was being watched.

"He isn't gay, is he?" Theresa asked.

"Not as far as I know."

"How long were you married?"

"Long enough," Kate said. The best way to defuse Theresa's curiosity, she decided, would be to introduce her to Carl, knowing he would be haughty and aloof with her, as he was with anyone who had neither power nor connections. "Carl is restoring the house next door, so he'll be around for a while. Want to meet him?"

"That's okay," Theresa demurred. She looked at Kate. "I thought that you owned all the houses in the compound."

"Just two of them."

"But this is your family's estate, not his."

"It's complicated." Kate opened the front door. "The whole sordid story would make an R-rated movie, seventeen and under admitted with parent only."

"You mean, ask my dad."

"Right."

"Or my grandmother," Theresa said. "I talked to Grandma this morning. She's bringing some kind of cranberry salad and pies on Thursday. Aunt Teri is bringing hot vegetables."

"I didn't realize Thanksgiving could be so easy. With everyone bringing food, all we have to prepare is the turkey."

"Nana, my great-grandmother, won't bring anything. She doesn't have a kitchen in her apartment at the retirement home." Something uncomfortable seemed to occur to Theresa and she turned away.

"Is something wrong with Nana?"

Theresa shook her head. "You didn't invite Carl, did you?"

"I didn't want World War III."

"Or my mom?"

"She's in New Mexico," Kate said, wishing that were answer enough. Theresa hadn't seen her mother for over a year, and as Kate understood the situation, wasn't likely to see her for another. Kate hurt for her. There were times now when she missed her own mother. Even though Mother had been a difficult personality, sometimes when she needed someone to talk to, only her mother would do.

"If Mom was here," Theresa said, "could she come for Thanksgiving?"

"Of course," Kate said, tightening her fists inside her shorts pockets. "We'd make her bring the rolls or something."

"Doesn't matter." Theresa went off toward the Chinese vase in the foyer. "She won't come."

"Maybe next year." She hoped Theresa couldn't see through her; she had never been a very good liar. But there were some truths that didn't bear addressing.

Kate picked up the briefcase she had dumped on the table after school and carried it upstairs.

In her room, Kate opened her briefcase and spilled its contents onto the bed. The late edition of the local paper ended up on top. She tossed it aside, let out a long breath, then began sorting the exam blue books into piles: easy-to-read handwriting in one stack, illegible scrawls in another. It was a beginning, she thought, but the reading was tedious.

She had been so distractible all fall that she could hardly sit down long enough to read through two papers at a time. Always, it seemed, swirling around in the background like a high-powered buzz saw was a sense of impending horror. Of one thing she was sure: the core of her fear was not, as Tejeda's was, a recurring memory of what had happened to them. It was instead the realization of how much worse it all nearly was.

She looked down at the exams and tried to estimate how long this chore would take. Then she killed a few minutes searching for the best red pen. And when she ran out of delays, she stripped off her clothes and ran a hot shower.

Two hours later, when Tejeda came upstairs looking for her, she had managed to grade only a depressingly small number of blue books.

"Dinner in half an hour," he said.

"Okay."

As far as he could tell, Kate wore nothing except bikini underpants, his marathon T-shirt, and her reading glasses. She sat cross-legged in the middle of the bed, a charming island in a sea of midterm blue books. She marked an exam and tossed it against the ancient carved-oak headboard that depicted either the Battle of Waterloo or the tragic story of Tristan and Isolde— Tejeda couldn't decide which.

When she looked up, her wide pale eyes seemed tired. "Eddie Green called."

"What did he want?"

"He'll call back."

"I'm sure." Tejeda dropped to the bed beside her, crushing a pile of exams.

"Don't lie on those," she said, gently pushing him over. "I have some hope for those people. You can sit on the other pile."

He thought about offering her a match, but managed to make space for himself beside her. He kissed the inside of her exposed thigh and rested his head on the crook of her knee.

As she read, she scratched between his shoulder blades with the end of her pen. "I think Eddie misses you."

"Does he?" Tejeda pulled an exam from under his hip and flipped it open. " 'Andrew Jackson was a very great man,' " he read aloud. " 'He fought a duel for his wife, which was already married to someone else. His boot filled up with blood and he became President.' Sounds good to me. Why'd you give him an F?"

"He forgot the part about Jackson's friends getting drunk and vomiting in the White House during the inauguration party."

"Is this what you teach them?"

"He had special help from the football-team manager."

"How can you stand to read this stuff?" He tossed the exam aside and picked up the newspaper lying beside her briefcase. He read the headline to her. " 'DEATH VISITS SANTA ANGELICA BAY.' Well, hell," he said, "and Monterey only got the pope."

"Lydia thought that article would upset me." She took the paper and scanned down the paragraphs about the severed head of an unidentified young man and the few details available from the police. Since there wasn't enough information for a feature story, they padded with a rundown of all the bodies and parts thereof that had floated up in the bay during recorded history. Some of them, Kate was sure, were folklore passed along and embroidered upon in the bar around the corner from the newspaper offices.

When she found the paragraph she wanted, she pushed her glasses up on her nose and read: " 'Cornell Byrd, playboy son of one of Santa Angelica's most prominent families, was another victim of the seemingly peaceful waters of our city's bay. Byrd's disappearance while sailing his yacht prompts some to wonder whether the mysterious conditions at work in the infamous Bermuda Triangle might also be at work off our own coast.'

"Playboy?" Kate took her glasses off and rubbed her eyes. "That's a new one. I suppose that if they had called Dad a drunk it would have ruined their Triangle theory. Lots of drunks get lost at sea."

"The story makes good fill between their ads. Bus-stop reading." He rolled up on one elbow. "Theresa said what's-his-name was around today."

"Who? Sean O'Shay?"

"Sean O'Shay?" He tried to force something out of the blank space in his mind. "Sean O'Shay? Sounds like a brand of deodorant soap."

"He's the college freshman Theresa wants to go out with."

"Won't he ask her?"

"He did. You said no." She stretched forward and kissed him, a sort of consolation prize, he thought. "Sean is on the swimming team. Remember now? Shaved off all his body hair? You said that if he had so much body hair he had to shave it, he probably had an oversupply of hormones and she should watch out for him."

"I said that?" Recognition failed him.

"He was over the day you had your last seizure."

"Ah." He closed his eyes as she wrapped her arms around him, knowing he couldn't hide his chagrin from her. He had had two seizures since his head injury, both when he had been overtired and overstressed. About them he remembered nothing except the wonderful euphoric aura that preceded them and the bottomless void that followed.

"Okay, so it wasn't Sean who came over," she said. "Who was it?"

"Name's gone. Doesn't matter."

"Sure it does. The doctor said to think of your brain as a flabby muscle that needs exercise. Come on. Try to force it."

"You know." He had a picture in his mind, but the label wasn't there. "Damn."

"Twenty Questions, then. Give me a hint."

He made a circle with his thumb and forefinger.

"Round?" she asked. He shook his head and put the circle to his eye. "Hole," she said. "Doughnut hole? Keyhole? Asshole?"

"Right." Then he made a larger circle with both hands.

"Big asshole?" She thought for a moment. "Carl?"

"That's it."

"I saw him. He's started work on Uncle Miles's house."

"He going to live there?"

"I don't know."

"What will you do if he does?"

She shrugged, trying to seem blasé, but he saw her expression harden.

"Kate?"

"Honest to God, I don't know. It would be so . . . presumptuous, I guess, for him to move in."

"Because he was your uncle's bastard son?"

"Because he wasn't."

"So?"

"So, I'll wait until everything clears probate, get our property settlement finalized, then I'll sell out and move to Tahiti." She made a fist and rested her chin on it. "You like Tahiti?"

"We could stay at my place." Then he wondered whether, like his car, some disposition had already been made of his house. No. He was still making mortgage payments. He stretched and yawned.

"Tired?" she asked, capping her pen.

He shrugged, smiled. "I forget."

Slowly she raised the hem of her shirt, giving him a glimpse of round, pale breast. "Remember this?"

"No," he said.

6

Kate moved the can of shaving cream aside to make room for herself on the edge of the sink in front of Tejeda. When she was situated, she held a letter on thick cream-colored stationery in front of him. "See this?"

"Wait a sec." He rinsed his hands before taking the letter from her. "Apology from the bank?"

"Hand-delivered, accompanied by flowers. They're afraid I'll transfer my accounts somewhere else."

Strange world she lived in, he thought. No bank had ever sent him flowers or apologized for a gaffe. Nor was ever likely to.

"I'll let them stew for a while," she said, "but I won't move any funds. If Carl tries another stunt, the bank won't be so fast to comply."

"Good idea," he said, not knowing what else to say. Money was a potential bugaboo between them. As far as he could tell, Kate never thought much about money; it was always just there. But her indifference was a luxury he—first as the son of schoolteachers, then as a cop supporting a family—had never been able to afford.

Both he and Kate lived simply, well within their means. But there was a vast difference, he thought, in the scope of their means. This month, after making a house payment and sending some emergency funds to his son, Richie, in college, Tejeda had about a hundred and eighty dollars left in his checking account. Kate spent almost that amount every week just to have the three cars in her garage washed, even though one of them, a Mercedes belonging to her one surviving uncle, was never driven beyond the turnabout in the driveway.

Maybe it was time to talk about money, he thought with resignation. When Kate had brought him here from the hospital, no one had mentioned finances, only how practical a solution this living arrangement was, for a number of reasons. Tejeda watched Kate rinse whiskers out of his razor. It was time to talk, he decided. Then she looked up and smiled at him, her face still rosy from her shower, and he changed his mind. They'd hack out the money thing soon. But not now. Talking about money meant talking about permanence.

He handed the bank letter back to her. "I'm glad you got it settled so easily."

"Too easily, if I know Carl. Oh, look, you've nicked yourself." She held his face in her warm hands and carefully pressed a tissue against the tiny cut under his jaw. He watched her in the mirror as she took the tissue away, leaned forward to check the bleeding, then refolded the tissue and put it back on the nick. She was very gentle, very matter-of-fact, and he found himself very moved.

Without warning, he felt an uncomfortable pang thinking about her gentleness. He knew it had something to do with Cassie, an unexpected reminder of their early married years together, her sweetness, before the reality of life with a cop, the never-ending obligations of raising children, and a lot of nights alone had snapped her. Kate, he thought, was tougher, certainly more independent. Maybe she would have made it. Then he glanced at the bank letter, soaking up a puddle of water on the sink, and wondered if he and Cassie might have survived if they'd had the buffer of an inherited fortune. Though it made him feel bad to even think it, he could understand why so many people resented Kate for her money.

"What time is Eddie picking you up?" Kate asked.

"Eight-thirty." He was still watching her in the mirror, feeling almost as if his thoughts of Cassie had been a betrayal. But the guilt faded as he followed the lines of Kate's straight back, admired the simplicity and grace of her every movement. Under the heavy lime scent of his shaving cream he found the delicate perfume she had dabbed on after her shower. When she leaned toward him, he felt a rush of warm air escape from the top of her robe. And with it came a heady scent that was uniquely hers.

"What?" she said, catching him staring.

He folded her in his arms and pressed her against his bare chest, leaving no room between them for ex-spouses or other ghosts. "You smell good."

She kissed his shoulder as she lightly ran her fingernails down the long muscles of his back. "What else?"

"If I say anything else," he said, nuzzling the smooth hollow at the base of her throat, "you'll miss your nine o'clock class and I'll miss the inquest."

"I could call in sick."

"I could get arrested."

"Mister!" Trinh's voice carried through the door of the adjoining bedroom. "Sergeant Green is here!"

Tejeda leaned back and yelled, "Tell him to go find his own girl."

There was a small silence before Trinh said, "He wait downstairs."

Tejeda sighed and kissed Kate's smile. "Leave your name and number. I'll get back to you."

They talked as they dressed, side by side, in the cavernous dressing room that opened off the bathroom. Comfortable, Tejeda thought, just as if they'd been together like this for years.

"Reece has tickets for the Rams game Sunday," she said as she reached for a pair of fawn-colored heels. "Want to go?"

"Good seats?"

She smiled."You know Reece."

"Yeah." He nodded. Reece, Kate's cousin by marriage and also her closest friend, was in so many ways her opposite, Tejeda thought, his taste running to early Duke of Windsor. For all Reece's starched cuffs and designer picnic baskets, though, he was always good company and endlessly loyal. "Ball game sounds like fun."

"I'll tell him," she said. "Will your inquest take long?"

"An hour or two."

"Richie said he'll be here two hours after his last class this afternoon. About five." She came over and straightened his tie and smoothed the lapels of his navy suitcoat. "You've lost some weight since you wore that last. Make Eddie buy you lunch."

He put his arms around her. "I'd like to tell Eddie to take a flying leap."

"Then do it," she said as she stretched up to kiss him.

Eddie Green, never much of a talker, was quiet all the way to the County Hall of Administration. Tejeda stood beside him in the elevator to the fourth floor, waiting for his partner to spill whatever it was that was bothering him. But there was never a chance. As soon as the elevator doors slid open, the press of people hovering outside the door to the coroner's conference room surged toward them.

Tejeda took a step back, letting Eddie head the forward assault. The crowd circled them. He had expected this to be news hounds, but the crowd's equipment ran more to vinyl handbags than videocams. He had been looking at them in a generic way, as just a mass of people. But he shifted his focus and picked out more than a dozen familiar faces, each, in common with the others, with a mask of fear, anger, and unrelieved sadness.

A man, about fifty, with a fringe of steel-wool hair, stepped forward from the group. Tejeda knew him, but couldn't name him.

"We're glad to see you again, Lieutenant," he said.

Tejeda stayed behind Eddie's shoulder. "Exactly who are 'we'?"

"Silver Threads," the man said. "We've organized a support group for the families of Arty Silver's victims. We've sent a representative to every single one of Silver's pretrial hearings."

"Very commendable," Tejeda said. "But why are you here? This inquest has nothing to do with Arty Silver."

Eddie nudged him as if he'd made a gaffe. "What?" he asked, but Eddie only rolled his eyes. There was more going on here than Eddie had told him about, and it was making him feel uncomfortable, like coming into a joke just before the punch line.

"Haven't you heard?" The man raked his wiry hair nervously. "Arty's attorney has asked for another trial postponement. He says this case is so similar to Arty's that there's a good possibility Arty was wrongfully accused, 'cuz there's no way Arty could have done this one. He wants full disclosure and time to study."

"That's just more of Arty's bullshit," Eddie fumed. "Trial's going to start Monday."

A tall, hard-faced woman pushed to the front. "Maybe we should let him postpone."

"Velma," the man said, aghast. "What are you saying? We been waiting five years already."

"My son's murder isn't among the charges against Arty Silver," she scolded. "All the D.A. has is one photograph of my boy found at Arty's house. He can't even prove whether he was dead or alive. Maybe if he had a few more weeks . . ."

Tejeda expected the crowd to shout her down, but instead they seemed to draw around her supportively. A plump little woman stretched her short arms around Velma and drew her head down to her shoulder.

"No, honey," she said, offering a handkerchief to the woman softly weeping into her neck. "We agreed. None of us will ever know the whole truth about what happened to our kids. The important thing is helping the D.A. fry Arty."

Tejeda could almost see this motherly little woman dropping the cyanide pellets under Arty's chair. He wondered which of the counts on the indictment represented her son. When she looked up at Tejeda, there were no tears in her eyes.

"Get this killer, Lieutenant," she ordered. "You came through for us once, trapped that little bastard. We're asking for your help again. Find him fast. Don't let Arty Silver ride to freedom on his back."

"Take care of each other," Tejeda said. He grabbed Eddie's elbow and began moving with him through the crowd. "We'll take care of Arty."

He was grateful that the Silver Threads didn't follow. Apparently they were keeping their vigil, and their presence, out in the hall.

"Remind me to call the marshals," Eddie said as

they walked into the coroner's conference room. "We need metal detectors outside courtroom eight on Monday."

"Yeah." Tejeda was only half-listening. He saw in front of him another room full of people and he broke out in a sweat; all this pressure, he couldn't remember a single name. But as he followed Eddie deeper into the room, he felt a tremendous burden lifted. He raised his eyes and said a silent thanks to Mrs. Otis Washington; the coroner's wife had made name cards for all of the participants in her fine script. With everyone labeled for him, at least he wouldn't be stumbling over names. He grinned at Eddie. "Otis' wife must be feeling better."

Eddie nodded. "She's just back from two months drying out at the Betty Ford Center. You want coffee?"

"Yeah, thanks," Tejeda said. He found his place at the table and pulled his chair back so that he would be sitting beside but just behind Eddie so they could talk more easily during the proceedings. Anyway, if he was here in an advisory capacity only, as Eddie had assured him he was, then he wasn't about to take a seat among the official witnesses.

While Eddie waited for a turn at Mr. Coffee, Tejeda watched the chairs around the table fill up. Like waiting for a symphony, he thought, the sound level rising, changing tone, as each player entered and tuned up for the performance to follow.

The preliminary inquest was official, but informal. Which meant that Vic Spago, who came into the room sharing a joke with Coroner Otis Washington, was wearing a tie with a loose knot and an open collar.

Tejeda exchanged nods with the people he recognized, but he stayed in his chair, his long legs stretched in front to define his personal territory. He felt wary, nervous. This room, and the situation, were too familiar; this was where the official quest always began, the dropping-off point beyond which there were monsters.

Otis Washington, born politician that he was, stopped to greet each little group in the room. Then he broke away and came over to Tejeda. He turned Eddie's chair around and sat facing Tejeda.

"Glad you could make it," Otis said. When he sipped from a steaming mug with "Caffeine PRN" printed on its side, Tejeda got a whiff of bourbon.

"I had a choice?" Tejeda said. "There's nothing I have to say that you don't already know."

"Humor us." Otis winked at him. "Makes people feel happy to know you're here. You're our star when it comes to floating heads."

"Nice way to talk, Otis," Eddie said. He was wrestling two overfull mugs of coffee and a stack of files that someone had thrust under his arm along the way. As he put a cup in Tejeda's hand, he pointedly measured his partner's distance away from the table with his eye. "You want field glasses?"

"Come on, Spud," Tejeda said, leaning forward. "What aren't you telling me?"

Eddie looked down at Otis, waited for a desultory nod, then turned to Tejeda. His voice was low: "We need your expertise—that goes without saying. But we need something else from you too."

Eddie blew on his coffee as a delaying tactic. Then he cleared his throat. "Otis, Vic, me, some of the others, have seen enough of this case, and enough of cases like it, to know that this kid's killing is part of a series. The technique suggests it wasn't the first. And unless we catch our perpetrator, it won't be the last."

"So?" Tejeda asked. "You know how to proceed."

"Yeah, if we had the budget," Otis said. "The mayor and half the city council are up for reelection this spring. They get a lot of *image* per enforcement dollar busting street-corner drug pushers," he said. "They took three detectives per watch away from homicide and assigned them to narco. You know what sort of caseload that leaves the rest of us with."

"That's standard political bullshit," Tejeda said. "You'll find ways to survive."

Otis pulled his chair closer. "Except that Monday morning the most expensive trial ever mounted in this state begins—Arty Silver. The D.A. got budget for seven full-time new staff to handle the evidence load, and carte blanche on investigator time. You know what that leaves for the rest of our cases? Shit, Roger, there's simply no fudge money left in the department."

"That's where you come in," Eddie said.

"What?" Tejeda laughed. "Fund-raising?"

"You got it. We bring you in, parade you around, let the public think there's some tie-in to the Arty case, and bingo, we either get our men back or we get access to the investigators assigned to the D.A. for the duration."

Otis tapped Tejeda's knee with his ham-size fist and grinned into his face. "Already I've had calls from the L.A. *Times*, the San Diego *Union*, and KTLA: someone leaked you were subpoenaed for the inquest. The mayor invited me to sit beside him at his business-men's prayer breakfast tomorrow." Otis sat back and preened. "And he wants me to bring you."

"Like hell," Tejeda said loudly enough to turn a few heads.

"If you love me," Otis said, "or love your old department, you'll just tag along with Eddie now and then and look busy when you see the press. I figure every mention you get us on the six o'clock news is worth another day or two of investigator time. *Capisce*?"

Tejeda chuckled to himself; he should have guessed. Maybe he was worth millions after all.

"Heads up," Eddie said, jutting his chin toward the door.

So, he thought, the Silver Threads weren't waiting outside after all. Or had they only sent a delegation? The woman called Velma and the Brillo-haired spokesman flanked a middle-aged couple who walked numbly, as if anesthetized. Tejeda didn't recognize them from the Silver interrogations or hearings.

The woman held his eye, she was so strikingly plain. Stuck somewhere between forty and fifty, he guessed. Her dress, though clean and pressed, was so near to being both formless and colorless that he wondered where she could possibly have acquired it.

While the woman looked tired, haggard even, the thin man clinging to her arm seemed absolutely beaten down. The pair moved toward the conference table, propped up by the Silver Threads pair as if they were marathon dancers trying to hang on until midnight. Just looking at them, Tejeda knew that whatever circumstance had brought them here wasn't the first tragedy in their lives.

He nudged Eddie's foot and nodded toward the couple.

"John Doe's parents," Eddie said. "Wallace and Lillian Morrow. Little Lake, Iowa."

Otis was watching the Morrows too. He shuddered, took a big gulp from his mug, then got up from Eddie's chair. As he stood, he leaned close to Tejeda. "It's show time," he said, and Tejeda hoped Otis had a strong mint in his pocket; coffee wasn't enough to cover the booze on his breath.

Tejeda pulled his legs in and moved his chair closer to Eddie's. "Why are the parents here?"

"Their request."

"Pretty brutal." Tejeda studied the Morrows again.

"Get out the smelling salts. They don't look up to this."

"We'll see." Eddie shrugged as Otis gaveled the inquest to order.

While Otis went through the preliminaries and his usual pontificating about the tragedy before them, Tejeda surveyed the group assembled around the long table. Most of the official types from the initial discovery on the beach were here: Angelo Tibbs from harbor patrol, Rebecca Farmer from lifeguards, Vic Spago, and so on. There were also two uniformed Marines; one seasoned brass, a captain, and the other a very young enlisted man. Tejeda had a hunch that they used the same barber as had the object of this inquest.

He was thinking about how much easier the investigation was when the head was found, rather than other body parts, because it carried identifiers in hair and teeth and facial features, when he noticed Maria Cosretti, the assistant D.A., trying to get his eye, smiling at him. He waved, then moved his attention to the man sitting on the far side of her. Tejeda recognized the man, even though he was camouflaged here in a gray three-piece suit. This was one of the joggers who had discovered the head.

The jogger was the first witness called.

"Now, just relax," Otis told him. "This is not a trial. We simply seek to learn the truth about the demise of the young man known officially as John Doe—Santa Angelica number 003.

"Now, sir, will you please identify yourself for the record?"

The jogger stood up and looked around, apparently not knowing where he should go or what he should do.

"Just sit right there beside our pretty Miss Cosretti," Otis said. Then he turned to the assistant D.A. "Maria, am I in trouble with local or federal law if I call you pretty?"

"You might be, Otis," the D.A. said in firm court-room tones. "Perhaps a more androgynous adjective would be preferable, for example 'nice-looking,' 'hand-some,' or, the always safe 'damn fine.' "

"Thank you, counselor," Otis chuckled, and the atmosphere in the room seemed palpably lighter. "Now, sir, for the record, will you identify yourself?"

"Gregory Joiner."

"Occupation?"

"Certified life underwriter." Then he gave an address in a new, upscale housing development in a nearby suburb and was sworn.

"Mr. Joiner," Otis said, "I believe you made the initial discovery of the remains on Monday last. Will you describe how you came to be at that spot and what you found?"

"Mondays and Thursdays I jog with my partner." Joiner made an effort to relax. "It's the only way we can talk without interruptions. Anyway, we saw this Christmas box in the surf and we opened it. And . . ."

After waiting for Joiner, who seemed about to lose out to some powerful emotion, Otis offered encouragement. "In the box you found the remains?"

"Just the . . ." Joiner glanced at the parents and stopped.

"What time was the discovery made?" Otis asked.

"At four-ten P.M."

"Had you passed this place earlier?"

"Yes," Joiner said. "At around three-forty-five."

"Was the box there at three-forty-five?"

"Definitely not. We would have seen it."

"Exactly where on the beach was this?"

"You mean the address?"

"If you can."

Joiner took a breath and held it while he thought. "Below the bluffs that run along Ocean Avenue. I don't know the closest cross street, but it was opposite those mansions that were in the news this summer. There was a murder or something." He looked up at Otis. "You know where I mean?"

"Lieutenant Tejeda," Otis said. "What's the address there?"

"Twelve-hundred Ocean," Tejeda said, looking at the back of Eddie's head.

"Thank you," Otis said. As Otis continued questioning Joiner, Tejeda noticed a spark of life flicker between the Morrows of Iowa. What made him uncomfortable was that *he* seemed to have ignited this spark for them; it was obvious from the way they peeked up at him that he was the subject of their whispered conversation, the source of some sort of hope.

Gregory Joiner was followed by the lifeguard who had relayed the discovery to harbor patrol, who then radioed the police. Each person in the chain offered another nugget, but little of it was information that Tejeda hadn't already heard or seen for himself. Until Otis called on the Morrows of Little Lake, Iowa.

Mrs. Morrow pulled a half-full packet of Kleenex from her vinyl purse and self-consciously tried to extract one without rustling the plastic wrapper. This was a churchgoer's reflex, Tejeda thought, this fear of making noise and interrupting the word of God. Then he sat back with his arms folded across his chest and studied the woman for what she might reveal about her son. He wondered whether the closest she had ever come to an official proceeding was in her church in Little Lake.

"Mr. and Mrs. Morrow," Otis said in his best fatherly voice. "You know you can forgo this inquest.

We have your sworn depositions, and unless or until this case goes to trial, that is sufficient."

"We want to be here," Wallace Morrow said as Mrs. Morrow dabbed at her eyes. "We'll do anything we can to find out what happened to our boy."

Otis looked down at the notepad in front of him before he spoke. "Were you asked to identify the remains known here as John Doe—Santa Angelica 003?"

"Yes. He is . . ." The man blinked twice. "He was our son, Wally. Wallace Lee Morrow, Jr."

"Did he have any identifying marks?"

"Yes," Mrs. Morrow said, her voice soft, her control tentative. "He had a bad case of chickenpox when he was three. Left him with scars. He had four of them on his forehead. Made a perfect little square."

Tejeda turned away as she choked back her sobs. Wally for her at that moment, he suspected, was a vulnerable three-year-old sick with chickenpox. These were people without great expectations, and it seemed to him that what little leavening this world had offered them may have been snuffed out with the death of their son.

Otis cleared his throat. "Would you like to be excused?"

"No," Mrs. Morrow said firmly.

"Then please tell us a few things about your son, in hopes some light can be shed on the circumstances that brought his death." Otis glanced at Mrs. Morrow. "How old was the boy?"

"Nineteen."

Otis shook his head. "The evidence indicates your son was involved in a homosexual act before his death."

"My son was no homosexual," Mr. Morrow said with quiet ferocity. "No matter what they say."

"Wall," Mrs. Morrow said, laying a hand on his arm.

"Mrs. Morrow?" Otis encouraged.

"Now, what my husband told you was the truth," she said. "But there was an incident when Wally was in high school. He was real close to his wrestling coach, so when the coach died the authorities questioned our Wally."

"How did the coach die, Mrs. Morrow?"

"You may never have heard of this," she said, her fierce blush adding appealing color to her face. Tejeda for the first time got a hint of what she might have been if she'd been dealt a different hand.

"Go ahead," Otis encouraged.

Mrs. Morrow was looking at her folded hands when she spoke again. "Autoeroticism, it's called."

Otis dropped his folksy smile and took a long drag on his coffee cup. "Why did they question your son?"

"Wally called the police."

"Was he with the coach when he died?"

Mrs. Morrow nodded. "The juvenile-court judge let him join the Marines instead of going to the honor camp."

The Marine captain sitting at the far end of the table seemed to be flexing his jaw muscles. When Otis called on him to testify, he seemed more than ready to express himself.

"If I ever met Lance Corporal Wallace Lee Morrow Jr. personally, I don't remember it," the captain said. "But I have familiarized myself with his records. He had good ratings as a mechanic, as a Marine. There is only one negative mark during his eleven months in the Corps. Three weeks ago he was found to be in possession of an unauthorized substance."

"Drugs?" Otis asked.

The Marine glanced at the Morrows. "Amyl nitrite."

Eddie whipped around and looked at Tejeda."Pop-pers?" he mouthed.

"As a result of this infraction, Corporal Morrow was restricted to base until last Sunday," the Marine continued. "He was given a twelve-hour pass, com-mencing at oh-nine hundred hours, terminating at twenty-one hundred hours. He failed to report at roll call Monday morning and was listed as absent without leave."

The excruciatingly young Marine beside him was called next. Wally Morrow was his bunkmate and friend, he said.

"Was he homosexual?" Otis asked.

"No, sir," the Marine responded, glancing at the captain to his right. "There are no homosexuals in the Marines."

"When did you last see Corporal Morrow?"

"Sunday, sir."

"Will you describe Corporal Morrow's activities on Sunday?"

"We got a ride into Oceanside," the private said. "Got something to eat, dropped off some laundry, hung around."

"Hung around where?"

The boy looked again at the captain before he an-swered. "Clyde's."

Tejeda had half-expected the answer as soon as he had seen the uniforms: this case that seemed with each revelation to be an echo from his past had to begin with Clyde's. He noticed how straight the captain was sitting, armored against some slings and arrows from the different reality of the world outside the Corps. If there were no gays in the Marines, then there was also no Clyde's.

"What happened at Clyde's?" Otis asked.

"Nothing. We shot some pool, had some beers."

"Captain," Otis said,"you know this place, Clyde's?"

The captain nodded. Tejeda noticed how his face glowed with fresh sweat. "Clyde's is a popular restaurant with the men."

Tejeda wondered what sort of coaching the captain had given the young private during the drive up from Camp Pendleton. He knew from past experience that the Marines liked to handle any situation that involved their own.

Tejeda moved his chair up beside Eddie and caught Otis' eye.

"So, Lieutenant Tejeda . . ." Otis smiled. "You have something to add?"

"May I ask the private a few questions?"

"You may."

Tejeda turned in the direction of the young man, leaning forward so he could see his face better. "Were you in uniform at Clyde's?"

"No, sir."

"Why is that?"

"The place is off-limits for enlisted personnel, sir."

"Why is that?"

The young Marine lost some of his starch."It's a gay bar, sir."

"Had Corporal Morrow been to Clyde's before Sunday?"

"Yes, sir."

"Often?"

"Every chance he got, sir."

"You last saw him Sunday?"

"Yes, sir."

"What was the very last thing you saw him do?"

"He got in a car with some guy, a civilian, and drove away with him, sir."

"He got into the car voluntarily?"

"Yes, sir."

"Thank you," Tejeda said as he leaned back in his chair.

Otis grinned. "Anything else, Lieutenant?"

"No. Sergeant Green here is going to take this man into custody as a material witness. He just might have some information that will help shed some light on a series of unresolved cases that may be related to the circumstances which brought about the unfortunate death of Wallace Lee Morrow Jr."

Otis beamed at him. "It is the finding of this hearing that Wallace Lee Morrow Jr. met his death at the hands of another. I thank everyone for their participation. This hearing is adjourned."

He turned immediately to the stenographer sitting behind him. "You get everything the lieutenant said, Fred?"

The stenographer nodded. "If I didn't, it's on the tape."

Then Otis beckoned toward a youngish woman who had been sitting in a far corner writing furiously during the entire proceeding. "You from the *Times*?"

"No," she said, "the *Register*. Can I ask a question?"

"Go ahead," Otis said.

"Did Lieutenant Tejeda say this was a serial killing?"

"It's a possibility," Tejeda said.

"Similarities have been noticed between this case and the Arty Silver case that comes to trial Monday. Do you suspect they are connected?"

"Too early to say," Tejeda answered. "Too early to rule it out."

The reporter wrote something quickly, then glanced back at Tejeda. "And are you in charge of the investigation?"

Tejeda looked at Otis, who was nodding, obviously hoping for an affirmative answer. Then he turned to Spud, who only grinned.

"No comment," he said.

7

"Nineteenth-century Europe to me is like one of those little glass balls you shake to make a snow scene." Kate appealed to Lydia. "You know what I mean. Do they have a name?"

Lydia nodded. "They're called little glass balls you shake to make a snow scene."

"Thanks." Kate smirked. It was ten minutes before the end of the class hour. Lydia had already moved off the lecture-hall stage and was leaning on the wall near a side exit, prepared for a quick retreat. There were gaps in the student crowd; about a quarter of the class of a hundred and fifty had taken an early start on the long Thanksgiving weekend. Among those dedicated enough to show up, Kate noticed an unusual number of clock watchers. "I think of Europe in the early nineteenth century as a scene in a glass ball that was given a good shaking. People from every European nation were scattered, eventually landing in clumps in the U.S., Canada, Argentina, South Africa, Algeria, Australia, Siberia. During the century before World War I, something like seventy million Europeans left the continent and settled permanently elsewhere."

Kate acknowledged a hand waving furiously at the back of the lecture hall. "You have a question?"

"Yeah." A tall kid with spiky lemon-yellow hair

struggled out of his seat, clutching notes and textbooks against his chest. "Is all that on the final?"

"Who asked that?" Lydia demanded. "Kolofsky, is that you?"

"No. It's not me."

The class laughed as the blond head dropped into anonymity among the other students.

"About the exam," Kate said. "Professor Callahan and I were discussing it only this morning." She turned to Lydia. "Right?"

"Must have been."

"Last semester we had a student who wrote the best essay either of us had ever seen. It was so near perfection that it makes any other response less than useless. To save you the embarrassment of failing to come up to that standard, and to save us the bother of reading your attempts, we're considering duplicating that essay for you to copy into your blue books. Give you a chance to touch greatness."

"Anyway," Lydia said, "we have reservations to be on a plane an hour after the final."

"But just in case the department Xerox goes out again before exam week," Kate said, "maybe you should go ahead and study *all* of this."

Kate expected to hear Lydia's rejoinder over the din of moaning and laughter; Lydia usually had the last word. But Lydia seemed to have become involved in a tug-of-war with someone who was trying to come in through a side exit. Kate wondered why the struggle; they often had auditors, though it was against college rules. There were only a few minutes left of the class hour anyway, so why bother? Why not just let him in?

A woman student rose on the far side of the room and Kate had to strain to hear her soft voice. "Is the exam comprehensive?"

"Yes," Kate said, distracted by the activity at the

door. Lydia seemed to have lost her battle over control of the door, and sight of the man who oozed in past her made Kate's face burn. Craig Hardy, the local-news reporter for the *Daily Angel*, came far enough inside to put himself out of Lydia's reach. He was slowed in his progress toward Kate by students who were prematurely leaking away from their seats and heading for the side exits.

Kate forced her attention back to the woman who had asked about the exam. "Don't panic yet; the final is weeks away. Now, everyone go away. Have a good holiday."

Lydia shouted over the end-of-class rustlings: "The library now has three copies of Gorky's *Lower Depths* and a variety of G. B. Shaw on overnight reserve. Take one home for the weekend. See you Monday."

Kate had lost sight of Craig Hardy among the tide of bodies streaming toward the exits on the north side of the hall. Lydia had once claimed that the record for clearing the hall after class was thirty-eight seconds on a Friday before a three-day holiday. Kate shuffled her notes together and looked for a clear path: on Thanksgiving Eve the class might break their old record, leaving her only seconds to find an alternate route out before Hardy could snag her.

Fielding questions, comments, greetings, she made a dash off stage right and headed south toward the door that led into the faculty-offices corridor. Just as she reached the south door, she felt a hand on her elbow. She spun around and was surprised to see the fresh face of Zack Kolofsky.

"Are you keeping office hours today?" he asked.

"No, sorry." Kate saw Hardy puffing toward her. She put an arm behind Kolofsky and propelled him along beside her, planning to use him as cannon fodder if Hardy outran them. "Can it keep till Monday?"

Kolofsky, though he looked more than fit, was nearly out of breath and glanced sidelong at Kate as if he thought she were rather strange. "It's about my paper."

She had lost sight of Hardy again. "Are you working on the paper this weekend?"

"No. I'm going skiing."

"Great," Kate said, releasing him. The corridor leading to her office was still a clear shot. "We'll talk about it Monday."

She sped away, chagrined somewhat by the puzzlement on Kolofsky's face. She'd explain on Monday, she assured herself. Anyone who had read Craig Hardy's twice-weekly column of gossip and speculation would understand how imperative it was for her to get shed of him. And she thought she had. But Hardy proved he was too much a pro. He must have doubled back, she thought, as he careened around the corner and skidded to a stop half a yard in front of her.

Grinning, he thrust a newspaper in front of her. "Did you happen to see this?"

She saw the *Daily Angel* banner and tried to shoulder past him. "No comment."

"Come on. Be a sport."

"I don't know anything about anything."

He was quick, but Kate managed to sidestep him. She had to give him credit for tenaciousness; he stuck close beside her, sidling through the crowd. She sighed as she glanced at him. "If you want information about the head that was found in the bay, you should be at the inquest now."

"It's over. Anyway, who cares? Wasn't even a local boy. I'm more interested in your reaction to this."

Again he thrust the newspaper in front of her. She snatched it from him. "These are classified ads," she said.

"You haven't seen it, then?"

"No." She tried giving the paper back, but he held his hands away like a child refusing a face-wash, so she let the paper drop.

He recovered quickly, snapping the paper off the floor before anyone stepped on it.

"Okay, then, listen to this. From yesterday's paper." He walked backward in front of her, springing on the balls of his feet as he read. " 'FICTITIOUS-BUSINESS-NAME STATEMENT. The following person is doing business as: Byrd and Teague, Attorneys-at-Law, a corporation. Signed, Carl Beaufort Teague, President.' "

Kate shrugged. "So?"

"Come on, give me more than that. This is a major coup. Your ex-husband has infiltrated your family's law firm, the oldest continuously operating business in Santa Angelica, and killed it off. How do you feel about it?"

"I feel great, looking forward to the holiday. Hope the weather holds."

"Better you should tell *me* than some outsider," he persisted. "Story like this could even be picked up by the *Enquirer*."

"There's no story here, Craig." She was walking as fast as she could, but he stuck close. "The old law firm has simply incorporated to take advantage of the new tax structure. No big deal."

"No big deal? My sources at the courthouse tell me your ex has filed to have his birth certificate changed from 'father unknown' to something that will knock the lid off the Byrd family."

"Stuff it, Hardy," she said as she reached her open office door.

"Okay." He threw up his hands in submission. "But remember, I'm only the first to ask."

She slammed the door in his face and waited to hear his rubber-soled retreat.

"Damn pest," she muttered as she yanked open the filing cabinet beside the door. She dropped her notes in and slammed the drawer shut. She wished she knew what Carl was up to this time and which would be harder, having him committed or hiring a hit man. She wanted him to stop. The tenaciousness she had once found exciting in him now reminded her of persistent, blood-sucking sand fleas in summer. She opened the drawer again just so she could slam it. "Damn, fucking, stupid pest."

"Excuse me?"

She jumped at the sound of the quiet voice behind her. Sucking in a breath, she turned around slowly, looking for something to use as a cudgel along the way. Had someone let the *Enquirer* in?

Though she had a notebook open on her lap, the middle-aged woman sitting half-hidden in the corner beside Kate's desk was just about the most harmless-looking person she had ever seen. She was small, thin, faded. There was a sadness about her that seemed to have leeched the color from her eyes so that the beige wall behind her showed through.

"You're not from the press, are you?" Kate asked, not yet ready to let her guard down.

"No." The woman looked at her lap. "I don't blame you for being careful, though. I know how they can be."

"Have we met?"

The woman shook her head. "I shouldn't be here, bothering you. But I thought that as a mother you might be willing to help."

As a mother? Kate thought. The woman was beginning to spook her with her quiet intensity. "Whom are you looking for?"

The beige eyes darted up. "Aren't you Professor Byrd?"

"Yes."

"Your husband gave your address at the inquest this morning. I know it was pretty high-handed, but I went to the house to talk to you. I couldn't figure out how the gates work," she said. "Are those condos in there?"

"No."

"Oh." There was a pregnant pause. "Anyway, this man finally came out and I told him I wanted to talk to you, so he said I should come here. Told me the name to ask for."

"I see," Kate said, though she didn't see at all. As a precaution, she reached over and opened the office door. When no one, including Craig Hardy, bled in, she went over to her desk and sat down facing the woman. She folded her hands on the blotter and took a deep breath. "The man you talked to, was he tall, blond?"

"No. He wasn't very big. Had a dark beard."

"You haven't told me your name."

"Lillian Morrow. Most people call me Lily."

"Mrs. Morrow," Kate said slowly. "I have neither a husband nor a child."

"Lieutenant Tejeda isn't your husband?"

"Did you want to speak with him?"

She shook her head. "I already tried."

"Mrs. Morrow, I think you had better tell me what's on your mind."

"I thought if you were a mother, you would understand and maybe help me. Get him to help." Mrs. Morrow took a tissue from her handbag and delicately wiped her eyes and nose. "It was my son, Wally Junior, they found down by your house."

"Found?" Carl's latest shenanigan still cluttered her thinking, so it took a moment to figure out what boy she was talking about. When she realized this woman belonged to the head in the bay, she almost wished to have Craig Hardy back as a diversion.

"Mrs. Morrow," Kate said, "I'm sorry about your son, but I can't imagine how I can help you."

"I don't know exactly, either. When the chaplain from the Marines called my husband and me and told us about our boy, he put us in touch with this group of parents, Silver Threads, whose boys were killed in ways like what happened to Wally Junior. These other parents told us about Lieutenant Tejeda and how he caught that Arthur Silver, found out what had happened to their sons. Everyone says this killing has something to do with Arthur Silver. But the police tell me Lieutenant Tejeda won't take on the investigation of my Wally's case."

"I'm sorry, Mrs. Morrow, but he can't. He's not well enough."

"Well enough?" The spark of a well-banked fire flashed in Lillian Morrow's eyes. "He looks well enough."

"Jeez!" Lydia seethed, kicking off her shoes as she came into the office. Her anger seemed to fill the small space left in their shared cubicle. "Next time I see that shit Craig Hardy, I'm going to deck him."

She tossed her briefcase into the corner behind her desk, opened a bottom drawer, and took out a pair of jogging shoes. She had her sweat socks halfway on before she seemed to notice Lillian Morrow.

"Oh, sorry," Lydia said, simmering down. "Am I interrupting?"

"No," Kate said, "I think we're finished. Mrs. Morrow, I'm sorry about your situation, but there is nothing I can do to help you. Eddie Green is in charge of the investigation and he's very competent."

But Lillian Morrow didn't budge. In fact, she seemed to plant herself more firmly on her chair.

"I'm sorry," Kate repeated.

"Professor Byrd," she said, "do you know what I keep thinking about?"

Kate shook her head.

"The devil's disciple who killed my Wally."

Lydia stood up and edged toward Kate. "Everything okay?"

Kate only glanced at Lydia, but she reached for her office mate's hand and squeezed it as she turned back to the desperate little woman pressed into the corner. "Mrs. Morrow, could I call someone from the parents' group to come and get you?"

"I keep thinking," Mrs. Morrow said, "that tonight that sick example of humanity who killed my son is going to sleep in a warm bed. Tomorrow he'll probably sit himself down to a Thanksgiving dinner and eat his fill. Can you imagine what knowing that does to me and my husband, when we don't even know where our Wally's remains are? Is he out in the cold somewhere, left for carrion like one mother told me her son was? Did he suffer that last night?" She had wrung her tissue into lint. "I have to know what happened to Wally."

Kate understood the agony of not knowing. She remembered the three-week vigil her grandfather had kept before her father's body had finally snagged on Byrd Rock and surfaced. He wouldn't eat in case his son was hungry, or sleep, or laugh, or show evidence of his own life spark when his boy might have lost his. She had been too young to understand much more than the raw pain of loss. But she had sensed early on her grandfather's guilt for having lived when the proper ordering of things demanded that he die before his child. In Lillian Morrow's face she saw the same mute grief her grandfather had carried for the rest of his life.

Kate leaned forward and touched the woman's arm. "You can trust Eddie Green to do everything possible."

Lillian Morrow shook her head, her mouth set in a stubborn pucker. "They told me Lieutenant Tejeda has the gift."

The gift? Lydia was dialing the telephone on her desk. Upside down, Kate watched her press the first three numbers—777. She pushed the cancel button before Lydia dialed the last 7 and alerted security.

"Are you sure?" Lydia asked.

"No." Kate stood and moved toward the door, hoping Lillian Morrow would follow. She had to be dissuaded. And she had to be kept from Tejeda. "I'll tell Lieutenant Tejeda about your concerns. He'll do what's best."

"I had hoped you had children of your own." Mrs. Morrow gathered her vinyl handbag and wadded the tailings of Kleenex; she had read Kate's dismissal. In the doorway, she paused and faced Kate. "Can I call you?"

"If you need anything, you should call Eddie Green."

"All right," she said, as if she hadn't the strength to hide her disappointment.

"Mrs. Morrow . . . Lily," Kate said, feeling trapped between the woman's grief and Tejeda's needs. "I'm sure Lieutenant Tejeda is already doing everything he can to help Sergeant Green."

Mrs. Morrow nodded. "Just ask him to imagine if it was his own son."

8

"Don't get no sand on my new clean floor," Rachel, the thrice-a-week cleaning lady, scolded Tejeda as he came through the back door. "Kate has me polishing the foyer now, so I don't have time to do this floor again."

"Yes, ma'am." Tejeda grinned. He kicked off his sandy Reeboks and dropped them outside, pausing for a long breath. The heat wave had devolved into cold, sticky fog, but he felt hot and prickly. The small headache he had brought home from the inquest now throbbed like an anvil chorus. And for once, a run on the beach hadn't helped.

"Dad?" Richie, his handsome son, came toward him through the utility room from the direction of the kitchen.

"I thought you had classes this afternoon?"

"You look great, Dad." Richie submitted to his father's habitual bear hug and squeeze. Tejeda held on longer than usual, trying to reconcile this bristly-faced man, who stood at least two inches taller than his own six-feet-two, with the boy he had sent away to college three years ago. Every time he saw Richie, which was fairly often, he noticed in his son quantum leaps toward adulthood. He missed living with him, being able to watch every nuance of his development. While he loved the tall, self-assured man Richie had become, he missed the boy he had been not so long ago.

Tejeda stepped back and grinned, but he had to swallow hard before he could talk. "So, what's new?"

"My roommate, Lance Lumsden?"

"Yeah?"

"He couldn't afford to fly home to Montana, so I brought him for the weekend," Richie said, bringing back images of pigeons with broken wings and stray kittens Tejeda regularly used to find hospitalized in the family garage. "Can he stay?"

"There's certainly room for one more in this inn," Tejeda said, wrapping an arm around Richie's muscular shoulders and walking him back toward the kitchen. "But check with Kate."

"I did." He opened the kitchen door. "She said okay."

Lance Lumsden, the Nordic-blond roommate, was sitting at the kitchen table with Trinh, polishing silver and trying to quiz her about her escape from Vietnam.

Tejeda held out a hand. "Nice to see you, Lance."

"Thanks for letting me come," Lance said, wiping his hand on a flannel cloth before extending it toward Tejeda. "Rich said you didn't mind the occasional stray."

"The more the merrier."

"Sergeant Green called." Trinh took a bead on him down the blade of a daggerous silver carving knife, looking for spots on the stainless blade. "Say he call back."

"Tell him I'm not here." Tejeda clapped Richie on the shoulder. "Think you two big strong men can help me put leaves in the dining table?"

"Sure." Richie held the swing door for his father and Lance.

"There's a gizmo here." Tejeda went over to the

massive mahogany table and groped the underside for the spring release. When he pressed it, the table popped open at the center.

"Speaking of strays, Dad." Richie picked up a polished table leaf and seemed to give it a lot of attention. Tejeda recognized the avoidance of eye contact and half-expected to find a puppy in a box somewhere. "Jena's family is going up to see her grandparents, but she has to stay down for a modeling job Friday. Any problem if she comes for dinner tomorrow?"

"Jena?"

"Jena Rummel."

"Little Jena Rummel from high school?" Tejeda said as he helped Lance fit the second leaf into the table.

Richie's cheeks took on color. "Jena and I have been seeing each other again."

"She's at Santa Barbara?" Tejeda asked.

"San Diego State."

"San Diego," Tejeda repeated. Richie had dated a lot of girls—his friends said, enviously, that he had a gift—but he had never been serious about anyone. Except Jena. Richie had never been able to be casual about Jena. Such a beautiful couple, Tejeda thought, slim, tawny-blond Jena and Richie, who was tall and dark-haired like himself, but with Cassie's fair Irish skin. He could still see them together, their heads bent close, oblivious of everything except each other. And then the young woman he held in his mind's eye turned and the smiling face he saw was Cassie's. He shuddered as if he had been caught cheating, and tried to push Cassie away. He hadn't seen Cassie for a long time, had hardly given her a thought since he had met Kate. So why, he wanted to know, was she suddenly crowding his thoughts?

Tejeda looked over at Richie. "San Diego is over two hundred miles from Santa Barbara."

"If we leave after our last lab section on Friday," Lance offered, apparently oblivious of Richie's scowl, "we can usually beat the traffic through L.A. and get to San Diego in four, five hours."

Tejeda put his hand over his throbbing temple. "We need to talk about the car."

"Okay," Richie sighed. "But can Jena come tomorrow?"

"Everyone will be here, Grandma, Nana, Aunt Teri."

"I know."

"If it's that important, then I guess she better come." Tejeda went over to the sideboard and picked up the place cards he had coerced Otis Washington's wife to make for him. "Make her a place card, and one for Lance."

Trinh came in from the kitchen carrying a towel full of silver. She glanced at Tejeda as she spread it on the sideboard next to him. "Now how many for dinner?"

"Let me see." He went through the stack of place cards and checked them off against the list Kate had given him over the coroner's telephone: himself, Kate, Theresa, Richie, his sister, Teri, her husband and two kids, his parents and grandmother, Reece and Lydia, Eddie Green and his son, now Jena and Lance. He stopped when he got to Trinh, unsure whether she would sit at the table with them or would serve. But she was on the list. He restacked the cards and handed them to her. "I count eighteen, Trinh. When you set the table, would you put these around?"

"Who go where?"

"Doesn't matter." He shrugged. He had made it through the inquest that morning without a single name gaffe because of the labels in front of each seat. With place cards, he hoped Thanksgiving dinner would be as easy.

He was thinking about ordering I.D. jewelry for

everyone for Christmas when Kate's cousin, Reece, came in from the hallway with Rachel hurrying behind him. Barefoot, in cutoffs and a starched, monogrammed dress shirt, Reece was struggling with a heavy pail and an armload of bright gold chrysanthemums.

"Kate told me the drones were around here some-where." Reece handed the flowers to Trinh and bent to set the pail on the Bokhara rug.

"Don't put that nasty thing down in here," Rachel ordered, sweeping in behind him. She snatched the pail and glared at him as she backed through the kitchen swing door, bending under the weight of the pail. "I don't know why everyone can't leave a person to finish cleaning through before they start messing up again."

"I counted those oysters, Rachel." Reece pointed an accusing finger at her. "And I know them all by name. I'll know if any are missing."

"Don't want no smelly oysters," Rachel muttered as she disappeared through the door. "Like eating snot."

"Give them a beer," Reece called. "And send one out for me."

"I get beer," Trinh said, hurrying toward the door. "Rachel gets in refrigerator, I never get her out."

"Did Trinh just tell a joke?" Reece asked. He pulled out two chairs, sat on one, and put his bare feet on the other. Reece seemed to be in his element here, Tejeda thought, so comfortable, easy with the hired help. Not that Tejeda felt uncomfortable living in Kate's house, but it was, he decided, comfortable like staying at a resort hotel.

"Reece, you know my son, Richie," Tejeda said. "This is his roommate, Lance."

"Rich has told me about you." Lance thrust a hand toward Reece. "He said you have a sixty-seven Keyo

Plastic Machine. Man, that's a real collector's item.
An antique.''

"It's just a surfboard." Reece looked up at Tejeda
with a grimace that pulled his freckles together. "God,
do I feel old."

"I'd love to try a Plastic." Lance had the grace to
seem chagrined. "Could we take your board out sometime this weekend?"

"It's too long for the waves on this beach," Reece
said. "Anyway, I don't recommend going in the water
here until Roger finds the rest of John Doe."

"He's not in the water," Tejeda said with the assurance that comes from experience. "Probably dumped
in a canyon somewhere. I doubt we'll ever find much
more of him than coyote droppings."

"Oh, shit." Lance shuddered.

Trinh came back in with a pair of beer bottles on a
tray, and two lemonades. "Sergeant Green called again.
I say you say you not here."

"Thanks." Tejeda could smell the sharp bitterness
from the mums on her hands as she gave him a glass
and a bottle of beer. He smelled chopped onions, too,
as she bustled back toward the kitchen.

Trinh had been a blur of activity all day, excited, he
knew, about her first Thanksgiving and helping Kate
to get ready. The entire house was abuzz with cleaning, deliveries, people in and out. The constant hum
of Rachel's vacuum, the heat in the room, and the
pressure he felt coming from Eddie all seemed to bear
down on him. He wanted to escape to the quiet upstairs, but he heard Kate's voice out in the hallway
and he needed to wait, to see her face and exorcise the
stray and unwanted images of Cassie.

He sat down next to Reece and took a sip of his
beer, then pressed the cold bottle against the scar on

his temple, as if this spot were the direct route to the source of the pain in his head.

"I thought you were resting." Kate appeared in the open door and gave him a worried glance. There were two men in the hallway behind her, both with their heads craned back awkwardly, apparently intent on the ceiling.

Reece nudged Tejeda. "How many rings does this circus have?"

"It's endless."

The older man—the architect overseeing Carl's house-restoration project and whose name Tejeda couldn't dredge to the surface—rubbed his neck as if he had a cramp. "German?" he asked.

"Scots or English," she said. She glanced again at Tejeda, then turned to the architect. "Could you come back later?"

The man sighed. "Not easily."

"Kate," Tejeda said, "it's okay. Come on in."

She hesitated before she led the two men into the dining room.

The architect stretched for a closer look at the ten-foot ceiling. "They look German."

"Could be," Reece chuckled. "But according to family legend, Kate's grandfather shipped these moldings as cover for a boatload of bootleg Scotch."

"Could have been a German craftsman, though." The second, younger man who had come in with Kate was making notes on the edge of the sketchpad he carried. Tejeda couldn't place him, but he knew for sure that, with his well-brushed beard and shoulder-length hair, he couldn't be the body-shaven Sean O'Shay Theresa would be bringing over for dessert tomorrow. The man dropped his head back and stared at the ceiling.

Both Lance and Richie, like suckers to the old practical joke, looked up too. But Tejeda's head hurt too much.

The bearded one glanced down long enough to display his disinterest in everyone. Without asking if it was okay, he pulled out a chair, kicked off his worn Top-Siders, and climbed up to trace the whorls and leaves carved in the dark oak with his index finger.

"These are the finest I've seen. Should be in a museum," he said, looking accusingly at Tejeda. "Not as old as the Spanish choir panels in the study, but better workmanship."

"Roger," Kate said, and then indicated the architect. "You remember Harry Miller. Harry, this is my cousin, Reece Sumner, Roger's son, Richard, and his roommate, Lance."

"How's it going?" Miller said, exchanging nods with them.

Kate indicated the bearded one. "This is Harry's construction foreman, Mike Rios."

Rios shrugged bare acknowledgment. Tejeda thought he worked awfully hard at his rudeness.

"What do you think, Mike?" Harry Miller asked.

"Take too long and cost too much to duplicate," Mike Rios said. "But we could make a poly-resin form and cast them in plaster. With the right finish, the effect would be close enough."

Tejeda turned to Kate. "Are we building something?"

"No. Harry asked to see our moldings," she said. "Carl wants his restoration to be authentic."

"Doesn't he have fancy moldings of his own?"

"Ruined by termites," she said. "Came from a colonial palace in Vera Cruz."

When Lance looked at her doubtfully, she smiled.

"Rum shipment," she said.

"What a great place." Lance nudged Richie. "Why didn't you tell me?"

"I didn't know."

"Your history profs haven't told you about Archibald Byrd?" Reece teased. "Kate's grandfather put a Prohibition wrinkle in the old triangle trade: rum, real estate, senators. By the time of repeal, he owned almost as much coastline as William Randolph Hearst."

Kate smiled. "Salt of the earth, my grandpa."

"Salty, anyway," Reece chuckled.

Rios was examining the mitered edges where two strips of molding met at the corner. He shook his dark head in disapproval. "See, the pattern's messed up here because this originally came from a much larger room." He turned his pad sideways and continued sketching, every movement crisp.

"They could have done a better job cutting it down," he said, getting down from the chair. "I'll make some adjustments in the molds, fix the pattern."

Miller seemed cheered. "It's a go, then?"

"I have to get some materials. Could start the molds tomorrow." He glanced at Kate. "You home in the afternoon?"

Reece laughed aloud. "Tomorrow is Thanksgiving."

Tejeda saw a flush rise under Rios' dark beard. But when he spoke, his voice was steady. "Friday morning, then?"

"You're presuming a lot," Kate said evenly. "I agreed to let you take a look. But I don't much want to be bothered by your workmen."

Rios challenged Miller. "Harry?"

Harry Miller seemed embarrassed, the normally aloof professional caught in something that smacked of passion. He took a deep breath and rubbed his aching neck before he made eye contact with Kate. "It's like a chain," he said. "If one of the three houses in your compound isn't up to standard, isn't authentic, then the value of the other two will be diminished."

"Is Carl planning to sell?" Reece asked.

Miller shook his head. "He hasn't confided in me."

Kate had crossed the room, away from Miller and Rios, as if removing herself from any taint of alliance with Carl and his plans. Tejeda held out his hand for her and she came to him. She stood behind his chair and put her hands on his shoulders, gently at first, her grip tightening as she spoke.

"You want authenticity?" she said. "Let me help you."

Both Miller and Rios seemed to relax, but her fingers held firm.

"There are eighteen rooms in this house," she said, "and twelve apiece in both of the others. The woodwork in every room, from floor to ceiling, is unique. Each represents camouflage for a different shipment of bootleg hooch made between 1920 and 1933. If you want authenticity, you'll go to Europe and buy the castle of some impoverished count, or the mansion of a bankrupt captain of industry, and dismantle it.

"Imitating this house might make Carl feel better, but it won't make his house authentic."

Mike Rios seemed not to be listening as he made another visual circuit around the ceiling. "Too expensive to go abroad," he said blandly. "Too time-consuming."

Reece threw his head back and laughed.

"If you can't make it to Europe, Mike," Tejeda said, "would you settle for some photographs?"

"Have to"—he shrugged—"if that's the best you can do for me."

Miller seemed relieved that nothing had erupted after all. "Flash would wipe out too much detail. Natural light's probably best in here in the morning."

Rios looked at Kate. "Friday morning about nine?"

"Someone should be around." She looked to Tejeda for confirmation. Then she said, "Eddie Green called. He said Arty Silver's attorney will let you talk to him Friday morning."

The room seemed suddenly filled with silence, making Tejeda's ears buzz ominously. Until he realized that Rachel had simply turned off the vacuum in the hall.

Kate put cool fingers against his face and looked at him closely. "You don't have to go with Eddie."

Mike Rios had his shoes back on. "Friday morning, then?"

"Fine," Kate said without taking her eyes from Tejeda. "Are you all right?" she asked him.

"Little headache." Tejeda smiled at her. He didn't want her to worry. With Miller and Rios going, and the cleaning apparently finished, there was quiet again and the panicky feeling was fading. Not preseizure euphoria, just calm. "Think I'll take a nap."

He tried to stand up, but there seemed to be nothing solid underfoot. When he grabbed for the table to break his fall, it slipped through his fingers like warm Jello-O. He could feel strong hands holding him, making him like a fixed point in a swirling miasma. He floated through darkness for what seemed like an age. Finally, when the room stopped spinning and he opened his eyes, he found himself lying on the floor with Richie's lap under his head.

Kate knelt beside him. Her face was ashen but she

smiled. "Want to finish your nap upstairs, or do you want to stay here for a while?"

He looked down at his hands, crossed over his chest like a corpse. "Where's my lily?"

She laughed. "Lilies are for Easter."

9

Kate eased up from the bed beside Tejeda, hoping not to disturb him. She couldn't see his eyes under the cold towel over his forehead, but from the slow, regular way he was breathing, she thought he had finally gone to sleep. The medication she had given him made him dopey, but he fought it. For the last month he had been having trouble giving in to sleep, as if, she thought, he were afraid he would never wake up again.

The antique bed frame creaked under her.

"Maybe I should call Arty's attorney," he mumbled.

She leaned over him. "Are you dreaming?"

"Just thinking."

"How's your head?"

"Okay." He moved only enough to peel the towel away. His eyes were closed. "Want to take a drive down the coast later?"

"If you feel up to it."

"Yeah." The word was hardly more than a deep sigh. She kissed his cheek and watched his face, but he was almost frighteningly still. Probably the medication, she thought. He rarely admitted to needing even an aspirin, but he had taken a precautionary dose of the antiseizure drug without complaint. If sleep scared him, what horror must he have for the convulsions that twice now had knocked him out? The doctor had tried to reassure him; they were only a transitory aftermath of the injury to his head. If he took it easy, watched for the warning signs, there would probably be no more. She listened to his slow breathing; she knew that for him, *probably* wasn't assurance enough.

Kate edged toward the side of the bed.

"Richie has a girl." His voice startled her.

"He told me. Jena Rummel. I know her family."

"You do?" He opened his eyes a slit and looked at her suspiciously. "How?"

"The usual. Yacht Club. Symphony Guild. Cancer Society. Her aunt and I were in school together."

"Does all that mean money?"

"Lots of it."

He was quiet for a moment, apparently thinking this over. Then he stretched the towel back over his head and pressed it in place. "Tough break."

She laughed because it was better than crying. "Be amazed, what obstacles love can overcome."

"Maybe." He seemed to be drifting off, losing his battle with sleep. "When you're young."

She wasn't sure whether he was aware of what he had said, but she still felt stung. When they had first gotten together, the rich-girl/poor-boy business had seemed only a minor hurdle, a sort of oddity for him to explore. Increasingly, as they skirted making a lasting commitment to each other, the issue of her money and his lack of it had escalated toward cold war. She had begun to think of his attitude as a form of bigotry she didn't know how to fight. What, exactly, did he want? she wondered. For her to seek forgiveness for having inherited a pot of money? Or three pots, if she counted all of her benefactors so far.

Sometimes she wished she had come from a more fertile family, for lots of blood relatives to divide the booty among. Then she thought about Carl, and his

strange campaign to be recognized as of the blood.
For a fleeting moment she considered giving up the
fight and turning everything over to Carl. But it was
only a fleeting moment; she didn't mind a pitched
battle, and in this one money was only a side issue.

Tejeda didn't stir this time as she slipped away from
his side. She left her shoes beside the bed and walked
softly in stocking feet toward the door. As she turned
the knob, she stopped to look at him again.

He was lying flat on his back, his long legs crossed
at the ankles. He had started to snore softly, but still
he reached one hand to the side and patted the inden-
tation she had left on the quilt beside him.

Dammit, she thought, watching his profile in the
soft light, of all the battles she had fought during her
lifetime, and there had been plenty, none had had
stakes higher than this one.

"Kate, what's wrong with my dad?" Richie was
waiting for her in the hall outside the bedroom door.
Behind him, a shadow in the deep pile of the carpet
defined the path he had been pacing. "He told me he
was better."

"He is better."

"He passed out," Richie pressed. "Dad passed right
out."

"He stood up too fast and got dizzy."

"Tell me the truth, Kate. How is he?"

"The real truth? The life-and-death truth?"

"Please."

"Okay. But come away from the door."

From the look on Richie's face as they walked down
the hall, she knew he had prepared himself for major
bad news. What could she tell him he didn't already
know? Since the injury, in spite of all the reassurance
the doctors repeatedly gave them, both she and Richie
had lived every moment with the fear that something

in Tejeda's patched-together head would burst and they would lose him. Whatever their fears, she knew that treating him as if he were an invalid was the worst thing they could do to him.

Kate looked up into the face that twenty-some years ago could have been his father's, they were so much alike. She took a deep breath and smiled. "The only thing wrong with your father is, he still thinks he's Superman."

"Come on."

"Honest to God, Richie, he's fine. Better than we ever expected. He's supposed to take it easy, but you know your father; he's into everything. Eddie Green has him involved with the Wally Morrow killing. Then there's all the fuss about Thanksgiving." The front doorbell chimed and she turned toward it, listening for Trinh's quick footsteps to cross the foyer downstairs. "Do you think I should call everyone and cancel dinner tomorrow?"

"He'd only fuss more," Richie said. "Dad gets off on family and holidays."

The doorbell was chiming again. For years she hadn't paid attention to the ridiculous song her grandfather had it play—the first bar of "Katy, K-K-K-Katy"—but now it seemed outrageously out of place, childish.

"Have you seen Trinh?" she asked.

"She went with Reece to pick up Theresa. Want me to get the door?"

"I'll go," Kate said, annoyed at the interruption. "Your dad never sleeps very long. Why don't you go sit with him? Talk to him when he wakes up. Maybe you can keep him quiet for a while longer."

He caught her hand as she passed him. His smile was shy, very appealing, and very like his father's when he looked down into her face. "I don't know how to thank you."

"No need," she said.

"You must love him a lot, to see him through this mess."

"I must," she said with a smile.

"If my mom . . ." Richie started, but got no further. Though he hadn't moved, she saw him brace as if some heaviness had descended.

"Don't be too hard on your mother."

Whoever was at the door was now insistently knocking and repeatedly chiming "K-K-K-Katy."

"Never ends, does it?" She took her hand from Richie's firm grasp, then headed down the long staircase.

"I'm coming," she called as she crossed the foyer. Her stocking feet slipped on the marble floor as she tried to hurry. By the time she reached the door, she had moved from annoyance to anger, thinking that any sensible person would have either gone away by now or gone back to the gate and called the house over the intercom to see if anyone was at home.

Through the stained-glass windows in the double doors she could see the watery outline of a not-very-tall person on the other side.

The windows pictured an elaborate clipper ship at full mast, outrunning a naval frigate across stormy seas—a family joke about her grandfather's occupation. The colored glass was barely opaque, except for the clear tip of a wind-whipped wave, and through this Kate saw an elbow clad in workshirt blue, the same chambray Mike Rios had been wearing earlier when he inspected the ceiling moldings.

Kate flung open the double doors, prepared to ream out Mike Rios for causing so much racket.

Her ferocity seemed to startle the woman standing on the steps. The woman took a half-step backward, clutching at the shark tooth suspended from a long

silver chain around her neck. Then she gathered herself and forced a polite smile, but Kate could see the
effort it took.

What had Lillian Morrow called the parent support
group? Something like Silver Threads, she thought.
She suspected that this woman was a second envoy
from the group; she shared a certain wounded look
with Wally Morrow's mother.

The woman had left an ancient Volkswagen bus
parked in the courtyard. Kate looked at it while she
waited for the pitch to come, the plea for Tejeda's
help with one investigation or another. She liked the
bus. It looked like a throwback to the sixties, a thick
crust of road grime nearly obliterating the Indian sun
symbol painted on the passenger door. It seemed of a
piece with the woman, with her long cotton print skirt,
squaw boots, and lashings of silver and turquoise jewelry around her neck. She was so slender and willowy
that she could have been a young hippie girl fresh out
of a time machine. Except that her doll-like face,
wreathed in a shoulder-length tangle of steaked gray-
blond hair, had been cruelly abused by the elements.
The hazy sun seemed to hurt her pale eyes.

"I followed a workman through the gate," the woman
said. As she turned slightly, her face moved into
shadow, and in the softer light Kate could see how
pretty the woman had once been, very fair and delicate. Kate looked again at the bus, at its New Mexico
plates, and knew suddenly who had come to call. She
almost shut the door.

"Is it okay if I park there?" the woman asked.

"It's okay," Kate said. The words sounded brusque
to her, and she wanted them back. She had hoped that
when this moment came she would seem cool, poised,
charming beyond words. Instead she stood there inar-
ticulate, wearing cotton socks with a hole in the toe,

old shorts, and one of Tejeda's misshapen T-shirts. Her hair was still ruffled from sharing a pillow with him while he napped. Then she pictured him, his lower lip pouched out like a petulant child's as he slept, his arm across her place in the bed.

Kate pulled herself a little taller, offered her hand to the woman, and smiled. "Are you Cassie?"

She hesitated before she accepted Kate's hand. "Kate?"

"You've had a long trip." Kate's eye was drawn again to the dusty VW. Theresa had spoken to her mother on the telephone the day before yesterday. In New Mexico. Cassie must have started immediately afterward and driven straight through. Surely there were telephones along the way. "We didn't know you were coming."

"I didn't know myself," Cassie stammered. "My job . . ." she began, then started over, the words pouring out in a nervous rush. "The organization I work for markets native Hopi artworks to galleries. There's a major show in Phoenix scheduled for this weekend, but there was a delivery foul-up and no one else was available—you know how it is around the holidays—so I decided the only way I could get the stuff to Phoenix was to deliver it myself. Then I thought, since I was going that far, why not go on to L. A., follow up on some galleries we'd made contact with."

Cassie stopped suddenly. "I'd like to see Theresa. Is she here?"

"Not yet." Kate stepped back into the foyer. "But Richie's home. He's upstairs with his father. Would you like to come in?"

"Please." There were tears in her eyes, but she seemed to be winning her fight against them. As Kate led her through the foyer and into the book-lined study, Cassie took in everything quickly, dismissively.

Kate recognized the reaction, a stubborn refusal to be impressed by what she saw. It told her a great deal about Cassie.

"How long are you staying in the area?" Kate asked as she offered a seat.

"I don't know." Cassie sat stiffly on the edge of a deep velvet chair. "So much depends on the children."

"You must be tired. Can I offer you something?"

"I would love a cold drink."

Kate opened the mirror-lined bar camouflaged among the bookcases. As she got out glass, ice, ginger ale, she could see Cassie behind her, studying her. The room was filled with sunlight from the French doors. The brightness washed the color from Cassie's gray eyes, making them seem glasslike, disconcertingly huge and soulless. Soulless like Lillian Morrow's, Kate thought as she handed the ginger ale to her.

"You're not what I expected," Cassie said.

"I could say the same."

"Roger is doing well, isn't he? More like his old self." She sipped the ginger ale. "I can tell by the way he sounds over the phone."

"He's fine." Kate sat down opposite Cassie, wondering now about her ulterior motives; she hadn't asked about her children yet. "He's getting antsy, though. He misses his work."

"Don't let him go back," Cassie warned.

"Roger has a mind of his own."

"You'll lose him. The same way I did. He'll give himself to a case with more passion than most men give their mistresses. And there will be nothing left for you."

"Excuse me." Kate got to her feet. "I'll tell Richie you're here."

She was halfway across the foyer, headed for the stairway, before she remembered to breathe. What

Cassie said was true; she had seen Tejeda passionately consumed by a case. But it had been Kate's case, and it had brought them together. Somewhere in the back of her mind she had tucked away any notion that when the case was finally resolved, the injuries healed, Tejeda would move on.

As she passed a side table, she saw a puddle of water growing under a vase of mums. She mopped it with the toe of her sock and then gave the foyer and the rooms opening off it a quick inspection; she was in no hurry to get Richie, to start the cycle of confusion that Cassie's arrival had made inevitable.

Trinh and Rachel had done a beautiful job on the house, she thought, everything polished and fresh and brightened with arrangements of fall flowers, cattails, and leaves. There was expectation here, subdued excitement for the holiday.

Kate reached into an arrangement and snapped off a wilted mum that spoiled its perfection, and thought about Cassie and her intentions. She crushed the mum in her palm. Why, after two years, had she come now? Had she planned her grand reentrance for Thanksgiving, making sure she had a full audience? Or had she simply, and naturally, needed to be with her family?

Kate began to feel Cassie's presence, threatening her in a way she couldn't yet define. Sooner or later, she had known from the beginning, Cassie was destined to reappear, just like the rest of Wally Morrow's body.

Lance came in from the kitchen passageway, silent on bare feet, his damp hair finger-combed, a red beach towel wrapped around his middle.

"How's the water?" she asked.

"Cold." He fell into step beside her. "Reece loaned me a board so I could try the surf in the bay."

"What do you think?"

"Pretty wimpy." He shrugged. "I don't get it—when I was a kid, there was a five-foot curl here."

"Probably no breakwater then." She stopped. "I thought your family came from Montana."

"They do," he said, but she had noticed the pause before he answered.

"When were you in Santa Angelica?"

He seemed embarrassed, as if caught in a lie. "I was born in Santa Angelica."

"Is that so bad? I was born here too."

"No, it's not bad. It's the reason we moved away that's bad."

"Why?"

"My older brother died. I wanted to finish junior high with my friends, but my parents couldn't take living here anymore. So we moved to Montana."

"I'm sorry," Kate said. "Was there an accident?"

"My brother was a Marine."

"I'm sorry," she said again, touching his arm.

"It's okay. It's been a long time."

From the corner of her eye, she saw Cassie standing in the study door. She gave Lance's damp arm a squeeze. "Excuse me, I need to get Richie."

"Yeah, sure," he said. He hung back as she walked away.

As she walked, Kate was doing a little quick arithmetic in her head. Lance had been in junior high maybe seven or eight years ago. What had the Marines been involved with then? She stopped in her tracks and turned to him.

"Where did your brother die, Lance?"

"I don't know."

Cassie had taken a step into the foyer.

"How can you not know where your brother died?" Kate pressed.

Sadness dropped over him like a cowl. "I don't know where he was killed, but they found his body here, in the bay. His head, anyway."

The sound Cassie made was somewhere between a cough and a sob. Lance glanced at her and his face flushed.

"He was murdered?" Kate asked.

Lance nodded. "He's counts seventeen and eighteen against Arty Silver."

"Does Richie know about your brother?" Kate asked.

"Only that he was killed," Lance said.

"If Arty Silver killed your brother, you had to know about Richie's father."

Lance straightened himself and looked at her almost with defiance. "Look, I'm not using Rich. I heard at school—at Santa Barbara—who he was, so I got close to him. Just to keep posted about Silver. If he ever got out, on a technicality or something, I wanted to be there."

Kate saw Cassie dart toward the front door and was afraid she was going to bolt. But after a few steps she stopped, turned, and fled back into the study.

"I'm sorry," Lance said. "I'll leave if you want me to."

"No," Kate said, watching Cassie's shadow cross the study wall. "I think this is where you belong."

10

At first, when Tejeda looked out the window, he thought he was still dreaming; the scene below had to be a continuation of the bizarre, convoluted stream of images that were always part of his drugged sleep. He kept watching them on the beach, his former wife and his two kids playing chicken with the surf. Too bizarre even for Dilantin.

Where had she come from? His head felt foggy and he couldn't remember her name. He could remember her naked: thin and naked, pregnant and naked, sun-blistered and naked. He just couldn't remember her name and he could never let her know that he couldn't. She had warned him too often what would happen if he didn't quit police work.

He started to panic at the out-of-control feeling not remembering gave him. But he caught himself, forced his breathing to slow, sat down, and concentrated on tying his shoes. It helped, but not enough. He had to find out her name before he could confront her.

"Kate!" he called as he ran down the back stairs. There was no answer. He found the housekeeper in the utility room ironing dinner napkins and watching a TV talk show.

"Ah . . ." he started, but no name followed. "Ah . . ."

"Trinh," she said, pointing to herself.

"Right. Trinh. Where's Kate?"

Trinh shrugged. "She got call and went out."

"Damn." He pounded his fists together. "Look, did you meet my wife?"

"Yes. Very nice lady."

"Good. What's her name?"

"Mrs. Tejeda."

"No. Her other name."

Again Trinh shrugged. "Mrs. Roger?"

"You don't know where Kate went?"

"Just out." She snapped another napkin from the laundry basket. "She was in hurry and she didn't take purse."

"Thanks." He grinned at her. "You'd make a great detective."

"Better than cook?" he heard her call after him as he ran out through the back door.

The estate covered so much ground and had so many buildings that he had learned a long time ago that the fastest way to find out whether Kate had left the compound was to count the cars in the garage, see if one was missing. Looking through the garage window, he saw her three: the Jag, the Rolls, and her uncle's Mercedes. And an extra, his own gray Cutlass, back from Santa Barbara with Richie. He didn't know why, exactly, but he felt relieved to have everyone home and safe. Then it occurred to him that someone might have come and picked up Kate. She could certainly take care of herself. Still, he wished he knew where she was.

From where he stood, he could see the top of Byrd Rock, white-capped from sea-gull deposits. If his ex-wife had heard anything about Wally Morrow, she wouldn't be down there.

He tucked his shirt into the top of his cords and set off along the walkway that led to the beach stairs.

Except for the gap in his head where his wife's name should be, he decided that he had no reason to put off at least saying hello to her. Best to get this first meeting out of the way while Kate wasn't around.

The feeling had nothing to do with Kate, really. It was him. He couldn't imagine ever being happy again with anyone but Kate. That didn't stop him from carrying a load of guilt, the living root of an idea planted in his childhood that he was entitled to only one spouse, till death and all that. Maybe he could have tried harder, somehow held his marriage together. It was too late to do anything now. And had been since he'd met Kate.

On the beach below, his kids were walking with their mother. From the way she was gesturing, she seemed to be doing all the talking, her hands punching the air for emphasis. So things were okay, he thought. When she was upset, she grew sullen and quiet. When she was really mad or hurt, she took off.

So maybe this was a good time to drop in on them, he thought. Before she got up a head of steam.

He lost sight of the beach as he passed the landscaping around the gazebo that overhung the bluff. He dismissed the first movement he saw inside the gazebo as oleander blowing in the breeze, until he heard shuffling steps and something like gasping sobs.

"Hello, in there," he said, and startled when Kate came flying out. She didn't slow or seem to notice when the tail of her sweater snagged on a hedge and tore. She just ran.

He ran to her and pulled her against him; he had seen Kate upset before, but never like this. Something had happened, and all he could think of was his ex-wife and what she was capable of doing.

He patted Kate's heaving back. "It's okay, babe."

"Kate," she gasped, and he almost laughed, the reminder was such a reflex reaction.

"I *know* your name. What happened to you? Did she say something?" He let out a long breath. "Oh, God, Kate. What's her name?"

She wiped her red-rimmed eyes and looked up at him in puzzlement. "Who?"

"The mother of my children."

"What are you talking about?"

"Never mind. Just tell me what happened."

"Come with me." Holding on to him, she seemed calmer as she led him through the oleander hedge and back to the gazebo. She talked all the way, gasping for breath. "The department secretary called while you were sleeping. Said someone had left a message for me."

As soon as he smelled it, he tried to hold her back. But she wouldn't be held.

"Said I could find my baby in the gazebo. I didn't know what it meant, so I came out here to look." She went straight to a wicker rocker in the far corner of the gazebo and picked up a bundle wrapped in a fuzzy yellow receiving blanket printed with ducks and giraffes. She brought it to him as if she were passing off a wet baby. "Take a look."

He took it from her and set it on the window ledge, trying to close his nose against the sweet stench. "You shouldn't have touched it."

"I'm sorry." She folded back the top of the blanket anyway. "Who is it?"

Where the baby's head would be there was a hand, or rather a claw, tinged the peculiar green-white of decomposing human flesh. Its heavy plastic wrapping made it seem artificial, but the smell made it obvious this was no joke prop.

Tejeda tweezed an edge of the blanket and peeled it

away to see how much arm was attached to the hand. It was all wrapped in a clear plastic bag that ended in a wire twist-tie just about where the elbow should have been. The forearm was thickly muscled and covered with curly dark hair.

Kate's hand on his shoulder was admirably steady. "Smells."

"Who left the message for you to come out here?" he asked.

"I don't know. Winnie took the call at school and just passed it on."

"What time?"

"Winnie called here maybe ten, fifteen minutes ago. I don't know when *she* got the message." Her breath caught as she glanced at the arm. "Is it Wally Morrow?"

"Could be." He flipped the blanket back over it, leaving only one retracted finger showing. "Look, someone has to stay here with Junior, and someone has to go inside and call Eddie Green. Your pick."

"How's your head?"

"Fine."

"Then, if it's all the same to you, I'll go."

He walked with her out into the fresh air, but the heavy odor clung to the inside of his nose and throat. He had a sudden craving for one of Vic Spago's cigars. "Was Winnie going away for the weekend?"

"I don't know."

"Ask Eddie to track her down in a hurry. I don't want to wait until Monday to talk to her."

"All right."

"Kate." He reached out for her but didn't want to touch her; his hands felt polluted. "You're a brick."

"No I'm not. I'm scared to death."

He smiled. "Me too."

"Liar." She wrapped her arms around him. "Can you let Eddie take over?"

"It's his case."

"So you say. There are a few things I have to tell you."

"Like what?"

"I'll go call Eddie first." She kissed his cheek before she disengaged herself. "We can talk later."

"Tell Eddie to hurry," he called after her. "It'll be dark in another hour."

She started down the walk, but turned and called back to him. "Cassie. Your ex-wife's name is Cassie."

"Thanks." "Cassie" didn't quite register, but it would do. He probably had some sort of pet name for her that was better forgotten.

Watching Kate jog across the lawn toward the house, he thought how much worse this scene would have been if Cassie had been sent to the gazebo instead of Kate. To make sure she was still down on the beach with the kids, he walked to the edge of the bluff and squatted out of sight in a stand of eucalyptus trees. If they saw him, they might come up. He didn't want them anywhere near here until Eddie Green had taken charge of the remains.

He crushed a handful of dry eucalyptus leaves between his palms and held them up to his face, using their pungent oil as an antidote to the smell of rotting corpse, and watched his family like a voyeur. The scene on the beach held no nostalgia. Richie and Theresa had grown so much since he had last seen them with their mother that what he saw was three adults in conversation rather than a mother and two children.

They were sitting out of the wind now, sheltered behind an outcropping of Byrd Rock. Cassie had her skirt fanned out around her as if she needed a lot of personal space. Richie and Theresa sat close together; such a change from all the years when any touch between them inevitably led to a slugfest.

The kids seemed okay, he thought. Theresa didn't have her head bowed, so she wasn't crying. Richie wasn't pacing. And Cassie was still there. Miracle of all miracles, the reunion hadn't knocked anyone flat. Yet.

He put a couple of leaves in his shirt pocket and left them, feeling relatively comfortable that they would stay put for a while longer.

There was a variety of footprints on the gazebo's wooden floor, and he tried to step only where he could see the prints of his own shoes. Much of the case against Arty Silver had come from the forensic laboratory —hair, fibers, dirt samples—and he wanted extra care taken here. The first order of business, he felt, was proving conclusively, and quickly, whether or not what was going on here had any possible connection to Arty.

Tejeda folded the blanket away from the plastic-covered arm and bent for a closer look.

The coroner's report had listed Wally Morrow's height as five-feet-eleven. Tejeda didn't know where that measurement had come from: the Marines, his mother, or the gaps between the few vertebrae Vic had to work with. Whatever Morrow's actual height, there was general agreement that he was somewhat taller than average and fairly slender.

Tejeda measured the forearm against his own, and it came up both shorter and thicker. This was hardly scientific method. But until the forensic pathologist had stretched this human fragment across her osteometric board and made a pronouncement about its owner's height, he would tell anyone who asked his opinion that this man had been significantly shorter than young Morrow, maybe by as much as five or six inches, and was heavily built.

The cut end of the arm was difficult to see because

the plastic was bunched into the wire twist. Didn't matter too much, he thought, because what he didn't see told him plenty.

First, there was no apparent blood, not even pink ooze. He guessed from the condition of the plastic bag that the arm had only recently been wrapped: the plastic looked clean, there was no film on the inside from the outgassing of decomposition, and no discoloration. The skin didn't seem to stick to the plastic as it would if the arm had been inside for very long, the way rotting chicken sticks to supermarket wrap.

There were other details that would help identify the corpse if fingerprints failed. The nails were clean and unchipped, freshly manicured. He couldn't see how callused the palm was because of the way the fingers curled over it, but he suspected that the bulky brachioradialis muscle owed more to stevedoring than weight lifting.

He examined the blanket and had to chuckle. Maybe the one professional benefit of having been abandoned by his wife was that now, just by looking, he could tell that the blanket had been laundered a number of times. Yet that small fact meant the origins of the blanket would be harder to trace, since it could have come out of an attic box, a thrift store in Cleveland, or been stolen from a dryer in a laundromat at any time during the last ten or fifteen years. And who would remember one faded little yellow blanket?

"Whew! That your stink, Roger?" Vic Spago lumbered down the gazebo path with a heavy black case in each hand, trailing a plume of smoke from his cheroot.

"You got here fast," Tejeda said. "Where's Spud?"

"Up at the house getting an earful from the girlfriend."

"What is she telling him?"

"Dunno. They sent me out here." Spago put his

cases down and made an elaborate survey of the gazebo. "What's this, a bandstand?"

"No. It's a summerhouse. A gazebo."

"I don't know much about the arrangements up
here in high-class heaven, 'cuz I've been invited to
visit you exactly two times." Spago inhaled a lungful
of smoke and leaned over the plastic-wrapped arm.
"Two bodies, two visits."

Tejeda smiled. "What are you doing for dinner
tomorrow?"

"Going to my mother-in-law's." He put his glasses
on and talked while he studied the arm. "But I'm free
Tuesday."

"So come."

"Okay if I bring Spud and Otis and a deck of
cards?"

"Sure."

"About seven?"

"Fine."

"Good." Otis had taken a lighted magnifying glass
from one of his cases and held it over the fingernails.
"How long has this been here?"

"I don't know. Kate found it about twenty, twenty-
five minutes ago."

"And it was here in the window?"

"No. She found it in the rocker and carried it over
here."

"Bad girl." Spago didn't look up from his glass. "If
this goes on much longer, we'll have to give her a
basic course in police procedure. Hand me that camera, will you?"

Tejeda played assistant while Vic Spago spent three
rolls of film on the arm, the rocker, and every inch of
the gazebo. They were marking the area off with police-
line tape when the white mobile forensics laboratory
van came bouncing across the lawn toward them.

Eddie Green bounded from the front seat and cut Tejeda out of the massing crowd of technicians. "We have to talk."

"Something Kate told you?"

"No. She'll tell you all that herself. Let's go into my private office."

While Spago's forensic team set up mobile floodlights and began dusting for prints, vacuuming for fibers, Eddie gripped Tejeda by the arm and marched him out of the circle of activity.

"How far we going, Spud?" Tejeda asked when they had reached the top of the beach stairs. "Maybe I should have packed a bag."

Eddie stopped. "Tell me the truth—how are you?"

"I'm okay. Why? Did Kate say something?"

"What, you two have a fight or something? You keep asking about Kate."

"Spud," Tejeda said slowly, "you have ten seconds to tell me what's on your mind."

"The Police Commission met this afternoon."

"Yeah? So?"

"So they voted to cut off your disability pay unless you stay off the case."

"We have more than one case going here. They mention any case in particular?"

"Yeah. Any case." Eddie jammed his hands in his pockets and slouched as if he had an elephant on his back. "They said that if you're well enough to make press statements for the coroner, you should be well enough to come back to work."

"Or I should shut up, right?" Tejeda asked softly as he clapped Eddie on the back. "They may be right."

"It's my fault. I asked you to chime in at the inquest this morning to help Otis finagle more budget. And maybe that worked for us—the City Council's been fielding calls and wires all day from taxpayers demanding that more be done about the killing. But for you I think it backfired. Couple of councilmen are really pissed because giving more to us means pulling back some of the gang and drug task force. And Thanksgiving is a heavy media weekend."

"So what are my options?" Tejeda asked.

"All these politicos really want is some attention. Their problem with you is that whatever you do anymore is heavy media," Eddie said. "So I think you have two choices. One, you take Kate on a trip around the world and stay away until the dust settles. Two, you come back to work full-time, jump into the investigation with both feet, and invite certain councilmen to stand with you at the photo opportunities."

"I'll have to think about it." Tejeda chuckled. "Of course, I might come back if I could get Richie and Theresa to stand in front of the cameras with us. We need a good picture for the family Christmas cards."

"You're incorrigible." Cassie's voice cut through the general buzz of activity and unnerved him. She had been eavesdropping from the stair landing. "Any sensible person would have had enough."

"Hi, Cassie." Tejeda ignored her scolding and opened his arms to her. "How've you been?"

"Oh, Roger." She came to him for a hug. He ran his hands down her back, taking a sort of inventory, or looking for the on switch. He couldn't seem to find it. He was surprised how little residual feeling he had. He remembered, too clearly sometimes, their tender moments together, that he had loved her. But this woman in his arms was difficult to connect with the Cassie in his memory. Now she was just another woman. The scent of her wasn't even familiar.

Cassie took a step back. "You've no right to look so good."

"Hey, Cassie." Eddie seemed nonplussed but he

composed himself enough to stick his hand out to her. "Didn't know you were back."

"Just arrived. How's Libby?"

"We split up last year," Eddie said. He seemed as embarrassed as she did. "Excuse me, I have to get back. Hope to see you before you leave, Cass."

"You'll see her at dinner tomorrow," Tejeda said.

"Will I?" she asked.

"Of course. Tomorrow's Thanksgiving."

"Well, then." Eddie shuffled his feet a bit more. "Until tomorrow."

"Nice to see you again, Spud," she said.

"Yeah. See you tomorrow." He punched Tejeda's shoulder. "Until you decide, staying away means don't even help Kate serve coffee to the crew over there."

"Thanks for the warning."

Eddie turned and walked away into the circle of bright lights around the gazebo.

It was nearly dusk, but there was enough light coming from Spago's portable floodlights for Tejeda to get a good look at Cassie. He didn't like what she had done to her hair, it was an uncontrolled mane of permed kinks, but he liked that what she had done was none of his business. Otherwise, she looked fine, a little older, but fit, healthy. If she seemed nervous, he thought, it was only because of the uncertainty of the moment and not because she was ready for another emotional collapse.

"Where are Richie and Theresa?" he asked.

"They went for a walk. Richie said his girlfriend lives down by the marina."

"You talked to the kids for a long time. Everything okay?"

"They're great, Roger. You've done a good job."

"So have they."

"I know." She looked away. "I expected them to be angry with me. But they seem . . . They seem very mature and accepting."

"Cassie, they're mad as hell at you. Just give them time to get used to you again and they'll tell you all about it." He gazed off down the beach, looking for some sign of them. After what had happened in the gazebo, he didn't want Richie and Theresa out in the dark, even together. When he turned back, he caught Cassie staring at him.

"How long are you staying?" he asked.

"I have some time off from work, but I had forgotten how expensive everything is in California."

"Save your money. Our old house is vacant. You might as well stay there."

"I don't know."

"The house is half yours, Cass."

"I guess I still have a lot to sort out."

"Yeah." He had noticed how many times she said "I." Maybe it had always been that way; he couldn't remember.

"Does Theresa get along well with Kate?"

"They're good friends."

"I wondered. Theresa didn't seem to know anything about the party tonight."

"What party?" he asked.

"We were watching the caterers set up from the beach."

"What caterers?"

Cassie shivered and wrapped her arms around herself. "Maybe I made a mistake coming back like this. I think I'm in the way."

"Dammit, Cassie." He wheeled on her. "Did you hear what Eddie said to me about going back to work?"

She nodded. "Most of it."

"As I see it, you have the same two choices Eddie

gave me. You can either hop it back to New Mexico and stay there. Or you can jump back into this family with both feet. You call it. If you're ready, you can be Mom again. Or you can go back to being a stranger. But no more hovering around the edges, grilling them over the telephone like some long-distance voyeur. It's too confusing for the kids."

"What about you?" she said.

"I don't figure in this except as a sideline coach. You call it. Are you in? Or out?"

She was looking off toward Kate's house. "What time is dinner tomorrow?"

"Three."

"I need to think. Tell the kids I'll see them tomorrow. Now, you go tend to your guests before Kate comes looking for you."

"What guests?" He turned to see what she was looking at. The portable floodlights and yellow garlands of police tape made the gazebo and the lawn around it look very festive. There was quite a crowd now, loud voices, some laughter. But the trays coming out of the white van didn't carry fancy hors d'oeuvres or cocktails.

"Look again, Cassie," he said. "There's no caterer. Just the coroner. And his guest of honor is in no shape for a lawn party."

11

"You said, 'Let's take a little drive down the coast, clear our heads.' " Kate slid her hand from the gearshift knob to Tejeda's knee. "I was thinking maybe Laguna. This is Oceanside."

Tejeda put his hand over hers and moved it further up his thigh. "Two blocks ahead on the right. There's a parking lot in back."

"You said, 'Let's get a drink.' I'm thinking candle-light, groping under the table." The Jag purred to about 3500 rpm before she took her hand from his to shift into third. "But a gay bar?"

He laughed softly. "We'll grope later. And talk. I heard you gave Spud an earful. Anyway, you'll like Clyde's. Be a new experience for you."

"I've been to a gay bar before," she said defensively.

"Finocchio's doesn't count," he said.

"No, a *real* gay bar."

"Yeah? Where?"

She slowed for the light. "Berlin."

"Berlin?" he mocked. "East or West?"

"You know, that's the third crack you've made about my sheltered past since we left the freeway."

"Third crack, huh?" he said. "But who's counting?"

She pushed his shoulder. "You want to take a taxi home?"

"No. I only have twenty bucks in my pocket."

"Keep that in mind," she said as she pulled into traffic.

Traffic was heavy for a Wednesday night, especially in the off-season. Though there were sprinklings of civilians, the sidewalk traffic for the most part seemed to be very young men with very thick necks and very little hair. She had to keep her eyes open: a surprising number of pedestrians careened out into the street from between parked cars or tilted into walls as if they had only a tenuous relationship with either gravity or the sidewalk. The yellow sodium lights made them all look jaundiced.

Kate had found Oceanside to be an odd combination of beach resort and military town. California Highway 1, which did duty as Main Street, split at the north end of town. One branch turned into a state-beach parking lot, the other ended abruptly at the guarded entrance gates to the vast Camp Pendleton Marine Base.

Kate drove past Beach Mania Custom Surfboards, tucked into a slot between a karate studio and an enormous all-night laundry advertising military alterations, and wondered how peacefully this coexistence worked.

"Eddie told me about the Police Commission hearing," she said, interrupting Tejeda's silence. "Does this trip to Clyde's mean you've made a decision about going back to work?"

"I just needed some air." He pointed toward the right ahead. "If Clyde's lot is full, you can park next door at the dry cleaner's."

Clyde's stood by itself in the middle of its block, an unadorned green-stucco square surrounded on three sides by a parking lot jammed with souped-up pickup trucks and macho little Samurais. Kate pulled into the lot and found a space near the building's back door.

As she got out of the Jag, she could hear loud country music and the peculiar deep bass of men's voices when there were no women's voices to temper the sound.

Unlike other bars she had passed along the street, here there was no slopover of noisy patrons onto the sidewalk and street in front. The men she saw coming and going, most of them wearing tight Levi's and boots of one sort or another, were a surprisingly subdued group.

Tejeda put an arm around her as they walked toward the front. "Good place to look for a guy."

"If you *are* a guy." She reached for the brass lasso that served as the door handle.

He pulled her toward him, his face washed yellow under the street lights, and started to say something, but two well-muscled men in matching Stetson hats pushed through the door past them. Anything Tejeda had intended to say was lost in the noise pouring from the open door.

The barroom inside was well-lit and heavy with smoke, sweat, cologne, and the scent of leather. Tejeda held her by the hand and opened a wedge through the crowd as he made their way toward the bar at the far side.

Kate had expected some of the decadent, flamboyant display she had seen in Berlin. But this was a group of jocks, most of them young, many with military sidewall haircuts, whose dress tended toward macho-western or weekend bike club. Nothing that would turn heads on the street. She had the sense that there was enough testosterone loose in the air to bottle.

The room was packed, the clusters of men even denser around a pair of pool tables and in front of a row of video games against the far wall. A few heads turned as Kate squeezed through a path that seemed lined with thick, naked, sweat-shiny biceps. She real-

ized that she was more than a little put off; she had
never walked through a congregation of men before
and gathered no more than the occasional disinter-
ested glance.

Tejeda found space for them at the long movie-
western-style bar. She stood in a pocket of space in
front of him while he waved down the rotund, balding
man behind the bar. Kate watched the man with fascination as he worked his way toward them, trading iced
beers for outstretched pairs of dollars, fielding jokes,
and laughing in what seemed one long, continuous
manic gambol.

According to the pressed-tin sign on the mirror behind the cash register, "MITCH is serving you tonight."
But the sign seemed at least a generation older than
the bartender. She wondered about it because, except
for a Chamber of Commerce sticker and an unframed
business license, it was the only ornamentation in the
place.

The bartender scrubbed at the bar in front of them
with a damp rag, grinning as if he knew a secret.

"So, Lieutenant," he said. "Haven't seen you around
in a while. Heard you was busted up pretty good."

Tejeda pulled Kate in toward him. "How are you,
Fred?"

"No complaints," he said. Then he nodded toward
Kate. "You bring a chaperon?"

"This is my partner." Tejeda grinned. "In drag."

"Naw. I talked to your partner couple hours ago.
Told Sergeant Green everything I know about a certain deceased corporal. Maybe you should talk to him."

"Maybe you forgot to tell him some little thing,"
Tejeda said. Fred shrugged as he went to replenish a
tray for his waiter to circulate among the standees.

Tejeda hadn't said anything about it during the drive,
but Kate had known that this trip had something to do

with the death of Wally Morrow. Probably, she thought, he had asked her to drive him only because he couldn't drive himself while he was on Dilantin. And since the Police Commission's hearing, he could hardly have ridden down with Eddie Green without risking his disability status. She didn't much care *why* she was here; she was just glad that she was. Not only because Cassie's reunion with Theresa had begun to shoot some sparks and Kate didn't want to be used as a referee, but also because she was still damn scared. And with Tejeda she felt safe.

Fred, the bartender, wended his way back toward them, mopping the bar and doling out bottles of beer as he came. He stopped to stuff a wad of damp bills into the cash register and deal some change next to a pyramid of empties. Then he turned, looked at Tejeda, and threw his hands up. "Honest, I didn't see nothing."

"I'm not here as a cop," Tejeda said. Kate saw the edge of a folded bill under his hand on the bar. "I'm just a citizen who doesn't want to see Arty Silver maneuver himself another postponement or get himself walking papers on a technicality."

Fred's bar rag quickly swept over the bill, then dipped under the counter. "What are you drinking?"

Tejeda turned to Kate. "Beer okay?"

Kate glanced at the beefy forearm resting on the bar next to her. The blue tattoo said "USDA Prime." She looked back at Fred. "Milk, please."

"Yeah, sure," Fred chuckled. He put two drippy bottles of Moosehead in front of them and flipped off the caps. Then he spent a lot of time wiping his hands on his rag.

"Arty Silver did a lot of damage to my business, you know," he said finally, squinting up at Tejeda. "I've always kept my place quiet, decent. Guys can come here to relax, maybe meet a new friend. But I don't tolerate no overt shit. For that they have to go off the premises. You could bring big Marine general what's-his-name from Pendleton in here, and he'd never see anything could get a recruit in trouble.

"The Marines don't want to hear about their guys going to gay bars," Fred continued. "But they never gave any kid a hassle about coming to Clyde's, until Arty Silver started picking up new material here and doing what he did to them. Soon as my place got in the newspapers, the brass made me off-limits."

Tejeda looked around at the crowds. "Looks like business is pretty good."

"Getting back up there." Fred shrugged. "But it was me, myself, and the jukebox for more nights than I care to remember. Anything like what Silver done gets started up again, it'll kill me."

"Then help me," Tejeda said. "What do you know about Corporal Wallace Morrow Jr.?"

Kate felt USDA Prime pressing into her space. When she looked up at him, he opened his mouth and slowly, obscenely ran his tongue over his lips. He pointed at her, then at himself in a question: you and me?

"Thanks just the same," she said, and turned her back.

Tejeda seemed only to shift from one foot to the other, but he managed to put himself between Kate and the tattooed arm. He snagged one end of Fred's rag and reeled him closer. "You have a quiet place we can talk?"

"Sorry. I got just the one waiter—the other one quit Monday." He slid some bottles down the bar and talked to Tejeda over his shoulder. "I can't even take a piss."

"Go piss," someone down the bar called out. "I'll watch the register."

"Yeah, Fred," the man next to him laughed, "and I'll go with you, hold your lizard for you while you drain it."

"Shut up, grunt." Fred playfully slapped the man on the side of the head. "I just told the lieutenant what a respectable place I run."

A dozen heads craned to check out Tejeda, then there was suddenly more room at the bar around them. Kate found space to stretch and take a deep breath. When she looked around, she saw the top of USDA Prime's close-cropped head swimming away through the crowd.

Fred leaned in close, his eyes betraying his amusement. "Don't like brass around here."

Kate heard a collective stifled laugh, as if the preacher had dropped an off-color remark into his sermon.

Tejeda seemed to ignore them as he squared a studio portrait of an excruciatingly young man in uniform on the bar in front of Fred. "Tell me what you know about Wally Morrow."

Fred sighed. "He'd come in maybe once, twice a week. Usually with a couple friends, usually on weekends."

"Hey, Fred!" An arm waved over the bar to Kate's right. "I'm still waiting."

"So wait some more," Fred said, but he slid half a dozen bottles of beer down the counter in each direction, pausing only long enough to note which hands gathered them in along the way, like a ballpark peanut vendor. When he brought his attention back to Tejeda, he seemed serious, concentrated. He lit a cigarette, blew out some smoke, then slouched his bulk against the bar.

"I see a lot of young kids in here," he said. "Join the Marines to prove they're real men, or prove it to the folks back home. But they get out in the world a

little and find out it ain't so bad being gay. At first
they don't know what to do about it. So they come to
my place, or a place like it, looking for a big brother
who can show them what goes where."

"You think Wally Morrow was inexperienced?"
Tejeda asked.

"When he first come in?" Fred said. "He was raw.
Completely uncooked. I can't say that he was a virgin,
you know, but the kid looked like he needed a relief
map to find his own ass."

Kate noticed that a silent crescent of men had formed
behind them, a few listening more intently than the
others. Not nosy, just interested. Without being too
obvious, she tried to single out those whose interest
seemed most keen. Looming behind the ring of men
was the bulk of USDA Prime, with his back to her.

"Tell me about Sunday," Tejeda said. "Did you see
who Wally left with?"

"Who can keep track?" Fred asked.

"Had he been with anyone in particular on Sunday,
or before?"

Fred scratched under his chin, thinking. "Besides
his bunkmate, he cuddled up to two, maybe three
guys. But like I said, in here they just talk. Coulda
made a date to meet someone later. I just wasn't
paying much attention."

Fred walked away, seeming distracted, to take care
of some customers.

"Except . . ." he said, stopping on his way back to
light a second cigarette from the first. "Except I pegged
him for a poacher, guy goes off base looking for game."

"He liked civilians?" Tejeda asked.

"Some guys do. Think it's safer." Then he winked
at Kate. "Till they hear about Arty Silver."

"Had you told Wally Morrow about Arty?" she
asked.

"Not me."

Someone propped open the back door to let in fresh air, and a few men spilled out into the parking lot.

"Sunday," Tejeda said. "What was the crowd? Mostly regulars? Convention in town? What?"

"Your partner already asked me," Fred said with exasperation. "I don't remember. Sunday was Sunday. Marines get weekend passes, come into town, drop off their laundry, get a beer. It's crowded. Who has time to notice one snot-nosed grunt?"

"It was hot Sunday," Kate said. "Remember, Roger? Beach traffic was so heavy we decided to stay in."

"Stayed in, huh?" Fred grinned and set another beer in front her, even though she hadn't touched the first. Then he looked over toward the open back door, the row of cars under the lights outside. "Yeah, it was nice Sunday. We had the doors open all day. Like summer."

A kid who should have been carded stepped forward and propped himself up with a pool cue. "We opened the door because the power went out. Wasn't that Sunday?"

There was general agreement among the crowd that it had been Sunday.

"Someone hit a pole or something down the highway. P.G. and E. repairman came."

Tejeda handed the boy Kate's beer. "Where was Wally Morrow?"

"He was shootin' pool." A tall, slender redhead took half a step forward. His hair was too long for the Marine Corps. "He took his shirt off, Fred, and you told him to put it back on, remember?"

"Yeah." Fred shrugged. "Vaguely."

"Who was he shooting pool with?" Tejeda asked.

"All comers." The redhead frowned, drawing his freckles together. "He got pretty loaded."

Fred reacted to that. "I didn't sell him much."

"He kept going out to the parking lot," the redhead said. "The guy from the electric company had a cooler of beer in his car."

"Shit." Fred pressed his wet rag to his forehead. When he looked up again, Kate saw he was pale. "That's how Silver used to work it. I don't want to go through all that no more."

Tejeda turned to the redhead. "You said he had a car. Not a San Diego P.G. and E. truck?"

"No, a car. The kind Daddy uses to drive the kiddies to Sunday school. We teased the guy about it."

"What did he look like?"

"Didn't see his face much—had a hat and shades on, stayed outside the whole time. But I'd recognize his rock-hard little buns if I saw them again."

"If the power line was out down the highway," Tejeda said, "what was the repairman doing here?"

"Yeah," Fred said. "The power was only out five minutes. What was the guy doing all that time?"

Kate watched heads dip together, listened to a general murmuring. But no one offered an answer.

Tejeda took in a deep breath. "Did anyone actually see Wally Morrow leave?"

"I did," the boy with the pool cue volunteered.

"With the man who said he was the electrical repairman?"

"Yes."

"Describe the car."

"Light gray, maybe beige," the boy said. "Olds Cutlass."

12

K ate seemed all crisp and businesslike walking on the sand beside him, the way Tejeda remembered her from the first time they had met, listening to him politely, showing interest. The gap of night sky between them was small enough to be friendly, but too big for anything else, the way it would be dancing with a stranger for the first time. He understood what was happening; it wasn't the first time she had slipped behind a barrier of awfully good manners to keep him at a distance. Everyone needed space now and then, but tonight it rankled him because he was afraid her formality was cover for things she needed to say but wouldn't. If his hands hadn't been loaded with firewood and the picnic basket Trinh had packed, he would have tossed her to the sand and tickled her, just to loosen her up.

"Trinh found that blanket in the laundry-room closet," he said. "I hope sand won't hurt it."

"I'm sure it won't," she said, smoothing a fold in the plaid wool draped over her arm. Her voice hardly carried over the rush of breaking surf.

There was no moon, and the only light came from the phosphorescence of the waves in front and the muted neon glow of Oceanside behind them. When Tejeda glanced down at Kate, her hair was so dark against the black sky that her face seemed luminous.

But her eyes, sometimes so pale in daylight they were almost colorless, caught no light and he couldn't see them, couldn't read them. She shivered a little but didn't say anything.

When they reached the first concrete fire ring, he put down the bundle of firewood. She dropped to her knees beside it and wrapped the blanket around her shoulders.

"I thought Clyde's would be more exotic," she said.

"Berlin was better, huh?"

"More theatrical, more absurd."

There were a few fires scattered at a distance along the beach, disappearing toward the horizon like a spill of red beads. Tejeda wondered what brought other people out in the night chill. Unless they were lovers.

"Now what?" she asked.

"I make like a Boy Scout and light the fire."

"I meant, what are you going to do about the investigation?"

"Tell Spud what we found out."

"Then what?"

"I don't know." He busied himself laying the fire: wadded newspapers, kindling, split fir logs. "Richie's tuition for the spring quarter is due next month. I can't pay it until my next disability check comes."

He had to light three matches before he managed to shield one from the wind long enough to catch the edge of a newspaper. The sudden flare of fire washed Kate's face in sharp contrasts of hot red and deep, cold shadow. He couldn't take his eyes from her; she was so beautiful at that moment as to seem almost unreal.

The kindling raged fiercely, briefly, shooting sparks into the dark; then the fire settled into a low, crackling burn. He opened the basket and took out a bottle of wine and poured two glasses.

"Roger," she said, raising the ends of the blanket and holding it open for him. "Let's get away."

"If you want." He moved into her arms, shivering as her warmth inside the blanket enveloped him. "We could borrow Reece's boat, sail to Catalina for the weekend. If the weather holds."

"No. I meant we should get *way* away." She unbuttoned the top of his shirt and slid her smooth hand inside over his chest. "There's a little Romanesque village in the south of France, Conque, not far from Limoges but up in the mountains, very isolated."

"I don't think so."

"Right, might be cold this time of year. How about the southern hemisphere? It's spring in Australia, almost summer."

"Slow down a minute," he said, covering her hand to hold it still. "Richie's talking about graduate school in the fall. After Theresa graduates next year, I'll be paying two college tuitions."

"Assuming you don't lose your disability before you're healthy enough to go back to work."

"I'm okay."

"Remember who scraped you off the dining-room floor this afternoon? Don't try to play tough guy with me, Roger."

"Tough guy, huh?" he said. "What's your point?"

"What do you really want to do?"

He started to undo her shirt. "What I really want to do is strip naked and make love in the sand."

"I know that," she laughed. She pulled open her shirt and bared her breast to the firelight. Watching his face, smiling but calculating, she made a slow circle around the taut nipple with her finger. "Answer my question, and this is yours."

"What was the question?"

"You should be able to choose whether or not you

want to investigate this case without risking either
your income or being forced back into the department
before you're ready." She laid his palm over the goose-
flesh on her chest. "If money weren't a factor, what
would you choose to do?"

"But money is a factor."

"Doesn't have to be." Her thigh moved slowly against
his crotch.

"Foul," he said, pulling her against him and wrapping the blanket tighter around them, like a cocoon.
"Unfair holding tactics."

She laughed. "So?"

"What are you offering?"

"Freedom of choice. You can tell the Police Commission to shove it. All you have to do is sign a
signature card at the bank."

"Yeah? What if I cleaned out your accounts?"

"Then I'd learn something about you I should know."

"Thanks anyway," he said. "I'm old-fashioned about
living off a woman's money."

"No you're not. The problem is that you haven't
made up your mind about us. Talking about money
means talking about the future."

"Is this a proposal?"

"No." Her hand was working at his belt buckle.
"It's a proposition."

Out of the corner of his eye he saw a column of
darker sky on the far side of the fire.

"That you, Lieutenant?"

Tejeda spun into a crouch, knocking Kate back onto
the sand. He had a split log in his hand. "Who's
there?"

"Take it easy," the deep voice urged from the dark.

Tejeda firmed his grip on the splintery wood as an
enormous skinhead loomed out of the night beyond
the fire.

Kate came up beside him, clutching the front of her shirt together. "It's USDA Prime. From Clyde's."

As soon as she said it, Tejeda recognized the tattooed beefcake who had stood next to Kate at the bar. The man's hands were out to the side and empty, but still he missed the reassuring weight of his service revolver tucked into the back of his jeans.

Though the guy was big, tough-looking, he seemed more cautious than threatening. Tejeda thought his own appearance was fairly silly, pants and shirt gaping open to the frigid night air. He had to choose between hanging on to the log or buttoning up. He dropped the log.

"What do you want?" he asked the intruder.

"You're the guy arrested Arty Silver?"

"Yes."

"I don't make it no habit of helping cops. But that Silver dude offed two guys I know." The big man held his hands out to the fire and stared at Tejeda. "I got something maybe you should know."

"You have a name?"

"Don. Don Kelley."

"Can you show me some I.D.?"

Tejeda watched Kelley's hands as he reached for the wallet in his back pocket. He held it out in front of him as he walked slowly around the fire ring, with his free hand out to the side as if he knew all about dealing with police requests.

The California driver's license behind the plastic window identified him as Donald Kelley, age thirty-two, of Carlsbad—a local.

Tejeda handed the wallet back. "What's on your mind?"

"They lied to you at Clyde's. That electrician? He's been hanging around for months. He puts on these phony-ass disguises and tries to get guys to talk to him."

"He tries to pick up people?" Tejeda asked.

"No. Everyone thinks he's a narc. They thought it would be funny to sic you on him." Kelley squatted next to the picnic basket.

"Mr. Kelley," Kate said, "would you like a glass of wine?"

He shrugged. "I don't mind."

Kate took out a glass and filled it.

"Alcohol's illegal on the beach." He grinned as he accepted the glass. "You'll get busted."

Tejeda smelled more than wine on the man; besides stale sweat, there was the gassy residue of amyl nitrite, poppers, a heart drug some people used for a sexual rush, especially during rough sex. He wondered how much of the rush came from knowing the drug could be lethal. Wally Morrow had been confined to base because he was caught with amyl nitrite.

Knowing this didn't make Tejeda feel any better; he wished Kate weren't there. How was he to know whether Don Kelley had more on his agenda than information, like maybe waiting for more troops to show up: Arty Silver still had a number of very loyal friends who were either convinced of his innocence or might have shared in his guilt.

Arty Silver had liked his sex rough and deadly. Don Kelley, from his crude appearance and tight-ass swagger, looked like rough trade himself.

Tejeda dropped another piece of wood on the fire. "You ever talk to the electrician?"

"No. Saw his car, though, a Cutlass, like they said."

"Hear a name?"

"Nope."

"Did he ever pick up anyone besides Wally Morrow?"

"No. See, that's the lie." He held out his glass for a refill. "What is this stuff?"

Kate looked at the label. "Cabernet sauvignon. B.V. Georges de Latour. Nineteen seventy-eight."

Kelley shrugged. "Is that good?"

"Do you like it?"

"Yeah," he chuckled, and slugged more down. He wiped his mouth with the back of his hand and squinted up at Tejeda. "Wally Morrow never went anywhere with that guy."

"How do you know?" Tejeda asked.

"Wally left first. He went out to the highway to thumb a ride. Told a friend of mine he had a date down at the shack."

"Is the shack another bar?"

Kelley snickered. "You don't know the shack?"

"Should I?"

"Yeah, 'cuz Arty Silver used to meet guys down there. I thought you knew everything there was to know about that dude."

Tejeda shook his head. Had he forgotten this place? Or had he never found out about it? Not knowing was too frustrating. Maybe, he thought, he should go home and learn how to grow petunias. Or go with Kate to Australia.

Kate asked, "Where is this shack?"

"Just this side of San Onofre. Maybe a quarter-mile past the wetback snatch." He brought his hands up. "Sorry. Guess you're a Mex, huh?"

"Nothing to be sorry about," he said. "Do you mean the immigration check station on the freeway?"

"Yeah. I never could figure that place out. How many illegals you think come into America on the freeway?"

Kate emptied the last of the wine into Kelley's glass. "Can you give us directions to the shack?"

He held the glass up to her. "You won't find any of this stuff there. When I said shack, that's what it is—an old storage shed of some kind on the Marine base."

"I'm sure it's charming."

Kelley laughed and looked at Tejeda. "Your girl's kinky."

"That's why I like her." Tejeda put his arm around Kate and pulled her close; Kelley was still too much of a wild card. He wanted Kate within reach if they had to leave in a hurry. "If she wants to go to the shack, I'll take her. Now, how do we find it?"

"Whatever." Kelley shrugged. "Like I said, about a quarter-mile past the check station, there's an access road. You have to look careful 'cuz it isn't marked. There's a barbed-wire gate you have to go through. Then you're inside Pendleton where you ain't supposed to be. You cross a wash, then look into the trees. There's a caved-in bunker. You can't see it from the road, but the shack's back of it."

"Thanks," Tejeda said. He looked down at Kate. "Eddie and I will check it out Friday."

"It's okay." Kelley put his empty glass on the picnic basket. "I'm not setting you up. If you like, I'll go along. You did a lot of us a big favor when you caught that Silver dude. He scared a lot of chickens, really cramped my style. Worse than all this AIDS shit."

"Gives new meaning to my job," Tejeda chuckled. "To protect and to serve."

"Yeah." Kelly got up and brushed sand from the seat of his pants. "I gotta go."

"I appreciate the information," Tejeda said, offering his hand.

"Yeah." Kelley's hand was like leather. "See ya."

Tejeda held Kate tight, waiting for Kelley to merge

with the darkness. But after a few steps, the big man turned and came halfway back.

"You heteros are such animals, always sniffing around each other." Kelley had a big grin on his craggy face. "But I'm sorry I interrupted you guys earlier. You can get back to it now. I'm going."

When he was no more than a shadow moving across the skyline, Kate cupped her hand under Tejeda's rump and squeezed. "Well?"

He laughed. "I think the magic's gone."

13

"I'm not staying here alone." Kate pulled the car in among a cluster of scrubby live oaks and turned off the ignition. "I saw that movie."

"What movie?"

"You know, the hero leaves the girl alone in the car and while he's gone some freak comes along with a chain saw and fillets her."

"There may be ticks in the chaparral," he said.

"Ticks are better than chain saws."

"Suit yourself," he laughed. He took the flashlight from her glove compartment and stepped out into the chilly night. The heavy smell of dry sage was almost overpowering.

While he waited for Kate to lock the car and put on her jacket, he tried to see a path to take across the weed-covered field to the shack.

The shack looked like an abandoned toolshed behind a collapsed earthwork of some sort. Two hundred yards beyond it, the elevated freeway was a slash of light through the inky midnight sky. The light from above skimmed the high points of the terrain, giving the corrugated-tin roof of the small building a dull gleam, picking out the tips of the sage and making it silver.

Behind him there was nothing but dark, a vast range of uninhabited scrub that was used by the Marines for gunnery practice and war games. Tejeda tucked the flash into his pocket; any light they showed while crossing the field would be visible for miles.

"All set." Kate came up behind him and hooked two fingers through his belt loop and hung on.

The going was treacherous because they couldn't see the ground under the weed covering. Every time Kate stepped in a rut or hopped a trench, Tejeda felt a tug at his belt loop. He liked the tugs, liked having her beside him. He would rather have been beside her at home in bed. But knowing he had that delight to look forward to, being with her out in the crisp evening air, forgetting for the moment the purpose of this little expedition, was pretty goddamned nice. She was quiet, as she had been off and on all evening, as if maybe she was afraid there was someone around who might hear them. He didn't mind. In fact, he thought, he felt a lot like a kid playing hide-and-seek with his best friend.

They landed in a patch of nettles, and when they were clear, Kate let go of him to pick stickers out of her socks. She whispered, "What if the Marines catch us?"

"I'll show them my badge."

"Did you bring it?"

"I'm not much worried about the Marines." He swatted at something that flew past his ear. "You okay?"

"Yes." She straightened up. "Do you know what time it is?"

"Vaguely."

"You should be home in bed."

"Kate, if doing this really bothers you, we can leave."

She looked ahead at the shack, a dark block in the feathery shadows of the chaparral, and took a deep breath. "We've come this far . . ."

They pushed ahead through the brush and finally

came out into a hard-packed clearing. The shack was no more than slabs of rough board tacked together.

"Want me to go in first?" he asked.

"Hell, no." She stayed close beside him, hesitating only when he stepped under a loose section of corrugated roofing that hung precariously over the single door.

He stood very still for a moment, listening. But all he heard was an occasional night bird and the constant oceanlike rush of the freeway.

Getting inside the shack would be easy, he thought: there was no knob or lock on the door. He held a hand up to Kate to keep her a pace behind him. Then he took a deep breath, and as he raised a foot to kick the door open he shouted, "Military Police. Everyone out."

The door banged open into something metallic and set off a scurrying of feet that sent both him and Kate diving into the bushes for cover. He risked a flick of his light, and laughed when he saw whom he had disturbed.

"Those aren't naked white hineys," he said, brushing twigs off his back. "They're skunks."

"Thank God," she said.

He offered his hand and pulled her up. "You were expecting maybe freaks with chain saws?"

"No. But I *was* expecting something else."

"Like what?" he asked, but she had jogged ahead while he searched for the bur that had burrowed under his collar. When he caught up to her, she was standing in the clearing watching the section of broken roof swing over the gaping door like a pendulous ax. She glanced at him, then walked up to the door, grabbed the hanging bit of corrugated tin, and pulled on it until it broke free.

She tossed it aside and turned to Tejeda. "Are we going in, or what?"

"Yeah, sure," he laughed, watching the tin bounce to a stop.

The first thing he noticed before he turned on the flashlight was the smell. It reminded him of a fraternity house after a big party—a sour combination of beer, semen, and piss. With a skunk overlay.

The only window was boarded over, and little outside illumination managed to get past the door, making the darkness inside seem dense as velvet, almost touchable. His flashlight could light only a small section at a time, so they saw the interior as a series of photographs.

The dirt was thick everywhere, but underneath it he found what had once been a cozy trysting place. The door had banged against an iron cot covered with a standard military-issue bed-ticking pad. It was stained, but it didn't seem very old. At least, it was untorn. On the far side of the twelve-foot-square space, beyond the bed, there were a card table and four folding chairs. A broken ice chest had been shoved into the corner behind the table.

Tejeda aimed his light down and heard Kate mutter something. The rough-board floor between the bed and the table was littered with crusty, used condoms. Here and there a scattering of colored ones as bright as party balloons stood out in vivid contrast to the dull gray of the general grime. Kate gave a low whistle, and he wished she hadn't seen this. Something about the wantonness of the sexual debris and the connection of the place with Arty Silver made him feel dirty by association.

Kate had gone to a box beside the bed and pulled out a stack of newspapers. She held them up to his light.

"July 4, 1984. February 14, 1983," she read. "When did you arrest Arty Silver?"

"Labor Day, 1984," he said. "Better put them back. Spago's people need to see things exactly the way they were found."

Directly opposite the door there was a tall chunk of log, maybe three feet high, he guessed, thirty inches in diameter. It seemed out of place among the other meager furnishings, whose one common feature was their portability. He nudged the log with his foot; he couldn't have hefted it alone. The top was scarred and stained.

Kate was brushing off her hands. "How's your botany?" he asked.

"Not so good. I can tell a palm tree from a geranium, but that's about it. Why?"

"Can you tell a redwood from a live oak?"

"Sure. Redwoods are big. Live oaks aren't."

"Right."

She looked over his shoulder at the log. "That's redwood?"

"That's my guess," he said, picking at a dry brown flake on the wood. "We're three hundred miles from the closest redwoods."

"Maybe someone brought it for firewood."

"No," he said, holding the brown flake to the light. "It's a chopping block."

He heard her retch as she ran out the door. When he caught up to her, she was leaning against the outside wall, gulping deep breaths.

"Sorry," he said. "Maybe the men who use the shack hunt jackrabbits."

"Don't patronize me," she snapped.

"Kate, what's going on? All night you've been . . ." What had she been? Quiet. A bit short-tempered, as if she had to bite off something that kept trying to get out. "I'm sorry I brought you out here."

"Forget it." She grabbed a handful of his sleeve and looked up into his face. "You asked me earlier what I expected to find."

"Yeah?"

"I keep half-expecting to find Lance."

"Lance?" He thought he must have come in late and missed something. "Richie's roommate, Lance?"

"I'm sorry, Roger, I should have told you earlier, but it just seemed like one more thing to bother you with."

He felt prickly all over, and it had nothing to do with his roll in the weeds. "Tell me."

"It's probably nothing."

"Dammit, Kate—" he started.

"That's why I didn't want to tell you. I didn't want you upset."

"You want to see upset?"

"No. Just remember that this is only wild speculation." She gripped both of his arms now, hard, as if he would drift if she didn't anchor him. "I started thinking about Lance when we were at Clyde's, when they told us that the electrician drove a gray or beige Cutlass. Like yours."

"Like eight or ten million others." He shrugged.

"Okay, but I remembered Lance saying that he usually drove to San Diego with Richie. Suppose that while Richie was visiting Jena, Lance had use of the car. To go surfing. Or to lurk around Clyde's."

"So he had opportunity. But why would he?"

"I don't know exactly. Except that Arty Silver killed his brother."

"Are we still talking about the Lance I know?"

"Yes. He told me about it this afternoon."

"Oh, God." Tejeda pulled his arms free and rubbed

his eyes with the heels of his hands, pressing hard. His eyes felt better but his head was no clearer. He wanted to get back to the car and call home, tell his kids to lock themselves in until Eddie Green could put them in protective custody. Protective custody from what, though? Richie's ditsy roommate? Or did Lance need protecting too? He shoved his hands into his pockets and blew out a shaft of air. Kate was looking at him expectantly.

"Anything else?" he asked.

"Not really. Lance was on the beach this afternoon about the time the arm must have been deposited in the gazebo. He had to pass the gazebo on his way back up to the house. Somewhere in all that are motive, means, and opportunity. But for what, I don't know."

"Right." His head hurt. "Anything else?"

"That's it. I can't imagine Lance being involved, he seems so ordinary. I mean, it must take a certain sort of warped creature to cut off heads and arms and carry them around town. But, my God, Roger, you can't ignore a certain volume of coincidence."

"No." So now he knew what she had been holding back. He hoped she was finished, but she took a breath and continued.

"I was trying to put Lillian Morrow and the Silver Threads group somehow at the center of the arm business. Mrs. Morrow is certainly spooky, and she seems to have a mission. I thought maybe she had done something to goose up her son's murder investigation."

"I hesitate to even ask," he said. "But how the hell do you know Lillian Morrow?"

"She came to my office this morning after the inquest. She wants me to intercede with you, make you take over the investigation."

"Dammit, Kate!" he shouted. "Why didn't you tell me all this earlier?"

"Because earlier it was none of your business!" she shouted back. "I've told Eddie Green everything except what we found out at Clyde's. I'll call him on the way home and tell him about *that*. And about this place."

He moved back a few paces and kicked at some dirt clods before he could trust himself to speak again, he was so nonplussed and angry. He hated being protected. When he turned to her again, she had walked over to close the shack door.

"How could you think this was none of my business?" he asked.

"Sorry. Maybe that was the wrong expression," she said. When a dirt clod skittered in her direction, she kicked it back. "Roger, you're being manipulated. And I don't mean by Lillian Morrow."

"But maybe by you?"

"That's different." Then she smiled shyly to herself. "I think."

"So?"

"Roger, my love, I think someone wants you dead. Or at least permanently out of the picture."

"So why doesn't 'someone' just put a gun to my head?"

"Too quick. I believe this whole crime has been set up for your benefit by someone who knows your health is still vulnerable. I think he, or she, wants vengeance," she said. "He won't shoot you. He wants to watch you twist in the wind for a while."

Tejeda made himself laugh, but he and Eddie Green had already covered this territory. "What have you been reading?"

"Human nature."

"And you're some kind of expert on human nature?"

"I'm no slouch." She was walking toward him. "Look who I fell in love with."

"Just tell me what picture you think I'm being gotten out of."

"There are so many possibilities," she said, and held up her hand to tick them off. "You said Arty Silver had friends. The case against him certainly wouldn't be as strong with you gone. Then maybe the family of a victim is enraged that you didn't get Arty soon enough to save their son. Or you got the wrong man and he's afraid you'll figure that out. Putting aside the garden variety of wacko who might think you're the reincarnation of Satan, there are more personal possibilities."

"Personal? Like what?"

"My ex-husband is up to something. And so is your ex-wife."

She had counted down all the fingers on one hand. He took the fist this made and pulled up one of the fingers. "Did it occur to you that I'm not the intended victim?" he asked.

"No." She furrowed her brow and looked off into the dark for a moment. When she brought her gaze back to his face, he could see more sadness than fear. "Do you mean me?"

"Think about it."

Kate leaned her head against his chest and he wrapped his arms around her.

"My offer still stands," she said.

"For Australia?"

"No. For financing. I know we're too far into this mess to back out. If you work as a policeman, there are certain procedures you have to follow. Certain niceties. If you work as an independent, you don't have to be so fucking nice."

14

"Where's breakfast, you say?" Rachel laughed. "You mean, where's lunch?" "Never mind." Kate had taken one look at what Rachel was wearing and headed straight to the pantry for a bottle of catsup. Keep it casual, she had told everyone in the house. The baronial trappings of a formal dinner in her dining room could be downright scary to the uninitiated. The day already promised to be like a picnic in a mine field, with a variety of potential combustibles that ranged from Cassie to the appearance of assorted severed body parts.

She carried the catsup back into the kitchen, looked at Rachel again, and debated whether to ask her to change into street clothes. But she didn't have the heart; Rachel seemed to feel very elegant, her hair fanned out from her face like Oprah's and a tiny gold heart glued to the nail of her left pinkie. That much of her appearance was fine. It was the other that set Kate's teeth on edge. Dress comfortably, Kate had told Rachel when she hired her to serve dinner. But sometime during a cleaning foray Rachel must have discovered the old store of servants' uniforms, because she was now garbed in black livery like Garbo's maid, with prissy white apron ruffles cresting her shoulders in stiff fins.

Kate sighed. Rachel *was* a picture, sitting in a straight

kitchen chair while she arranged radish roses around the edge of a satellite-dish-size silver tray. On ice in front of her were artful canapés composed of smoked salmon and beluga caviar—Trinh had used *Gourmet* magazine as a source for her English as a Second Language homework. A lovely picture, Kate thought, just not the one she had had in mind.

"You'll need Arnold Schwarzenegger to pass that tray around," Kate said.

"It won't be passed. Mr. Reece said to put it on the low table in the sitting room."

"I'm glad someone's on top of things." Kate slid a canapé from under the plastic wrap. It tasted about the way it looked—artful. "Have you seen Lance?"

"No. Mr. Roger came through here ten minutes ago looking for him too. I'll tell you the same thing: when I drove up about seven, Lance was walking down to the beach with a surfboard under his arm." She poked a fresh rosemary stem under a radish for garnish. "And yes, when I see him, I'll tell him you're all looking for him."

"You sound tired, Rachel," Kate said. "Take a break."

"I'm not tired." Rachel beamed. "I don't know when I ever had so much fun. Everything is so beautiful. Go look in the dining room."

With a sinking feeling Kate picked up the catsup bottle and slowly opened the dining-room door.

The fire in the grate cast a rosy light, an antidote to the gray afternoon sky. But it wasn't enough to dispel the chilly formality of the dining room. Outside of a china-shop clearance sale, Kate couldn't remember ever having seen such a display of china, crystal, and silver since the days when her grandfather had had a domestic staff of five. Someone would be up half the night washing dishes.

Trinh was helping Reece arrange champagne flutes on the sideboard for dessert. "Happy Thanksgiving," she chirped.

"You too." Kate handed the catsup bottle to Reece. "What happened to keep it simple?"

"You want this on the table?" He looked at the catsup and laughed. "William Randolph Hearst gave his guests paper napkins to take the edge off."

"Not a bad idea. I suppose I couldn't persuade you to use Grandma's crockery instead of the china."

"Not a chance." Reece reached past her to adjust the alignment of silver candlesticks. "People expect all this when they come here. You don't want to disappoint anyone, do you?"

"I just want people to feel comfortable," she sighed.

"They will. The bar is well-stocked and Trinh has some new jokes."

"Just promise me," Kate said. "No footmen. And no dinner jacket for you."

"Me?" He grinned. He wore tattered cutoffs and a creamy cashmere sweater. She suspected that if she looked closely enough, she would find a fair amount of beach sand clinging to the hair of his scrawny ankles. He was certainly casual now, but guests weren't due for another hour and she had seen Reece's garment bag hanging on a bedroom door upstairs; he could do a lot of dressing in an hour.

Kate took another look at the phalanxes of forks and spoons aligned beside each plate. "After what's happened, do you think all this is appropriate?"

Reece shrugged. "What's happened?"

Trinh drew a finger across her throat. "You know."

"Oh. That." Reece seemed to weigh the problem quickly. Decision apparently made, he drew Kate into a quick, hard hug, then turned her toward the hall door. "Go bother someone else. Trinh and I are having fun."

Kate hesitated. "Have you seen Lance?"

"He came over this morning and borrowed my board, but I haven't seen him since."

"Where's Richie?"

"Stayed with his mother last night. She said the press people worried her." Reece put his hand against the middle of Kate's back and gently propelled her toward the door. "Theresa went up for a shower. Roger is on the telephone in the study. Lydia is on her way over. The queen is in her parlor and the king is in the counting house counting out his money. Now, beat it."

"I'm going."

Everything in the house seemed so holiday-ordinary, she thought as she walked toward the study. She yawned. On the way home last night, they had stopped by Eddie Green's house and ruined what was left of his night to tell him about the shack and Don Kelley. The sun had been up before they finally got to bed, and the house was already stirring before Kate finally managed to fall asleep. Now she felt somewhat disconnected, lost in a crack between the normal household hum and the Twilight Zone of the night before.

She hoped that what she wore—raw silk gray skirt, pale pink sweater with her grandmother's Tiffany dragonfly pin, low heels—was noncommittal, neither dressy nor overly casual. And not at all festive. She kept thinking about something Lillian Morrow had said, about the pain of not knowing where her son's remains were, while his killer was out there somewhere, probably getting ready to enjoy his Thanksgiving dinner. It was Lillian Morrow's grief and not her own, she reminded herself, but the boy's horrible death had touched this house, and there ought to be some acknowledgment.

Reece certainly didn't share her feelings, Kate thought as she walked toward the voices coming from the front of the house. She yawned again; maybe this morbid feeling was only a concomitant of too little sleep.

She found Tejeda and Eddie Green in the study, Bloody Marys in hand as they bent over a large ribbon-festooned carton and an enormous basket of long-stemmed red roses. To Kate the gifts looked straight enough, if somewhat extravagant, but Eddie and Tejeda found them awfully funny. When Eddie looked up and saw her, he gagged on his drink, trying to stifle a laugh.

"What's in the box?" Kate asked. "A gross of whoopie cushions?"

"Could be." Tejeda held out his hand to her. "Carl sent his construction person over with it."

"Harry Miller?"

"No. The little bearded one."

"Mike Rios," Kate said. "If Carl sent this stuff, it isn't whoopie cushions. Carl was never amused by intestinal gas. Or much of anything else. So, what's so funny?"

"I didn't know Carl was such a sentimental bastard." Tejeda reached into the flowers for a tiny florist card. "Read it."

" 'Happy Holidays.' " She started to laugh. " 'A pleasure to service your construction needs. From Angel Center Building Supply.' "

"He must have missed the card," Eddie said.

"Maybe the florist made a mistake," Kate said. "Or Rios delivered the wrong stuff. Carl's no saint, but this isn't like him. Unless he really is cracking up. What's in the box?"

"It's addressed to you." Tejeda nudged the carton with his toe. "Heavy."

"Yeah?" Eddie nudged it too. "About the weight of a dismembered corpse."

"Minus the head and left arm, right?" Kate knelt down to undo the ribbons.

"Sergeant Green?" Trinh hovered in the doorway, looking nonplussed. "Your wife is here."

Before anyone could react, Eddie's almost-ex-wife, Libby, swept in and planted herself squarely in front of Eddie. She clutched their ten-year-old son, Justin, tight against her. Justin looked thoroughly miserable. Kate didn't know much about what had happened to Eddie's marriage, except that the end had come during the investigation into Kate's mother's death. Eddie had carried the double burden of covering an extra load at work while Tejeda was out of commission, and of trying to pacify his own domestic muddle.

Ordinarily, Kate thought, Libby would be a pretty woman. But she seemed tired and grim, and barely in control. Not unlike Cassie.

Tejeda moved toward her. "Nice to see you, Libby. Have you met Kate?"

Libby extended a hand to Kate, a habit of good manners apparently boring through her shield of hostility. Justin used the break in his mother's hold to squirm free and run to his father.

Big, tough Eddie Green seemed to melt as he held Justin. He kissed him noisily, ruffled his hair, and turned him around. "Did you say hello, Jus?"

"Hi, Roger. Hi, Kate. Thank you for inviting me."

"Glad you could come, sport," Tejeda said, feigning a punch to Justin's shoulder. "Richie brought home his octopus collection."

Justin grinned, showing his full set of braces. Cleaving to his father, he looked at everything in the room except his mother.

"Eight o'clock." Libby glared at Eddie. "You get him to my mother's on time for once or I'm going to the judge again about Christmas."

"Jeez, Libby," Eddie said. "Not in front of Justin."

"Eight o'clock," Libby warned. Then she turned and left without bothering with good-byes.

Justin leaned against his father. "Did you bring your watch?"

"Don't worry, Jus," Eddie said. "Everything is going to be okay."

Kate felt awkward. She wanted to offer Eddie a private place to be with his son for a while, but Justin, still clinging to Eddie, had discovered the carton in the middle of the floor.

"Whose present?" he asked.

"Mine," Kate said. "Will you help me open it?"

He broke away and dropped down eagerly beside her. With only one chipped nail and one paper cut between them, Kate and Justin managed to pry open the top of the carton.

Justin sat back on his heels disappointed, but Kate smiled up at Eddie.

"Wine," she said. "A case of very good white wine."

"I knew that." Eddie drained his Bloody Mary. She noticed the deep circles under his eyes, a slight tremor in the hand that held the glass. How much sleep had he missed last night? And how early had he started on Bloody Marys?

"Dad," Theresa called. "Grandma's here. They just called from the gate."

"They're early," Kate said as they all walked out to the foyer.

"No they're not," Tejeda said. "On time is for guests. Family comes early to help."

"Now you tell me."

He nodded toward Reece, who was coming down the stairs. "I thought you knew."

"Touché," she said.

Reece still wore the cashmere sweater, but he had traded his cutoffs for beautifully tailored gray flannel slacks. She noticed that while he had slipped on cordovan loafers, his ankles were bare.

"You pass wardrobe," she called up to him. "Now it's show time."

A light rain had begun to fall. Tejeda took an umbrella from the stand by the door and ran down the front steps to meet his parents while Kate and the others waited under the shelter of the portico.

Kate watched him laughing, joking with his parents, exchanging noisy kisses and hugs while they got covered dishes out of the station wagon and umbrellas opened. She saw in the easy, loving rapport he had with his parents the source for his strong relationships with his own children. She felt a pang of emotion she hoped wasn't envy. No, she thought, it was something like what Goldilocks must have felt when the three bears came back from their walk; a fear of being engulfed, they had such a strong presence wherever they went.

Kate smiled. It was show time, all right. Today, during dinner at their son's lover's house, Linda and Ricardo Tejeda would have their first meeting with Cassie since she decamped for New Mexico, leaving their son and grandchildren to sweep up her dust.

"Told you so," Reece whispered in Kate's ear. She nodded; he had been right, the Tejedas were dressed for a party. Kate suspected that Tejeda's father, Ricardo, the Santa Angelica High School marching-band director, was always dressed for a party. He was a very tall, straight, commanding-looking man with a head of crisp silver hair. In his black three-piece suit he looked to Kate as if he should have at least a brace of drummers behind him.

Physically, Linda was a striking contrast to Ricardo: she was small, a bit rounded, her blue-black hair set off by a red knit costume that looked like about three months' worth of her teaching salary. She seemed soft, but Kate knew that after twenty-some years of managing high-school-English students, Linda had a granite core.

Linda and Ricardo seemed to bring light with them into the foyer.

"Oh, Theresa," Linda exclaimed, handing over her drippy umbrella. "You look so beautiful. Is that a new sweater?"

"No, it's Kate's."

"Watch her, Kate," Ricardo said, wrapping Kate in his arms and planting a wet kiss on her cheek. "Before you know it, there won't be anything left in your closet."

"I'll know where to look for it." Kate took a heavy crystal bowl from him and winked at Theresa.

Rachel came from the kitchen. She paused long enough to make sure everyone had time to see and appreciate; then, with the tiniest of curtsies, she collected the dishes Linda and Ricardo had brought and carried them away.

During the round of cheek-kissing and introductions, Kate glanced at Trinh, who stood just outside the family circle.

Trinh had changed into a deep blue dress and tied a matching ribbon around her long dark hair. She seemed so excited that she couldn't keep both feet on the floor at the same time. Kate went over and put her arm around her and drew her into the sitting room with the rest of the group.

"You look beautiful," Kate said.

"Yes, I am," Trinh said. Then she blushed. "I mean, everything is so beautiful."

"Thanks to you. Now it's time for you to be a guest."

Ricardo had found a station beside the canapés. "I love this place. Reminds me of the Ahwanee Lodge in Yosemite." He accepted a sherry from his son. "Remember, Rigo, when we went there?"

"I don't think so," Tejeda said.

"Of course he doesn't remember." Linda nibbled a canapé. "Little Rigo was only six months old."

"Nana's here," Theresa announced, leaving her seat by the front window. "Come on, Dad. Richie's brought Nana."

Tejeda left the room and returned shortly with Nana, his grandmother, holding her by the arm as if she were very delicate. It seemed to Kate that Nana tolerated this special care with good humor, but didn't need it. She was in her late eighties, very tiny and slim in a bright green dress. Her step was sure and strong, her back very straight. Her dark eyes shone with intelligence and an impishness that she seemed to have passed on to Ricardo.

Ricardo folded Nana in a hug. "You are lovely, Mother."

Nana laughed. "Only to you, *mijo*."

In one hand she held a nosegay of daisies, which she handed to Kate with a light kiss, in the other a box of peanut brittle, which she gave to Tejeda.

Linda waited for her turn to embrace Nana. When their heads were bent together, Nana whispered something and laughed in a way Kate could only describe as bawdy.

"Sherry, Nana?" Tejeda asked.

"Sherry?" Nana repeated. "Maybe a gin and tonic, Rigo dear."

"I know," he said. "Light on the tonic."

"I'll help you." Nana took his arm again and they went off to find the gin.

Richie had followed Nana in, self-consciously holding his girlfriend, Jena Rummel, by the hand. Cassie followed, looking tentative. Kate walked over to greet her, bring her into the crowd, but Cassie hesitated as if to put off their meeting. Then she seemed to steel herself. She tossed her rain-frizzed hair back and moved forward again.

Kate offered her hand. "Glad you could come, Cassie."

"Thank you. Where do you want this?"

This was a flat basket covered with shiny blue-black disks. Kate wished she knew whether to offer them as hors d'oeuvres or put them in the powder room.

"Well, Cassie." Ricardo loomed over Kate's shoulder. "What the hell is that?"

"Indian blue-corn cakes," Cassie said, with a hint of challenge.

Ricardo chuckled. "Cassie belongs to one of the ancient tribes of County Cork. She's helping them resettle in New Mexico."

Linda swept past him and took Cassie by the arm. "Everything goes to the kitchen. Come along, I'll show you."

Very smooth, Kate thought, grateful that Linda had taken charge. She would have given up Christmas to listen in on what they had to say to each other in the kitchen; they hadn't spoken to each other for a long time.

The rest of her guests clustered into groups. Theresa, Eddie, Justin, and Trinh played cribbage by the front window, while Reece, Ricardo, and Nana swapped

limericks. Richie and Jena were off together in a corner pretending to look at a collection of snuffboxes in
a small case. From a distance, Tejeda watched them.
Kate went to him and slipped her arm around his
waist.

"Ah, young love," she whispered.

He smiled down at her. "You'd think the rest of us
didn't even exist. No one can be in love like the
young."

"You're wrong," Kate said.

"Ricardo!"

Tejeda turned at the sound of his mother's voice.

"Ricardo, where's the cranberry salad?"

Kate reached up and turned Tejeda's face back to
her. "It's just that the young don't have so many
distractions."

"Could be," he laughed.

Linda was scolding her husband. "I put it in your
hand and sent you out to the car. What happened to
it?"

"I remember. I had the plate in my hand when I
went into the garage." Ricardo closed his eyes as if to
visualize the fate of the cranberry salad. "Then you
called out and said it was raining, so I put the plate
down on the dryer to get an umbrella."

"Ricardo!" Linda gripped him by the shoulders,
kissed his cheek hard, then threw up her hands. "I will
never understand how you can take a sixty-piece march-
ing band all the way across the country and never lose
so much as a baton. But you can't get one little salad
from the kitchen out to the car."

"No one in the band sends me to get umbrellas."
He shrugged. "I suppose we can't do without this
confection?"

"Thanksgiving with no cranberries?"

"I'm going." Ricardo flipped up the collar of his suit

coat. "It's raining, but I don't mind driving all the way back to the house, because what is Thanksgiving without my wife's lovely salad?"

"Grandpa." Theresa bounded over, smiling deviously. "I have my learner's permit. Can I drive you?"

"Let you drive?" he said with mock horror. "Let you use my own car to kill me?"

"Kate?" Theresa sidled closer, her hands clasped prayerfully. "The Rolls?"

"If Ricardo's game, it's okay with me."

Theresa alternately pushed and pulled her grandfather, who made a show of reluctance and fear, out to the foyer for raincoats and the car key. Laughing, Kate and Tejeda followed.

"You'll love this car, Grandpa. It's like riding in a boat." Theresa reached into the Chinese vase for the key. When she brought her hand out, she did a double-take, then held up a stubby aluminum key to Kate. "Haven't seen this before."

"Me either." Kate took the key and turned it over. The top was flat and square to accommodate some engraving.

"Silver's Meats," she read aloud. "Locker one-oh-nine."

Tejeda grabbed her wrist. "Hang on," he said as he reached for the red silk handkerchief in his father's pocket. He draped the silk over the key and lifted it from Kate's fingers. She watched a full range of emotions cross his face, from sheer terror to flushed anticipation, as he bent his head over the key.

"So?" she said.

"So? So, Theresa, ask Eddie to come out here, please. Then you stay with the others."

Theresa balked. "What about Grandma's salad?"

"We can do without cranberries for one Thanksgiving."

Cassie was there suddenly, hovering in the background like the ghost of Christmas past. "Do what your father said, Theresa."

Theresa gave her mother a quick vacant glance, then hurried off on her errand.

Ricardo was quizzing Tejeda about the significance of the key, but Kate couldn't pull her attention away from Cassie. She had an eerie gleam on her face; triumphant, Kate thought. And ethereal, as if she might evaporate. There was a lot more going on behind Cassie's doll-like face than a simple, sudden urge to see her family again. She was gathering information, Kate decided, remembering how she had watched and eavesdropped yesterday while Lance told Kate about his brother. Just as she was now. But information for what?

A surge of panic shot through Kate's unease. "Where's Lance?" she asked.

Tejeda rubbed the scar on his temple.

Eddie Green came on the run. "What is it?"

"Silver's Meats." Tejeda showed him the locker key. "Someone put this in the vase here."

"Jesus," Eddie spat. "Kate, will you look after Justin? If I'm not back by eight, will you take him to his grandmother's?"

"Of course, Eddie. He'll be fine."

"Damn," he said. "I finally get my kid away from Libby, and this happens."

Tejeda nodded. "You might ask Libby how close she came to the Chinese vase."

"Not funny," Eddie said.

"No, it isn't. Spud, I want uniforms posted on the doors." Tejeda turned to his father. "Until the uniforms get here, I want you to play sheepdog. Don't let anyone out alone, and be careful who you let in."

Eddie drew back. "Where do you think you're going, Rog?"

"With you."

"I can't let you jeopardize yourself."

"Like hell."

Cassie took a few steps closer. "It's happening all over again, isn't it, Roger?"

He wheeled on her. "Don't be so goddamn dramatic, Cass. I'm a cop. This is police business."

"You used to be a cop," she said. "Now you're crazy. I'm taking the kids back to New Mexico with me tonight."

"You better ask them first," he said.

Kate put her hand on his arm. "Do you have to go?"

"Yes. I *have* to go."

"Okay," she said. "The proposition I made last night still stands."

"Yeah?" He took a deep breath and looked off into space. Then he smiled. "Proposition accepted."

15

"What's the matter, you guys run out of ways to harass the Silver family, you gotta pull me away from my dinner?"

"Just unlock the door, Lou," Tejeda sighed. He'd listened to Lou Silver grouse for a solid half-hour, non-stop, from the minute he had been served with a search warrant for his butcher shop. Because he was Arty Silver's uncle, the whole routine was nothing new to Lou. So Tejeda wished he'd just open his shop and shut up about the turkey he had been preparing to carve, and about his widowed mother who had driven all the way from Van Nuys for dinner. No one else was complaining. In fact, Tejeda thought, the judge they'd rousted to sign the warrant would have come along if his in-laws hadn't shown up early. He'd been damned curious to see where Arty Silver had learned how to use a butcher's saw.

Once inside, they split up: Lou and Eddie to the tiny office for the locker-rental books while Tejeda went ahead to turn on the lights in the cavernous meat-packing room. The place was frigid. Tejeda pulled the collar of his windbreaker up around his neck, but it didn't do much good. He plunged his hands into his pockets and wondered how, in that cold, the smell of blood could be so strong.

Lou was close behind him. When he stopped swearing long enough to look around, he nearly sobbed.

"You leave in a hurry last night?" Tejeda asked. Lou only shook his head with dismay. Tejeda felt bad for him. He knew this meat business was Lou's life, and he was proud about keeping it clean to strict kosher standards. He would never have locked up and left the crusty brown mess that was coagulating on and around the big center butcher block.

"No more," Lou muttered. He went to the big stainless sinks, turned on the hot water, and picked up a scrub brush.

"You have to leave it, Lou," Tejeda said, and turned off the spigot. "Don't touch anything."

"I know the drill." Lou slammed the scrub brush against the wall. "Damn kid. Damn fuckin', stupid kid."

"What kid?" Eddie held the rental books in one hand and covered his nose with the other. "You know who made this mess, Lou?"

"No, I don't know who made this mess. But we all know who's responsible. Damn," he spat. "I try to do the right thing, give my brother's kid a job so he can earn money for college. What do I get? A bleeding ulcer and a never-ending bellyful of grief."

"Why do you blame Arty?" Eddie asked. "He couldn't have been here. I checked—Arty hasn't left the lockup."

Lou sagged against the sink. "Can you lock up the devil?"

Tejeda watched him grieve, feeling helpless. With the first kid he lured to his death, Arty had triggered an epidemic of grief. Every person touched seemed to deal with his affliction differently; some passively taking it as a scourge from God, others demanding retribution as if it were a curative drug. In the current round of events, Tejeda saw every stricken relative and friend as a wild card, an unpredictable free agent.

When he added everyone involved, from Arty's first victim to Wally Morrow, the possibilities loomed huge. Especially since the families of so many victims were in town for the start of Arty's trial on Monday. And so were his friends.

Tejeda shared some of Lou's desperation. Like many others, Lou wanted nothing more than to be released from the endless reruns of Arty's horror show.

Lou had had a particularly heavy load. After Arty's arrest, the police had found parts of three corpses frozen in Lou's lockers. And, like Fred down at Clyde's, Lou had come perilously close to losing the business he had spent a lifetime building.

Lou was a hothead, and Tejeda could see him doing something stupid and drastic to be shed of Arty. Then he thought again and shook his head; Lou was too much of a wild card to call. Tonight, when they had picked him up, Arty's parents had been seated at Lou's dining-room table.

Families of the dead, he thought, family of the killer; they all seemed to function from a sort of Sirhan Sirhan logic. Who could tell what any of them might do? Or why?

"Coroner's on his way over." Tejeda put what he hoped was a reassuring hand on Lou's shoulder. "We won't keep you long."

Lou made an effort to pull himself together. "Sorry I flew off. I just can't get used to the idea that Arty . . . Out of my brother's three boys, Arty was always the good one. Honor student, track star. Everyone liked Arty."

"Not everyone," Eddie said. "You come in this morning?"

"No," Lou said. "We worked late last night, getting our turkeys delivered." He glanced at the mess on the chopping block. "Last thing, like always, I cleaned up."

"According to your books, locker one-oh-nine is rented to the Santa Angelica Gun Club."

"Was. The gun club rents a tier of lockers every fall for game birds they go out and shoot—you know, pheasants and quail and like that. Last couple days they been coming in to get their birds to have for Thanksgiving. That whole tier's empty now. And it'll stay that way till I can clean it—you never know what wild birds might leave behind. Like I said, we worked late last night. I was too tired to do the books."

"Where do you keep the keys?" Tejeda asked.

"Rack, there by the freezer door." Lou's face clouded over. "But how did he get inside? I wasn't that tired—I know I locked both the outside doors."

Eddie shrugged. "You still keep an emergency key somewhere in the neighborhood?"

Tejeda watched Lou seem to fold in on himself. The breath he took before he answered took some effort. "There's a key behind the toilet in the all-night market next door."

Vic Spago's cigar stench announced his arrival. He came in arguing with his snappish crew of two about holiday overtime. When he saw Tejeda, he stopped in feigned shock. "Lieutenant, my friend, I thought you got the word. You can't play with us anymore."

"I can do anything I damn well please," Tejeda said, liking the way that sounded. He still wasn't clear about the details, but the more he thought about it, the more sense Kate's offer made. "As of Monday morning, if the Police Commission doesn't promise to stay off my back, I'm taking early retirement."

Eddie gasped. "Like hell."

"Yeah." Spago grinned. "Like hell."

"Exactly," Tejeda said. "So, Vic, what's first?"

Spago exhaled a black plume. "Otis Washington always says he can smell human blood the instant he comes into a room. I can't. I mean, I can smell blood, but I can't tell what sort of beast it came from."

Vic scratched his balding head as he made a slow circuit around the butcher block, stumbling twice over Mark, his number-one assistant, who was taking flash pictures. "Anyone give me time parameters?"

"I locked up at eleven last night," Lou said.

"And everything was spic and span?" He scraped a congealed pool with a scalpel blade. "Mark, get a blood titer here. Do tissue, hair, et cetera. Same shit we did in Oceanside this morning."

"Maybe you should look in the locker first," Tejeda said. "If anything's in there, you might want to see it before it gets any harder."

"What locker?" Vic snapped.

"I told you on the phone," Eddie said. "Roger found a key to locker one-oh-nine at his house."

"You said he found a key to Silver's Meats." Vic picked up a black evidence case. "You didn't say anything about a locker. Come on, Mark. That'll keep."

He stopped and thumped Lou on the back. "Is this déjà vu, or what?"

"Shit, Doc." Lou shook his head. "You know where the freezer coats are."

Mark went ahead like the king's vanguard for pictures. Tejeda stood in the doorway outside the huge walk-in freezer and watched him through a fog of condensation.

"God, look at the prints," Mark said. "Ask Vic if the laser fingerprint unit will work in a freezer."

"Tell him, who knows?" Vic yelled. "We never tried it."

Vic was pulling on a pair of heavy gloves. "You

know, Lieutenant, I was hoping the Commission would lay you up for a while."

"Why's that?"

"I need a little rest." He crushed out a spent cigar and lit a new one. "I was up a good part of the night with Otis, working on your limb. Thought I'd get a little sleep before the family came over, but Eddie here dragged me down to Oceanside."

"You didn't tell me, Spud."

"Why ruin dinner?"

Tejeda chuckled. "Find anything?"

"Inside the shack?" Vic shrugged. "Possibilities. Old stains, old papers; too early to tell.

"Now, the arm . . ." Vic beamed. "That was a piece of cake. But weird. Very weird. Couple weeks ago, a transient lay down on the Southern Pacific tracks outside town for a little nap. Then the nine-ten Amtrak from L.A. came along, snagged him on the undercarriage, and deposited him piecemeal between here and San Diego. You may have seen the story in the papers."

"Must have missed it."

"Otis reassembled as much of him as he could locate, had him bagged for a pauper's burial. But someone who read about him donated money—anonymously —for a funeral, so he was sent to a local mortuary. They cataloged him in on Tuesday. But when they went to put him in a coffin Wednesday afternoon, they found an arm missing."

"Careless of them," Tejeda said. "Any idea how the arm got from the mortuary to my backyard?"

"Maybe." Vic shrugged. "Mortuary had a power failure Wednesday morning. Mortuary people were scurrying around, trying to keep their paying guests iced. Anyone could have come in unnoticed. And gone out."

"Anyone notice an electric-company worker?" Tejeda asked.

"Yep." Vic grinned. "Drove a big gray American-made car. Like a Cutlass."

"Hey, Vic," Mark called from the freezer. "Give me a hand, will you?"

Definitely a wild-card play, Tejeda thought. Someone who hadn't the stomach to generate his own cadaver parts had gone to a lot of trouble to find some already rattling around loose. But why? He took a step into the freezer to watch Vic and Mark open the locker.

"Full house," Vic said, his cigar gripped between his teeth. "Tell Lou to bring me a meat tray."

Eddie Green, watching Vic pull freezer-wrapped white bundles from the locker, handed Tejeda a tiny plastic evidence bag.

Tejeda held it up to the light. "Sand?"

"Beach sand," Eddie said. "Quite a bit of it on the floor around the butcher block."

Vic had plunged a meat thermometer into one of the larger bundles. "Hey, Lou, how cold's your freezer?"

"Zero," Lou said. "Minus ten when the door isn't opened for a long time. Right now it's zero."

Vic extracted the thermometer and held out the bundle to Lou. "Weigh this for me, will you?"

"I ain't touching it. Weigh it yourself."

"No sweat." Vic helped Mark roll out a meat tray mounded with white packages, some long and thick, others no more than a handful. While Mark and Vic meticulously weighed and recorded each bundle, Tejeda stood back and tried to judge the total bulk of the load. About the same size as an Eagle Scout in a sleeping bag, he decided.

"What the hell is going on?" Otis Washington swept

in, carrying a gust of fresh outside air. His cheeks and
nose glowed with a shiny bourbon flush. When he
spotted Tejeda he grinned and tottered toward him.
"And what the hell are you doing here?"

"Just tagging along." Tejeda suffered through a boozy
hug.

"I knew you wouldn't let us down, Roger," Otis
wheezed. "That fuckin' City Council can take a flying
leap, right? I called that asshole down at the paper,
what's his name, Craig Hardy. Told him to wait up for
a big story. I figured if there was nothing here, we
could fill him in on the mortuary caper. That'll hold
the Council off through the weekend." Otis found a
half-pint flask in his coat pocket and took a dose.
"After Monday, when Arty's trial gets under way, the
public will think we're saints and we'll be back on the
budget A-list."

Tejeda just smiled. Otis' budget problems had nothing to do with Tejeda's reasons for sticking to the
investigation. He thought about setting him straight,
but after a whiff of the vapor Otis exhaled, he knew it
was pointless. Anyway, as long as he was there, what
did it matter why?

Vic had hardly looked up when his boss came in. He
had been busy slitting the end of each paper-wrapped
bundle and sorting them according to some plan.

Eddie stood beside him, a bit green around the
mouth, making notes and listening to Otis. Occasionally Eddie would nudge Vic and they would mutter
something, as if sharing a long-standing private joke.
Twice Tejeda overheard "Betty Ford Center," where
Otis had spent his summer vacation drying out.

Refortified from the flask, Otis shuffled over to the
scales and leaned heavily against the counter. "Tell
me what you found, Vic."

"This is just preliminary, right?" Vic said, thumbing

through the notes. "We have here the dismembered remains of a Caucasian male, well-built, well-nourished. Rough guess makes him maybe five-eight to six feet tall, one hundred and seventy pounds.

"Take a look, Otis." Vic opened the top of the largest bundle. "Abdominal fat's white, fairly soft. I'd say he was young. Certainly well past puberty, but under thirty. Once we get a look at his epiphysis in the lab, we'll get closer on the age. Right now it would help if we had the head."

Feeling prickly all over, Tejeda moved in. "No head?"

"No head in locker one-oh-nine," Vic said. "Mark, maybe you and Lou could go check the other lockers in the tier."

Otis had peeled the freezer wrap further down, exposing a bare torso. Frozen and bloodless, it looked to Tejeda like a fragment of a Greek statue carved from white marble. The skin was smooth, shiny, the muscles firm. It suggested a perfect young male form. Until he looked at the raw edges.

"How old was Wallace Morrow?" Otis asked.

"Nineteen," Vic said.

"Think this is a match?"

"Consistent as to size, age, coloring . . ." Vic flipped the torso over. "But look: we're missing only the first five cervical vertebrae."

"Only five?" Otis' flask reappeared. "Damn."

"Morrow had vertebrae one through six attached," Vic said. "I've never seen a body with two number-six vertebrae. Anyway, this corpse is too fresh."

The room started to spin. Tejeda pressed a hand against the hammering in his head and broke out in an icy sweat as a surge of nausea rose through him. Black fog swirled through his mind and he fought it, focusing on the sliver of light at the edge of his consciousness.

He knew he was losing it again, but there were things he had to do.

.By putting one foot in front of the other, he managed to get out of the packing room. He barked his shin on an office chair, sat down in it, put his head between his knees, and waited for the void to sweep him away. But nothing happened.

Taking deep breaths into his cupped hands, Tejeda felt the fog clear as the attack passed. His brain felt like scrambled eggs and the overhead light pricked his eyes like silver in sunlight, but the relief he felt nearly overwhelmed him.

Eddie Green hovered over him. "You okay?"

"Yeah." But his hands shook when he picked up a desk telephone and passed it up to Eddie. "Do this for me."

"Sure. Who you calling?"

"You know," he said, and hoped Eddie did, because he couldn't have come up with a name to save him.

Eddie dialed, waited a few moments, then spoke into the receiver, "Let me talk to Kate." He handed the telephone back.

"Kate?" Tejeda said when he heard an extension pick up.

"Roger, are you okay?"

"Yes. Did the kid show up?"

"Not yet. How did you hear?"

"Hear what? We've been looking for him all day."

"Oh," she said, and there was a pause. "You mean Lance?"

"Lance?" He gave it a moment to register. "Yes. Who else?"

"Lance showed up right after you left," she said. "He ran into an old friend on the beach, he said."

"Thank God." Tejeda let the image of the white-marble torso fade. "We'll be home soon. Save us some pie."

"Roger, wait," Kate said. "I thought maybe you had some news about Sean O'Shay."

"Who the hell is Sean O'Shay?"

"Theresa's friend, remember? He was coming over for dessert tonight."

Tejeda felt the fog rolling in around the edges again. "So?"

"His parents are frantic," Kate said. "First thing this morning he told his mother he was going to work out at the high-school pool. But he never got there."

16

Sean O'Shay's parents waited for Tejeda in the chief's office, their faces washed with a too-familiar blank shock. Tejeda refilled two Styrofoam cups with coffee, taking his time. He didn't think he could make it through one more set of parents, trying to explain how such a horrible thing could have happened to their much-loved son.

The questions they asked were simple, yet unanswerable. They had raised Sean for the future, but somehow he suddenly existed only in the past. They needed help to make the transition, something concrete to hold on to. Why? they wanted to know. What cause or event had been worth such a huge expenditure?

Tejeda had tried to explain how Sean's death fitted into the fabric of some maniac's plan, and how he was sorry as hell because that plan had something—what, he wished he knew—to do with himself. But nothing seemed to register.

Where was the logic? It was like when he was eight and he smashed his mother's Dresden lamp. "You'd better have a very good reason for this," she had cried. But there was no *reason* that was weighty enough to balance the loss; he had been goofing around with a football in the living room. She had demanded logic too, and all he could do then was what he wanted to do now: stand up and yell, "It's my fault, I'll fix it, please leave me alone."

He had swept the remains of the lamp into a bag and stuffed them behind old paint cans in the garage. Now, thirty-some years later, they had come spilling out, reminding him that some things, no matter how precious, can't be fixed. Ever.

"Lieutenant?" The sergeant on desk watch poked his head into the bull pen. "Couple people out front to see you."

"Who?"

"A Mr. and Mrs. Morrow."

Tejeda handed the coffees to the sergeant. "Take these into the chief's office, will you? Tell him where I am."

"Yeah, sure," the sergeant muttered as Tejeda, temporarily reprieved from one set of tragic faces, went out to face another.

The Morrows sat together in their neat Iowa clothes, as colorless as the institutional-beige wall. Only the glassy shine in Mr. Morrow's eyes showed life. He stood when he saw Tejeda.

"We saw on the news you found the remains of a boy," Mr. Morrow challenged. "Why didn't you call us? We was in the motel all night, so don't say you couldn't reach us."

"Mr. Morrow, I'm sorry you came down here." Tejeda pulled out a molded plastic chair and straddled it to face them. "I know how much you want us to find the remains of your son. Believe me, I would give anything if the body we found tonight was Wally."

Mrs. Morrow gasped. "You mean it isn't?"

"I'm sorry."

She gripped her husband's arm. "Another boy was killed?"

Tejeda nodded.

"Your address was on the police report," she said, startling him with this bit of inside information. "Was another boy found up at your place?"

He started to say no, but held it back; sometimes the truth was the biggest lie.

Mr. Morrow pulled his mouth into a rigid, lipless buttonhole. "Do you ever think about divine retribution, sir?"

Tejeda shrugged; he had learned from listening to the nuns in grade school when to turn his attention off. He was looking at Wallace Morrow Sr.'s stiff grimace, wondering how Mrs. Morrow ever managed to find enough lip to kiss, and gaining fast insight into why Wallace Jr. had gone outside looking for male affection.

"Back home our pastor, Dr. Johansen, tells us that people have to pay for their sins, in this world as well as the next."

Tejeda sighed. "I'm sure we'll get this killer behind bars real soon."

"I'm sure you will," Mr. Morrow harrumphed. "But I was referring to you."

Tejeda turned his full attention back on. "Excuse me?"

"My wife tells me you live outside the sanctity of marriage."

Tejeda got up and set his chair back against the wall. "It's getting late, Mr. Morrow."

"Has it occurred to you, Lieutenant Tejeda, that the carnage that has visited your home is a message from God? Who has died except sodomites? The Lord rained fire and brimstone from out of heaven on Sodom and Gomorrah and all its inhabitants."

"Go home," Tejeda said. "When we find anything about your son, we'll call you."

"Give it some thought, sir," Morrow said, stabbing a finger into Tejeda's air space.

Tejeda walked away, leaving the Morrows to gather their plastic raincoats and the thread of their fractured lives. Kate had said that Mrs. Morrow was spooky. But the woman didn't hold a candle to her husband.

Tejeda used a note from the D.A. as an excuse for a break from grieving parents. Hymie Osawa, the assistant D.A. prosecuting Arty Silver, wanted to see him downstairs in the forensics lab.

He found Osawa bent over a microscope at Vic Spago's compulsively neat worktable.

"This is great, Vic," Hymie said. "But it sure fucks things up."

Tejeda looked over Hymie's shoulder. "What's the problem?"

"Want the bad news or the good news?"

"You call it."

"Take a look. Some of the samples Vic got from that shed you found on the Marine base are human blood. So far, three are compatible with three of the victims on the indictment against Arty Silver: Frost, Martinez, and Fong."

"What's the bad news?"

"That *is* the bad news." Hymie rubbed his eyes and groped for his bifocals. "The timing couldn't be worse. I'm set for trial Monday morning and I don't need this shit. But you know the rules of discovery. I have to inform Arty's defense that Vic here has new evidence. You know what Axel is going to do with this? First he'll need six or eight weeks to study it all, during which time we'll probably lose enough jurors so that we'll waste a few more weeks trying to get a full panel again. We're looking at an Easter start date.

"That's bad enough. But Dick Tracy here has segregated semen samples from maybe two dozen different men. That's two dozen unidentified suspects Axel will bring into court if we try to put Arty in that shed.

"You know what you have here?" Hymie handed Tejeda a slide labeled O+. "You have here the germ of doubt that Axel will plant in the minds of the jurors."

"You have strong evidence and a silver tongue," Tejeda said. "You can overcome."

"Maybe," Hymie said. "Except for the good-news part of Vic's findings."

Tejeda looked down at Vic. "Tell me."

"I found positive, fresh blood samples in the shed too. It'll take five days, a week, for the results of a DNA print. But I'm laying book on Wally Morrow."

"You see?" Hymie leaned backed and sighed. "The seed germinates. Arty's been in the lockup for five years, but here is evidence of an ongoing series of murders."

Vic pulled out a stack of grisly color photographs. "I compared the hack marks on the vertebrae of O'Shay and Morrow to several of Arty's victims. The blades are different, but the patterns are similar."

Hymie groaned. "Put a lid on it, Vic."

Tejeda picked up two of the photographs, close-ups of the severed necks of two of Arty's last victims. It bothered him that he had lost the names of these boys, but he remembered the cases and how they fitted into Arty's scenario. He turned to Vic. "Do you think it's possible Arty is innocent?"

"Not for a minute," Vic said.

"Then what do we have?"

"A copycat," Vic said.

"You think Arty found himself another schnook like William Tyler?" Hymie asked.

Tejeda shook his head. "It's more than that. Tyler couldn't even make it through one killing and mutilation without folding. It would take someone with major problems of his own to pull off two. The first requirement for a serial killer is an obsessive personality, and what I'm seeing is obsession—obsession with the Arty Silver case or some aspect of it. Whoever he is, he has damned good inside information."

"Anyone in mind?" Hymie asked.

"Not specifically," Tejeda said. "Everywhere I've gone for the last five years, the families of Arty's victims have tracked me down, giving me clues they think they've dug up, demanding that I do more. Hymie, I know you run the same gauntlet."

"Yeah. The Silver Threads are worse than rock-star groupies sometimes. I know that Alma Pappas goes through my office trash. And Arty's family can be just as persistent."

"God, when I think of some of the stunts family members have pulled over the years," Tejeda said. "Murder can unhinge anyone whose bolts are a little loose to begin with. It's difficult for anyone to deal with that abrupt interruption in a relationship, but especially so if there were unresolved conflicts. We've seen siblings who had secretly wished their brothers, sisters dead since birth. When the sibling dies, two things happen. First he feels guilty about his thoughts, then he feels happy because now he can be the center of his parents' universe. But the parents are so involved with their grief, they can't even see him, so he wants to kill the sib all over again. It's frustrating as hell.

"Happens to parents, too, when they have ambivalent feelings for a problem child who dies. They sometimes do something drastic, take violent revenge, to prove to themselves that they loved the little bugger."

Vic chuckled. "See what happens when you give a cop a college degree?"

"Forget it," Hymie said. "He read all that stuff in *Dear Abby*."

"And that's the truth," Tejeda said. "Hymie, can you get me in to to see Arty Silver tonight?"

"It's late. Axel won't like it."

"See if he needs something we can trade for."

"That we have," Hymie said, glaring at a box of microscope slides. "I'll give it a shot."

Hymie went to a phone in the corner and tried to coerce Arty's defense attorney into leaving his Thanksgiving guests to go baby-sit with his star client. Tejeda understood from the tone of the conversation he overheard that Axel bore no real love for Arty. Tejeda sympathized with Axel; it would be next to impossible to defend a man who thought he was infallible.

Tejeda straightened a row of slides left beside the microscope. Arty's soft underbelly, the character flaw that Tejeda had used to trip him up, was his need to be in control: of the press, the police, the emotions of the community. If Arty hadn't learned by now when to shut up, it would get him the death penalty. Tejeda looked at the slides of fresh blood taken from the shack and hoped Wally Morrow's killer was as flawed.

"Vic," Tejeda said, "did you talk to Don Kelley when you were in Oceanside?"

"Couldn't. Landlady said he'd gone out of town."

Tejeda nodded. "Figures."

"All set," Hymie said, tearing off a sheet of notes as he came back from the telephone. "Axel wants time to finish his dessert, then he'll meet you. Jailer got the okay from Arty, and passed along a shopping list for you, Roger."

Tejeda looked the list over quickly, then folded it into his pocket. He had rearranged the rows of slides on Vic's desk twice, looking over the labels: Fong type O-, Martinez type A+, Frost type O+. Something rang a bell, something he felt he should be able to hear more clearly. He looked at the names on the slides again, then turned to Hymie.

"You wouldn't just happen to have a copy of the indictment against Arty, would you?"

"Never leave home without it." Hymie opened his bulging briefcase and handed Tejeda a manila folder.

Tejeda scanned through the indictment, skipping the first paragraphs of legal mumbo jumbo before he came to the charges, sixteen in all. He read the first:

Arthur Radley Silver is hereby accused by the district attorney of this county to whit: of violation of section 187 of the Penal Code of the State of California, murder, that on or about February 14, 1983, in this county in the State of California, that the said Arthur Radley Silver did willfully, unlawfully, feloniously, and with malice aforethought kill Erich Michael Fong, a human being.

Another thirteen charges were identical except for the dates and names of the victims. There were two charges under Section 286, forcible sodomy, tossed in, he suspected, as a reminder during jury deliberations that these were sex killings. Not that anyone who sat through the projected year of trial was likely to forget.

Tejeda took a pen from Vic's pocket and made a list from the indictment:

Frost
Martinez
Fong
Ricks

Kemmer
Le Nguyen
Ferraro
Pappas
Meyer
Kowolsky
Adams
Louis
Reynolds
Nightengale

Fourteen young men. Sixteen counts. He remembered the details of each case as he read the names and dates. And he knew something was missing.

He looked down at Hymie. "How many charges are you sitting on?"

"Eighteen. We'll bring them up during the penalty phase, but we brought them up too late for the trial."

"Have the names?"

Hymie took the pen and added to Tejeda's list. After Hymie had added the eighteenth, Tejeda still hadn't found what he was looking for.

Vic picked up the list. "What's wrong, Roger?"

"I don't know."

"Call me when you do." Hymie slid the manila folder back into his briefcase and took out a thick turkey sandwich. "Anybody else miss dinner?"

17

Arty Silver rattled his chains at Tejeda like Jacob Marley as he hobbled down the hall toward the interview room where Tejeda waited. "Did you bring it?"

"Yes," Tejeda said. "They're checking it out downstairs."

"You get all of it?"

"I got what I could. Not much is open this late on Thanksgiving night." Tejeda went over the list Hymie Osawa had given him. "I brought you three tacos, no lettuce, a pepperoni mushroom pizza, three Big Macs and fries, a chocolate shake, and a Diet Pepsi. You know what shape this shit will be in by the time it comes upstairs?"

"You know what I got for Thanksgiving?" Arty shuffled into the room, legs shackled at the ankles, hands attached to chains around his waist. "A Swanson's frozen turkey dinner and a Hershey bar from the Salvation Army. Even if the shit rots, it won't be any worse than that."

The two guards handling him were a little rougher than was maybe necessary, but Arty didn't seem to help them much. They maneuvered him into a chair that was bolted to the floor and locked down his leg chains.

Arty fussed with them to hurry, but his complaints

185

only seemed to make them move more slowly. Tejeda had time to take a good look at him, curious to see what five years in the county jail had done for Arty.

Arty's arrogance was certainly intact. He had lost some weight and gained some muscle. He seemed not older, but cannier, sleek in an animal way. For the most part, though, Tejeda thought, the remarkable thing about Arty Silver's appearance was how ordinary he seemed. If he were to walk out on the street this very minute, without his chains, people would see an unremarkable and not-very-tall forty-year-old man with a fresh eight-dollar haircut. Unless they could peer into Arty's soul, they wouldn't suspect that this was one of the most brutal mass murderers in California history.

When Arty's legs were secure, the guards released his arms and went out. Tejeda could see them hovering by the door, keeping a close eye on their prisoner. With his trial starting Monday, Arty was likely to try something desperate.

Arty rubbed his wrists, pink from the chains, and leered at Tejeda. "You look okay, Sergeant. I mean, Lieutenant. I keep forgetting you got a promotion off me."

"All I got from you, Arty, was a pain in the ass."

Arty threw back his head and laughed. "I'd like to show you a pain in the ass."

"Where's your attorney? I thought he'd be here."

"I told Axel you'd be a little late. I want to talk to you alone a minute."

"He's not going to like it," Tejeda warned.

"Axel? That asshole, who needs him? But the judge won't let me defend myself."

"Nice of you to see me on short notice. What's it going to cost me?"

"Depends." Arty glanced at the guards, then leaned

as close to Tejeda as the chains would allow. "They fried Ted Bundy. They shaved his head, plugged him in, and set the dial for well-done."

"You comparing yourself to Ted Bundy?"

"No way, man." He smirked. "I'm still alive."

"For now. You know, there's a book in Las Vegas saying your friend William Tyler will be the first man executed in California since the new law."

"So?" Arty shrugged. "The world will have one less asshole."

"So, the same book says you'll be number two."

Arty laughed. "Get me five bucks on that book, will you?"

"What do you want, Arty?"

"I need a personal favor."

"Ask your lawyer."

Arty shook his head, his posture suddenly all business. "Axel won't do it for me."

"What is it?"

"My mom. I don't want her at the trial."

"Tell her."

"Axel wants her to sit right behind me, to show the jury what a cute kid I am. Even told her what she should wear." He started to reach for Tejeda, but pulled back when a guard cleared his throat. "You tell her, from me, not to come."

"We'll see."

"Man, if I ever hear her say, 'You'll always be my precious boy,' I'll puke." Arty sucked in a deep breath. "What can I do for you?"

"Give me some information. But I think your attorney should be here."

"Fuck 'im." Arty grinned. "Shoot."

"I want to run some names by you, see what you know." Tejeda turned over the shopping list and looked at the names he'd written down, just in case he forgot them. "Corporal Wallace Morrow Jr.?"

"Only what I saw on the news."

"Sean O'Shay?"

"Rings no bells."

"Watch the news tonight?"

"You mean about my Uncle Lou's shop? I bet he had a fit." Arty laughed. "You know, Lou wouldn't talk to me for three years after I was arrested."

"Do you blame him?"

Arty smiled, a foxy gleam on his face. "Remember, I pleaded not guilty. What makes you think I left those boys in Uncle Lou's lockers?"

"Right. What do you know about Don Kelley?"

Arty started to shake his head, then stopped and furrowed his brow.

"Age thirty-two," Tejeda encouraged. "From Carlsbad. He's a regular down at Clyde's."

"Big guy?"

"Very."

"I sort of remember him. Not from Clyde's, though. What about him?"

"He sent us to a shack on the Marine base."

Arty waved him away. "Can't talk about that."

"How close were you and Kelley?"

"Not at all. We might have banged around a little, that's all. We knew some people in common."

"What people?"

"I don't remember. Just people."

"Did he know William Tyler?"

"Ask Will."

"I'm asking you. Tyler said at his trial that you directed him how to pull off a duplicate killing."

"I can't talk about that."

"Yes you can. You got immunity to testify against

him. Now I want to know if you're directing someone else."

Arty rolled his eyes. "I'm sure if I said no, you'd believe me."

"I might," Tejeda said. "Do you think Tyler knows enough about your methods to tell someone else how to copy you?"

"A. He doesn't have the guts. B. I didn't kill anybody, remember?"

"Yeah," Tejeda said. "So you told me. Look, Silver, did you ever confide in someone, tell him how you liked to have fun on Saturday night? Give me some help and I'll go talk to your mother."

There was a terrific clatter along the concrete floor somewhere outside the room, and a deep voice boomed down the corridor: "What the hell is going on?"

"It's Axel," Arty said.

Tejeda glanced up long enough to see Arty's attorney, dressed casually under his rain gear, puffing toward them.

"Silver," Axel bellowed, "don't you say one word."

Tejeda gestured for Arty to come closer. "I figure you have twenty seconds—max—before Axel gets in here. Give me something to work with or the deal's off."

For the first time he could remember, Tejeda saw real desperation in Arty's face. His voice broke when he spoke: "Talk to Will. Because I just don't know."

"You wangling for another trial postponement?"

The guards got Axel through the double-locked doors a whole lot faster than they had Arty.

"No. Honest." Arty's eyes shifted quickly from the door back to Tejeda. "I'm tired of this delay shit. I want to get under way. I want to get out of here."

"Lieutenant Tejeda!" Even when he was inside,

Axel screamed at top volume. "You know better than this."

"So sue me." Tejeda stood up.

"Wait." Arty tried to stand up with him, but his waist chains caught. "Do we have a deal?"

"You didn't tell me a goddamn thing, Arty."

Arty's eyes made a last feral plea. "I did."

"See you on Monday, Arty." Tejeda walked to the door and waited for the guards. "Say hi to your mom."

Tejeda didn't stay to listen to Axel bawl out his star client, though it might have been fun. Word was that Axel was having a helluva time keeping a tight lid on Arty. His first problem was that Arty acted like a loose flywheel. Early on in the case he had granted a pair of very damaging interviews to the press and left poor Axel to put his finger in the dike. Axel's second problem was more venal; rumor was that, though it was unethical and highly illegal, he was negotiating both book and movie rights to Arty's story to pay the bills. And he didn't want his best material floating out in public domain.

Tejeda chuckled to himself as he made his way back down to the sally port. Poor Axel, he thought. After five years of working with Arty, trying to maneuver him through the court system and keep him away from a death sentence, Axel had probably earned every nickel he got. And more.

He checked the wall clock. If Hymie drove him straight home now, he'd be able to get about three hours' sleep before it was time to leave for the airport. With a tail wind and a head start on rush-hour traffic in San Francisco, he might have time to grab breakfast before his nine o'clock appointment at San Quentin.

18

The house was unnaturally quiet, like the pause before the roller coaster starts downhill. Only the slap of gin-rummy cards and Eddie Green's snores broke the silence of the cavernous foyer.

The taller of a pair of uniformed officers discarded the ten of hearts and glanced up at Tejeda. "All's quiet, Lieutenant."

"Where is everybody?"

"Asleep, finally. Got pretty rough there for a while. But it toned down after the eleven o'clock news."

"How long are you on?"

"Till four." The officer looked at his watch and shrugged. "Ralph here has to get home, but I can stay on if you need me."

"We'll see."

Eddie Green's head lolled over the back of his chair at such an awkward angle that Tejeda shook him awake; they had a long day ahead and he didn't want to spend it listening to Eddie bitch about a crick in his neck.

"Mmmm?" Eddie growled, opening one eye.

"Go find a bed."

"What's the point?"

Tejeda shrugged. "Did you get Justin squared away?"

"Yeah. Kate took him home to Libby."

Libby throw a fit?"

Eddie started to shake his head, but grimaced and grabbed his neck. "Damn."

"I'm going up," Tejeda said. "Get yourself some aspirin."

Eddie massaged his neck. "Don't get too comfortable. Plane leaves at five."

"I know."

Tejeda walked up the stairs in the dark. His eyes hurt and his head throbbed and he wanted nothing more than to sleep. But he didn't think it was possible, the way his mind was racing.

He had telephoned Kate earlier, and heard in her voice the effort it took her to sound composed. Though Wally Morrow's death had upset her, he was a transient corpse, as it were, a boy from the outside who had enough history of personal problems that she could assign to him some guilt for his own end. But Sean's death was something else entirely, a direct, personal attack on Tejeda and the people he loved.

Tejeda had some business to take care of in San Quentin first thing in the morning, but as soon as he got back, he would discuss with Richie and Theresa the possibility of going away as a precaution. Especially Theresa; some genius at a local television station had made her the focus of a news story, a sort of Juliet, the daughter of a famous detective working on a murder case, whose boyfriend had been killed by the murderer. The first time in his life Tejeda could remember seriously contemplating murder himself was while watching the local newscaster relate Theresa's "tragic" story; a thirty-second spot before the weather.

In the dark, he barked his shin on a roll-away bed Reece had pulled in front of Kate's bedroom door, guarding her like Cerberus, wrapped only in a down quilt and with a black satin mask over his eyes. Tejeda managed to open the door and climb over the bed without noticeably disturbing Reece. Some guard, he groused, rubbing his shin.

When he shut the door behind him, the bedroom was dim, streaked with long shadows from the lights outside along the bluffs. After counting the number of recumbent shapes in the room, he abandoned the hope of a little sleep and resigned himself to a hot shower and a pot of coffee.

He tried to discern who was where. The ball on the window seat under an afghan was Trinh. Kate slept at the edge of the bed with Theresa in her arms. On the far side of them, Tejeda recognized his mother, shoes off but otherwise fully dressed, softly purring in her sleep.

"Dad?" Richie reached out from the rocking chair beside the bed. "What time is it?"

"About three." He took Richie's hand and led him into the bathroom, closed the door, and turned on the light; no sense waking everyone.

"How's your sister?" Tejeda asked.

"Shook-up." Richie rubbed his eyes. "She's afraid to stay, but she won't leave."

Tejeda recounted the shapes in his head. "Where's Jena? You didn't let her go home alone, did you?"

"No. She's up in Carmel with her parents." Richie squinted up at his father. "I think I could get used to being rich. Kate called someone and got Jena on a private jet an hour after we decided she should leave town."

"Why didn't you go with her?"

"Theresa."

"Thanks." He wrapped an arm around Richie. "Where are the others?"

"Grandpa and Lance are sleeping in my room. Mom sort of freaked and went home."

"Home to New Mexico?"

"No. Our house. Lydia said she'd stay with her."

He could see Cassie with the doors bolted and the lights out, pots and pans all over the floor so she could hear anyone who got in. She'd freaked before, and he'd had the feeling that in a perverse way she enjoyed it.

His stomach growled. "Anyone get around to dinner?"

"Not really."

"It's late." Tejeda pulled off his shirt and started the hot water in the shower. "I need to talk to Kate. Would you ask her to come in here?"

Richie cut off a yawn and gave his father a worldly leer. "In here?"

"Please. And you go get some sleep."

Tejeda turned on the massage jet and stood under the hot water, letting it pound his back. He was tired and worried about his kids. He tried to focus his thoughts, but the questions he had for William Tyler at San Quentin ran in a continuous cycle through his head until they became nothing but a blur.

He was squeezing shampoo onto his head when Kate opened the shower door.

"You're letting out my steam," he said.

"Tough." She began to strip and he wanted to watch, but shampoo kept running into his eyes. When he finally had the stuff rinsed out, she was sitting on the tile bench at the end of the shower, looking sleepy and irresistible through the mist.

She yawned. "I suppose there's no point trying to talk you out of going to San Quentin this morning."

"None."

"You need to sleep, Roger."

"I'll sleep on the plane."

"Right," she said. "It's a fifty-minute trip."

"If there's no weekend tie-up on the Golden Gate

Bridge, I should be back by noon." He took her hand and drew her up to him. "After lunch, we'll take a nap."

"I've taken naps with you before," she smiled, picking up the bar of soap and lathering his belly. "And they never had much to do with sleeping."

He put his arms around her and held her close, the soap and the water slippery between them. "We have a whole lifetime for sleeping."

"When I arranged your airline tickets for San Francisco, I ordered you a car and a driver."

"Spud can drive."

"Better you should both rest," she said, rivulets of water coursing down her chin and onto her chest. "Especially you. I don't want you too tired for a nice long nap."

Kate managed to find space in the breakfront for the stacks of china dinner plates. Yesterday everyone had been so festive, and then after Sean was dead they had all seemed ashamed that they were ever happy. She wanted to get the last of the dishes put away before the others saw them, to spare them the reminder, the way a mortuary sweeps away the wilted flowers after a funeral.

It had been early still, barely six, when she got back from taking Tejeda to the airport. And, fortunately, everyone in the house except Trinh was still upstairs.

The mantel clock chimed once for the half-hour: six-thirty. Tejeda should have landed by now and be on his way up the Bayshore Freeway. In some ways she was glad he had gone. She wished he would stop challenging the obvious limits of his endurance, though she admired his gutsiness, because she wanted to have him around for a long time. She saw this trip as a break; in the back seat of a limo, under the protective wing of Eddie Green, how much trouble could he get into? By the time he got home, she hoped to have at least some of the extraneous problems out of the way.

In the meantime, there wasn't much she could do until people got out of bed. She took a sip of tepid coffee and despaired of squeezing in the candlesticks. It would be much easier, she thought, to stash everything left over into the pantry and close the door. But she needed something mundane to keep herself occupied, to keep her mind off what had happened until she could do something about it.

All of these dishes had come out of the breakfront, she thought, so there had to be room for them all to go back in. She picked up a candlestick and looked at the cupboard space: it was a matter of manipulation. Like what was happening to their household and the O'Shays and the Morrows. They were all being walked through some strange scenario like marionettes. And she hated it, hated being so easily manipulated.

She closed the breakfront, scooped up a load of silver, and carried it into the pantry. No more, she thought as she shoved aside boxes of cereal and canisters of rice and flour to make room; somehow she was going to cut the strings.

With only a modicum of care, she deposited the silver and went back to the dining room for another load.

" 'Morning." Mike Rios was taking camera equipment out of a bag on the floor. "Have a nice Thanksgiving?"

"You're out early." She stood holding the edge of the door for a moment, alarmed for no good reason she could think of. Then she remembered telling him he could come on Friday morning to take pictures of the ceiling moldings.

"Will you be long?" she asked.

"No. This whole exercise is a waste, anyway." He screwed a macro lens onto his camera. "Carl will never find a craftsman who will duplicate this in wood for less than thirty, forty thousand. Resin castings would be a hell of a lot cheaper and easier. And I wouldn't mind earning the money myself."

"If it will be too expensive, why bother with the pictures?" she asked, picking up another armload of dishes.

"He thinks he wants it. So I'll cost it out for him. Hell, anyway it's his money."

"Right." She backed through the swing door. "Excuse me."

Carl had money. If he wanted to duplicate the moldings badly enough, Kate thought, the cost wouldn't stop him. Then she shrugged; even if he didn't have money, if Carl wanted something badly enough, he would find a way to get it.

Mike Rios was up on a chair focusing his lens when she returned. He had made a space among the crystal goblets at the end of the table for his sketchbook. As she loaded the goblets onto a tray, she glanced at the top page of sketches he had made of the moldings on his first visit. They were exquisite, showing every detail of the carved patterns.

"You're very talented," she said. "Do you mind if I look through your book?"

"No." He nodded as if it didn't matter, but he flushed a deep red. After snapping a few more photographs, he came down and looked over her shoulder while she flipped the stiff pages.

His book was full of architectural sketches, many of notable old buildings around Santa Angelica. He had captured the personality of each building in clean, simple line drawings. The details of frescoes and friezes and peeling window frames filled the edges of his pages, like cameos, each one a tiny masterpiece on its own.

He had made studies not only of the grander buildings but also of a well-weathered barn, the ancient beach cabanas at the yacht club, a squatter's cottage up in a canyon beyond town.

When she was about halfway through the sketchbook, he took it from her and flipped to the back.

"You might recognize these," he said.

Her first reaction was a possessive lust. He had made a six-page study of her estate, the three houses, the garages, the beach stairs. The draftsmanship and detail were impressive on all of them, but his sketch of the gazebo framed by a stormy sky was absolutely masterful.

"I'm impressed," she said. "Where did you study?"

"Nowhere, really." He closed the book. "I had a pretty good teacher in high school, and I took a couple of architectural-rendering classes at the community college. But that's it. Art school's pretty expensive. And there isn't a good one around here."

"Did you look into scholarships?"

"Yeah." She heard bitterness in his laugh. "I always thought I had it made. My brother was supposed to graduate from college, get a job, and help me through. But it didn't work out that way, and now I'm helping him."

She smiled. "Life's full of curve balls, isn't it?"

"Yeah."

"Would you consider selling me the sketches of the estate? I would love to have them."

"Price would be pretty high."

"It should be."

"Yeah?" He was disassembling the camera, not looking at her. "I'll think about it."

Kate went back to the tray of glasses, thinking about

how perfect the sketches would be in the study, framed, hanging by the French doors from where the subjects of several of the drawings were visible. Especially the gazebo. She was trying to figure out a decent offer to make him when he snapped his camera case shut.

"Finished?" she said.

He shouldered the capacious bag. "You know, I never could figure what you had in common with that guy Carl."

"You're not alone." She smiled.

"I thought of one thing." His grin was sardonic. "Money's no object."

19

The uniformed limo driver held up a tastefully small card with "Little Rigo" printed in neat block letters. Tejeda took a look at the car and smiled, admiring Kate's restraint. This was no rock star's showy stretch Cadillac. She had arranged for a stately black Mercedes.

He nudged Eddie Green as they walked toward the passenger loading zone in front of the airline terminal. "Think the department will reimburse us for transportation?"

"Yeah. Fifty cents a mile."

"Should just about cover breakfast. I'll ask the driver to drive through the first McDonald's."

At that hour, the San Francisco airport was nearly deserted. The driver, seeing the only likely pair of men approach, opened the back door of the limo. "Lieutenant?" he said, touching his cap.

"Can you find your way to San Quentin?"

"Yes, sir," he said snappily, his posture Central Casting straight. "The trip should take less than two hours, giving you an hour to spare before your appointment. If you would like to stop anywhere along the way, perhaps for sightseeing, just buzz me."

"What's your name?"

"Peters, sir."

"Okay, Peters. We're hungry."

"I believe, sir, that you have been anticipated."

Tejeda interpreted Peters' bow as an invitation, and stepped into the car with Eddie close behind. The first smell was leather, the second was fresh coffee.

With the efficiency of an airline hostess, Peters leaned into the car, pulled down lap trays, and served them from covered dishes: steaming eggs Benedict, juice, croissants, coffee, with Godiva chocolate mints in a tiny silver basket.

"What?" Eddie said, tucking a starched napkin under his chin. "No Grape Nuts?"

Peters actually smiled as he closed the door and went around to the driver's seat.

Eddie dabbed at a blob of egg yolk on his chin as they accelerated up the freeway on-ramp. "Don't you think this is a little too much? Pass me the coffee, will you? A rental Ford would have sufficed."

"Kate wanted you to get some rest."

"She wanted *me* to get some rest? That's a hoot."

"Think about it. Who would be driving the rental Ford while I slept?"

"Right," Eddie mused, sloshing cream into his cup. "Tell Kate I think she's okay."

"Tell her yourself."

Tejeda finished his breakfast, popped a mint into his mouth, pushed the tray aside, and slid down against the deep seat. He was asleep before the mint was half-dissolved. He roused once, long enough to see hazy sunlight on the boats around Sausalito and to remind himself to take notice on the way back. Peters was a pro and the car rode like a baby's cradle; Tejeda didn't stir again until Eddie shook his shoulder.

"Next stop, San Quentin," Eddie said, pouring out the last of the coffee.

Tejeda sat up and tried to shake off the lingering drowsiness, the dull throb in his head. He sipped some ice water and held the cold glass to his head and watched the scenery slip by.

They were off the freeway, winding through the dry hills along the waterfront. Ahead, there was a cluster of dull green barracks wedged into the face of a stony brown bluff that overhung Richmond harbor. That innocuous cluster was San Quentin State Prison.

There had once been a village called San Quentin outside the prison walls, modest houses, a few bars and shops, a public school for kids whose fathers were locked up inside, and for the kids of their jailers. But it had been absorbed by time and the encroachment of chain discount outlets oozing off the southern edge of the city of Richmond. The prison was simply a part of the blighted landscape, no more noticeable, or ugly, than the electric-power plant below or the huge cranes off-loading cargo ships in the harbor.

Tejeda always thought that the walls of San Quentin seemed to sweat. Or cry. He blamed the climate of the entire Bay Area, too damp and cold for his taste. And today, altogether too far away from Kate.

The warden cut through the usual preliminaries quickly—a search, a fast exchange of bullshit—and had Eddie and Tejeda escorted to the cellblock that comprised California's Death Row. It was early and the prison was understaffed on the weekend; the interview was to take place in the corridor outside William Tyler's cell.

At last count, there were two-hundred and forty-one men waiting for their turn in the gas chamber. Walking along the catwalk toward an isolation area at the far end of the third tier of cells, Tejeda recognized at least a dozen familiar faces looking out through the bars, a sort of all-star lineup of California murderers. A few even nodded back.

William Tyler sat alone in an end cell in an area

segregated by an extra set of barred doors, waiting for his early-morning guests. While the jailer arranged two chairs outside his cell, Tyler watched with eyes so dark and cold Tejeda couldn't see his pupils. He had aged more than the three years he had been inside.

The last time Tejeda had seen Tyler was at his sentencing. Tyler had been defeated somewhat then, but he had still been a hard-muscled bantam cock of a man. Something had happened at San Quentin to loosen his tightly wound springs.

"I only get two visitors a month," Tyler said, sitting on the edge of his bunk and looking out through his green bars. "My lover's coming up today. I haven't seen him for a while. I hope this visit of yours hasn't fucked me up."

"Be nice," Tejeda said, "and we'll clear your boyfriend with the warden."

There was an almost tearful waver in Tyler's sigh.

"How have you been, Willie?"

"Not too bad, all things considered. Lots of time to read. I'm finishing another master's by mail. Physics this time. Not that I can do anything with it, you know." He shrugged, but he seemed less depressed the more he talked. "I miss getting around. I miss my lover. But I figure that at an average of six inches per, there are forty yards of dick on Death Row. Until I got sent down here to isolation, I probably took in fifteen yards of it."

Eddie crossed his legs. "Is that why you're locked up in Siberia?"

"Indirectly. I'm HIV-positive." He rolled up his sleeve and showed a four-inch patch of blue skin—a nasty lesion of Kaposi's sarcoma, an early symptom of full-blown AIDS. "Guess I have a double death sentence. It's just a matter of which takes me first."

"I'm sorry, Willie," Tejeda said.

"Don't be. What do you want?"

"Someone is trying to duplicate Arty Silver's murders again. Arty thinks you might know something about it."

"Not me."

"You never told us how Arty persuaded you to kill for him."

"I don't have to talk about that anymore. I confessed, I got sent up. As far as I'm concerned, it's over."

"It isn't over for us." Tejeda leaned closer to the bars. "What was your relationship to Arty?"

"Read my transcripts. We were friends in high school, in the math club together. He spent a lot of time at my house."

"Were you lovers?"

"No. I tried to help him come out. But he was so afraid of his old man, he kept it secret from his family until he was arrested."

"What did he think his father would do?"

"Kill him," Tyler said baldly.

"What sort of kid was Arty?" Tejeda asked.

"Ask a shrink. I only know what I saw. He was a good student—all the kids in the family are really bright, not that they ever did anything with their brains. He spent a lot of time in the library, or just hanging around, trying to stay out of his father's way."

"I heard all this a dozen times during your trial. You haven't been kids for a long time, Willie. And Arty hasn't lived with his father for twenty years. What I have never been able to understand is how he got someone as intelligent as you are to kill for him."

Willie shrugged. "I don't know myself. Guess I'm a loyal kind of guy."

"But you're not stupid."

"Don't be too sure."

The jailer took a call in his cubicle, then came out with a card in his hand. "Hey, Tyler. Put your clean shirt away. Your visitor can't make it today."

Tyler sulked. "I didn't want to see him anyway."

"Your lover?" Tejeda asked.

"Doesn't matter."

"Sure it does," Eddie said. "You were hot to see him."

"I'm tired. I don't want to see anybody."

"Who were you expecting?" Eddie pressed.

When Tyler didn't answer, the jailer looked at his card. "Donald Kelley," he read.

"Wouldn't you know?" Eddie took the card to read for himself. "The further I get into this, the crazier it gets."

Tejeda had been watching Tyler sink into a spiritless heap. "Are you trying to protect Don Kelley, Willie?"

"Why should I? He doesn't care about me."

"But he did once?"

Tyler only shrugged dispiritedly.

"Don know anything about the murder you were sent up for?"

"I thought he did, but I was wrong."

"Shit, Tyler." Tejeda rubbed his eyes. "What have you done?"

Willie looked up at the ceiling for a while; then he sighed and spoke in a very soft voice. "I'll tell you something I've never told anyone before. And if you repeat it, I'll deny I said it."

"Okay."

"I never killed anyone in my life."

"The fuck you didn't," Eddie spouted, but Tejeda put out a restraining hand.

"Go ahead, Willie," he said. In the back of his mind he had been expecting something like this for a long time. Almost every other man in this cellblock claimed his own innocence with boring insistence, and would likely continue to do so until the cyanide pellets dropped into the bucket under his chair. Anyone who had heard enough of them knew they were just blowing empty air. But with William Tyler, Tejeda felt, this profession of innocence was different. He had never been able to cast Tyler as a killer.

Tyler's cheeks were red, his breathing fast and shallow. Tejeda was afraid he would hyperventilate.

"Take it slow, Willie," he said. "Tell me what happened."

"I can't."

"What have you got to lose?"

"I mean, I can't tell you because I don't know. Don and I never talked about it. See, he used to be really close to Arty—that's how we met. The way he talked, I thought he had done the killing to help Arty get off."

"Something changed your mind?"

"He quit coming to see me. I thought he had deserted me, so I reminded him what I had done for him. He said he never killed anybody."

"Even if he had, why would you take the fall for him?"

"I don't know," he moaned. "Don wouldn't have lasted in here. He doesn't read, he gets into fights. I thought that if I was going to die from AIDS anyway, I might as well die in prison. If I had known I would live this long, I wouldn't have done it. Not even for Don."

"Have you told this to your attorney?"

"Sure. He won't believe me." He looked into Tejeda's eyes. "Would you?"

Tejeda thought about it a moment, massaging the pain in his temple. "Maybe I would."

"Then do something, because I don't want to die in here."

"Okay, Willie." Tejeda pulled his chair closer to the bars. "Start at the beginning, from the day you first met Arty Silver."

20

Kate dropped to her stomach in the ice plant and low-crawled into the oleander. The trail Lance had made dragging Reece's surfboard across the sand was clear enough, if she could just get to it without being seen.

The redheaded bimbo from the Channel 5 six o'clock news was showing her camera crew her war scars or something; at any rate, she had pulled her skirt up above the tan line on one leg and they were all certainly looking; even the soundman from Channel 2 was involved. Kate hoped that while they were distracted, she could slip down the bank behind them and merge unnoticed with a group of power walkers coming her way.

When she'd set out, she hadn't counted on the critters hidden under the ice plant or the slick green gel the plants oozed when broken. If she'd had time to rethink this move, she would have driven down to the marina and searched for Lance by boat. Or left him to fend for himself.

Something on the bluff above her caught the attention of the Channel 2 man, and she ducked, getting a faceful of oleander leaves. She was tired of chasing after Lance. He was a nice kid and she sympathized with the pickle he had gotten himself into, but when Roger got back she was going to ask him to lock

Lance away somewhere if he wanted to keep tabs on him.

Hymie Osawa had come over after breakfast and questioned Lance, who had managed to be at the same time contrite and evasive. He didn't know anything and hadn't been anywhere, he said, and the pressure of questioning had given him a headache. He needed some fresh air. So, once again, he had borrowed a surfboard from Reece's collection and managed to slip away.

The power walkers were directly below her. She waited for the clutch of newspeople to look the group over and lose interest in them before she moved from her cover. She slid down the last five feet of bluff, swallowing a scream when something dark and furry scampered over her bare ankle, and made it to the sand unseen; the walkers were rubbernecking the newspeople.

Lance had left an easy trail. The board he had selected this time was a pain to carry, a thirty-year-old that he was dragging behind him—it weighed well over a hundred pounds. Besides being cumbersome, the choice puzzled Kate. She looked from the deep track he left in the sand to the flat, lazy surf. Lance had presented himself to her as an expert surfer. At least, he seemed to know what he was talking about. This particular board needed two things: expertise and big surf. Kate was no surfer, but she knew there wasn't a wave this side of Hawaii big enough for that board.

So what was Lance up to?

Once she had passed behind the first outcropping of Byrd Rock, she was able to relax her guard a little. The beach was quiet, a nice break from the tension of a houseful of people in shock. The sky was still heavy with rain, and the wind off the water was stiff and bracing. As always, there were a few people around, the stalwarts who came out, no matter the weather, to walk or run or just sit and contemplate. It was a relief, even under the circumstances, to be out in the open.

Lance's trail scalloped around the pillars of Byrd Rock and ended suddenly where the rock flattened into a shelf that extended into the surf like a reef. She climbed up on the first shelf of rock and spotted the tip of the seven-foot surfboard tucked into an eroded fold.

The rock here was razor-sharp brescia, an aggregate of sandstone and shells, pitted everywhere with holes that ranged in size from thimbles to extensive interconnected pools of trapped water. Every pool teemed with tidal sea life—bright anemones, spiky black crabs, and tiny fish. It was a good place to lose yourself, she thought, if you had a lot to think over. Or something to hide from. And she thought Lance had both. She kept trying to make things Lance had told her mesh with what she knew from other sources, but they just didn't.

Coming around a corner, she spotted Lance. He squatted over a tide pool at the far point, just clear of the spray from the breaking waves. And he had company, she saw with dismay—Craig Hardy.

She hadn't given much thought to getting back through the gauntlet of reporters; if things got really bad, she could swim down to the pier to call for someone to pick her up. She bent down and rinsed some of the green ice-plant slime from her hands in one of the pools, and decided that a face-off with Hardy would be only slightly less uncomfortable than a quarter-mile swim in the frigid water.

The two men seemed to be absorbed with the tide-pool creature Lance was prodding with a Popsicle stick. As Kate approached, Hardy looked up and grinned at her, seeming smugly triumphant, while Lance kept his head down.

"Urchin or anemone?" she asked, bending for a closer look. "I never know the difference."

"I don't either," Lance said.

"You don't? I always thought you were in ocean studies of some kind, like Richie."

He shook his head. "Engineering."

Lance seemed either sulky or chagrined, it was hard to tell; he wouldn't look her in the face. Not that she cared, really, how he felt. She had only come to make sure that he hadn't taken a flying leap. Or worse; Tejeda had warned them all not to go off alone.

Hardy stood up and stretched out his knees.

"You two know each other?" she asked.

"Not really," Hardy said. "Just drifted toward the same tide pool."

"Lance Lumsden, meet Craig Hardy, reporter for the *Daily Angel*."

Lance looked up when he heard the word "reporter," but Hardy was unfazed by exposure.

"How are things up at the big house?" Hardy asked.

"Very sad. And you can quote me."

"How's the girl taking it?"

"Theresa?" she asked. "As I said, very sad."

Hardy nodded with the sort of trained sympathy morticians wore. "Does she feel responsible?"

"Responsible for what?"

"The death of Sean O'Shay, of course. Wasn't he chosen by the killer as a way to get a message to Lieutenant Tejeda?"

"That's absurd." She tried to laugh.

Lance stood up between them. "It was supposed to be me. The killer wanted to stop me."

Kate could almost see the light come on in Hardy's

eyes. But the tone of his voice remained very casual. "Stop you from what, Lumsden?"

Kate put a hand on Lance's arm. "Be careful."

"Nothing," Lance said. "Forget it."

"Lance," she said. "Get your board. Lunch is ready."

"Are you going to take that from her?" Hardy pressed. "You want to tell me something, don't let her stop you."

"Go ahead," Kate said. "Anything you say may be used as evidence against you."

Lance seemed confused. Then he took a long, shuddery breath and faced Craig Hardy. "Arty Silver killed my brother. I just thought maybe his friends would come after me next, that's all."

"She say your name's Lumsden?" Hardy narrowed his eyes. "This a stepbrother or half-brother?"

"No," Lance said. "My real brother."

Kate considered pushing him into the water to shut him up. "Don't say anything more until you talk to an attorney."

"I covered every Silver killing for eight years," Hardy said. "There was no Lumsden."

Lance choked something back, then dropped to his knees and covered his face.

"You better go, Hardy," Kate said, pulling him by the arm when he moved to hover over Lance. "Lance doesn't know what he's saying; you can see that."

"He seems lucid enough."

"Tell you what, you go away and give Lance some time to collect himself, and when he's ready, he'll give you an exclusive."

"I'd rather hear it now."

"Or I'll file harassment charges and get a restraining order against you. You know this is no bluff—I've done it before."

"I remember." He bowed in submission. "Paper

goes to press at eleven tonight. Get me a story by ten-thirty or the deal's off."

"Fine. I have your number."

Craig Hardy hesitated, giving Lance a long hard look; then he squared his shoulders, leapt the tide pools, and was gone.

While Lance settled down, Kate pried a mussel off the rock and flipped it into the air for a passing seagull. She watched the bird catch the mussel, then soar high with it before he dashed it to the rocks. The bird was picking the soft flesh out of the broken shell when she turned back to Lance. He, too, had been watching the gull.

His face was splotched but his eyes were dry. Roger had told her to trust absolutely no one, and not to go off alone. And here she was, alone with Lance, the most suspicious character of the day, well out of sight of the few people on the beach. It hadn't occurred to her to be frightened of him. If he had done what she suspected he had, he had gone to almost absurd lengths not to harm anyone. And "absurd" was the right word, she thought.

When he looked up at her, she asked, "Electrical engineering?"

"Mechanical."

"Close enough. I suppose that you don't have to be an engineer to know how to flip off a circuit breaker."

"You know about that?" When he stood up, his knees were pocked and bloody from the sharp surface of the rock. He didn't seem to notice.

"Lance, do you know an attorney?"

"That's what Mr. Osawa kept asking me. But why? I haven't done anything illegal."

"Last night Roger looked for your brother's name in every murder file in the county. Then he called

L.A. and San Diego," she said. "No one had heard of a Lumsden."

"I didn't lie to you," he said firmly. "I know Arty Silver killed my brother. And the police know it too. But they never found any evidence."

"Other than his head?"

"All right, I did lie to you." He looked absolutely miserable, like an injured kid who was afraid he was going to cry. "They never found any trace of him. He just disappeared. The Marines still have him listed as AWOL."

"Why do you think Silver killed him?"

"I just know. The police said his disappearance was a Marine problem, and the Marines wouldn't do anything. So my folks hired a private investigator. He traced my brother to Clyde's on the day he disappeared, talking to a guy who fitted Silver's description. Then he vanished."

"So years later you went to Clyde's and started asking questions. What did you think you could accomplish?"

"If you only knew what this has done to my folks—they might as well be dead. My mother keeps waiting for my brother to call. She can't live again until she has a body to bury."

"Did you think you could find him?"

"Maybe. But I ran out of time. I only wanted to delay the trial until I had *something*," he said. "It's real important that my brother get on the indictment against Arty Silver. I need someone to ask him questions about my brother."

"In the meantime, Lance, you've gotten yourself into one hell of a mess. I don't know if it's a crime to turn someone's power off, then masquerade as a repairman. But I suspect there's some law against stealing part of a corpse from a mortuary."

"You know about that too?" he asked. His surprise deflated into chagrin. "I'm sorry about everything. You've been so nice to me. But I don't think anyone can help me at this point."

She sighed. "Let's get the surfboard and go in. Lunch is ready."

She followed him over the rocks. "I hope you do very well in engineering, because you sure as hell wouldn't make it through drama school."

"Guess not." He actually laughed a little. He side-stepped a rough patch and reached into the hollow where he had left Reece's surfboard. Then he recoiled, protectively pushing Kate away.

Reece came out of the hollow, carrying the board and a big rock. He had ice-plant stains on his knees.

"Did you see the size of the rats on the bluff?" Reece asked, dropping the rock.

"You followed me," Kate said.

"Damn right. Whatever possessed you to go off alone?"

Kate pointed across the beach to a phalanx of approaching reporters. "Define 'alone.' "

21

"I thought I heard someone come in," Kate said, coming down the hall to meet him. "I was hoping it was you. How was the trip?"

"Productive. Thank you for breakfast." Tejeda folded her in his arms and kissed her, starting at the base of her neck and working his way up. "And for lunch."

"You're welcome."

"What's all the racket?"

"Come and see." She kissed him lightly on the lips and took him by the hand. "We've relented."

The dining room was a hive of activity, all apparently under the noisy direction of Mike Rios. The furniture had been moved aside to make room for a long tarp and three ladders. Rios was atop the middle ladder, flanked by Richie and Lance. Together they held a yard-long form against a stretch of ceiling molding. On the floor along the baseboard there were three similar forms with perfect impressions of the carved wood, except in relief.

Trinh, Reece, and Ricardo sat in the middle of the room and kibitzed, nursing beers and offering obviously unneeded advice. There was a round of elbow nudging when they saw Tejeda, and they all watched him closely for his reaction: Carl sat at the dining table opposite Hymie Osawa, passing a sheaf of legal-size documents between them.

Carl looked up. "How are you, Lieutenant?"

"No complaints. What's up, Hymie?"

"Rigo," Ricardo interrupted, "look at Richie's end. Don't you think his end is a little low? Mike, take a look at Richie's end. He's low, isn't he?"

"It isn't Richie," Reece chimed in. "It's Lance. Lance, your end is low."

Mike's attention to his two helpers and their mold seemed to lapse as he watched Ricardo get out of his chair to plant a wet kiss on Tejeda's cheek.

"No, Reece," Ricardo said, "it's Richie."

Tejeda wrapped his father in a bear hug, holding him stationary. "Don't pay any attention to Dad, Mike. He always has to be the conductor."

"Mike," Ricardo said, "you ever play the trombone?"

"Me?" Rios had leaned back to look at both ends. "I think it's ready. Careful now."

While Rios pulled the form away and struggled with his helpers to bring it down intact, Tejeda released his father and turned to Kate. "What brought all this about?"

"We did a little four-way bartering this morning," she said. "Carl wanted the moldings and Mike wanted the job of making them. So we made a swap: Carl is giving Lance some legal help and Mike is giving me some of his sketches for the privilege. The sidewalk superintending comes free."

"About what it's worth," Tejeda said, and went to help Lance set down his end of the mold. "Everything okay, son?"

"He shouldn't have any complaints," Carl offered. He ripped through a sheaf of notes, set them aside, then slid a document and a gold pen toward Hymie. "I'm not sure about the propriety of this arrangement, but it's certainly to Mr. Lumsden's advantage."

"What did you give away, Hymie?" Tejeda asked.

"The kitchen sink." Hymie read over the document. "Lance, think you'll be happy in Montana?"

"I'd rather be there than in jail."

"Same thing, as far as I'm concerned," Hymie said as he signed the papers. "You understand all this? You have immunity from prosecution on the body-snatching charge, on the condition that you go back to Montana with your family and seek professional counseling. If you enter the state of California, except under subpoena, during the next two years, immunity is automatically revoked. Capish?"

"Yes, sir," Lance said.

"Just to be on the safe side," Carl said, reading over the agreement, "I recommend you refrain from uttering the words 'Arty Silver' until you land in Billings."

"So?" Ricardo raised his hands as if cueing in the whole orchestra. "Is everybody happy?"

"Delirious." Carl collected his things and slipped on his suit coat. "Trinh, you have any more turkey? I only got one sandwich."

"Me too." Reece picked up two beer empties and was first man to the kitchen door. "Hymie? How about it?"

Tejeda watched the exodus until only Richie and Mike Rios were left. He draped an arm around Richie and watched Rios brush some extra material off a leaf whorl. "Nice work, Mike. Don't you want a sandwich? Looks like you earned one."

Rios looked up shyly. He seemed to have been watching the interactions of everyone in the room, spying almost, as if he were some sort of alien taking notes. "I don't eat meat."

"We have cheese and peanut butter," Kate said. "Trinh probably has some rice balls in the refrigerator."

Rios hesitated, watching Tejeda's face all the time, as if waiting for some clue. Then he began packing his tools. "I'm not hungry."

"Another time, maybe," Kate said breezily, and went into the kitchen.

Tejeda stayed behind, waiting for Rios to finish his packing.

"Did she mean that?" Rios asked.

"Kate always means what she says."

"Yeah?" Rios glanced at the swinging door as he stood with his tool bag. "Tell her maybe another time."

Tejeda put the last of the dishes into the dishwasher and dried his hands. He had hoped for a little quiet time with Kate before he had to leave again, but he didn't know how to get rid of Carl tactfully. Everyone else in their ongoing house party had moved on to other amusements—Reece had remembered an old set of boccie balls in the garage, and there was a noisy game in progress out on the lawn.

Carl had stayed behind to help Kate figure out what had happened to a property-tax payment she remembered making on a house they still owned jointly somewhere in town. It hadn't occurred to Tejeda while trying to figure out what to do with his own house that Kate might also have a house left over from her marriage.

Tejeda had never been able to imagine Kate and Carl actually living together, taking care of routine chores. Not that he thought Kate had lived in a vacuum before he had met her. He just couldn't imagine her with Carl, who was like a guy in a magazine shirt ad to him: great-looking, but when you turned the page, you found he had no backside.

He picked up a sponge and started wiping down the sink, a transparent ploy, giving himself an excuse to hang around a little longer. He knew from Carl's bland expression when he looked up that he saw right through him.

"Any more coffee?" Carl asked.

"Sorry, I washed the pot."

"I found it." Kate slid the check register in front of Carl. "October 20, check twenty-five-oh-eight. If it got to the bank around the first of November, then it was probably in the batch that bounced because of the hold you put on my accounts."

"Sorry," he said, taking a handful of his perfect haircut as he studied the register. "I didn't realize. I'll pick up any interest and penalties."

"Fair enough. How about these others?"

When they bent their heads together over the register, Tejeda had to admit to a little pang. They were a very attractive pair, Kate as dark as Carl was fair. Tejeda rinsed out the sponge and dropped it on the sink; what made him uncomfortable was the realization that Carl did have a backside, and a lot more depth than he had dared give him credit for. In fact, he admitted, the asshole could be downright nice. During his negotiations on behalf of Lance, Carl had shown himself to be tough, fair, and generous. Not that it made Tejeda like him any better; Carl had been a lot easier to dismiss as a factor in Kate's life when he was still a shirt ad.

He wondered how bizarre it would be if Carl actually moved into the house he was working on next door. The guy was quiet and neat and didn't spit on the sidewalk. But Tejeda didn't think he was modern enough to want his lover's ex parking his dirty socks so close by.

He filled a glass with water. "How's the house coming?"

"Great." Carl smiled. "I've never done anything like this before. I expected the whole enterprise to be a real pain, but I find I enjoy it."

"Mike Rios is an odd duck."

"Could be. But he walks on water as far as I'm concerned. Everyone told me my expectations for the house were too high. Everyone except Mike. His own ideas are usually better than mine, but if I want something, he'll move heaven and earth to get it."

"Where did you dig him up?" Tejeda asked.

"Actually, he dug me up," Carl said. "When he heard I was bidding the job, he got a mutual acquaintance to recommend him. He's worked out very well, I think, because we both have the same goal, to make the house as beautiful as it was before Kate's uncle let it go to pot."

Kate's eyes grew round. "Today he's my uncle and not your father?"

"Today, yes. After the mess I made of your accounts, I figure I'm skating on thin ice. And you did give me the moldings."

"And I got what I wanted." Kate closed the checkbook. "Mike's too young to have a teenage son. Does he have a younger brother?"

"I don't know," Carl said. "He's never mentioned family. Does it matter?"

"Maybe I'm getting paranoid," she said. "But I've met too many people lately who are the relatives of deceased young men."

She got up and came over to Tejeda, slipping an arm around him. "Theresa needs to get out of the house for a while, but every time she goes to the door, six telephoto lenses appear through the hedge. The pressure is too much. Can you do something?"

"Short of target practice, you mean?"

She laughed. "I'm not so sure I'd stop there."

22

"I brought you a present from my trip, kiddo," Tejeda said.

"Theresa," she said.

"I remember your name." He felt his face grow hot.

"Don't be so sensitive, Dad. Jeez." Theresa shook his arm. "What did you bring me?"

"A hat," he said, bringing Peters' chauffeur cap from behind his back. "If you're going to be my driver, I want you to look sharp."

"It's great," she laughed, the first spark of enthusiasm he had seen in his daughter all day. She piled her thick hair on her head and pulled the cap over it. "Do you think this will get us past the gate?"

"Worth a try."

She tucked the stray ends of her hair into the cap and straightened the tie she had borrowed from Richie. Even without makeup, there was no disguising that she was all girl. But the press would have no more than a few seconds to see her, and, with luck, they would be more interested in him, sitting in the back seat of Kate's Rolls like visiting royalty.

"Let me know when you get tired of driving," he said.

"Are you kidding?" she asked, hurrying him into the garage.

He let himself be led, buoyed by the rise in her

223

spirits. Kate had been right to insist that Theresa be gotten away from the telephone and the media. Theresa had taken Sean's death hard, as he had expected; she was always a sensitive kid. It broke his heart to hear her tell him how she felt responsible for Sean's death, how she had overheard someone say that if Sean hadn't been coming to see her, he probably wouldn't have been killed. The morning papers had only made Theresa feel worse by puffing two dates and half a dozen phone calls into a tragic romance.

Reece was waiting for them by the gates, helpful as always. He had instructed Theresa to stay on the turnabout beside the garage until the gates were open and he signaled that all was clear. Then she was to rev the powerful motor and make a fast getaway.

Tejeda steeled himself, searching for imaginary brakes in the back seat as Reece gave his signal. Theresa stomped the accelerator and stalled the motor as camera people began to ooze toward the opening gates. She got the engine restarted quickly, squared her shoulders, eased her foot on the accelerator, and sailed the Rolls out past the evening news and Geraldo's advance team with no problem.

Kate had asked him to sit in the back seat to draw attention away from Theresa in front. But he was beginning to understand that Kate, who had done a lot of driving with Theresa, had put him out of panic-reach distance from the steering wheel. When Theresa miscalculated a right turn and bumped a curb, he gripped the armrest until his knuckles were white. She grimaced and waited, but he didn't say anything.

After two blocks of smooth going, he unclenched his fists. "This has to be the most conspicuous car in town. How long do you think before those camera people catch on to us?"

"Reece said to call him if they bother us and he'll

come make a car exchange." She kept her eyes on the road. "What happened to the Cutlass?"

"Had to go to the shop." He didn't bother to say that the shop was in the basement of the county coroner's Forensic Science Services and that Vic Spago had taken it in charge. "You know where we're going?"

"Yes. Why can't I just drop you off and wait outside?"

"Because I like to make things complicated."

"That's the truth." She made a smooth left turn and glanced at him quickly in the rearview mirror, checking to see whether he had noticed. "I still don't understand what Lance did."

"You want me to tell you all about how he stole an arm from a mortuary? Better than Freddie Kruger."

"Dad, be serious."

"Seriously, he was a jerk. He thought he could delay the Arty Silver trial, first by finding new evidence on his own, then by faking a murder. He borrowed the Cutlass from Richie, cut classes, and spent his tuition money buying beer for men who let him think they had information. I can't imagine how he thought he could pull it off."

"Too strange. I always liked him."

"Me too." He opened the Thomas guide on his lap to the map page that included Angel Gardens, the postwar housing tract where Arty Silver had grown up. He counted the blocks between the shopping center ahead and the Silvers' house. Less than a mile, he figured, and an easy run unless it started to rain again.

"Park on the north side of the Broadway store. As close to the door as you can."

"Which way is north?"

"Left."

"Dad, I really don't think this is a good idea. Why do you want to talk to Mrs. Silver, anyway?"

"Because she didn't invite her kids over for Thanksgiving," he said, searching through his wallet for his Broadway charge card. "In what part of the store do you shop?"

"Juniors." She pulled into a space next to a tree two rows from the store. "Why?"

"Go up to Juniors, get an armload of stuff, take it into a dressing room, and stay there until I come for you. Here's the card. If clerks start to hassle you, buy something."

"This is weird, Dad."

He laughed. "I guess it is."

Tejeda took Theresa's hand and walked her to the store entrance, watching for the glint of telephoto lenses in the landscaping. "Stay away from the car, okay?"

She shrugged. "Okay."

"If you get scared or I don't come back in an hour or so, call Kate." He handed her a fistful of change. "Now, go have a good time. But don't spend more than a hundred bucks."

The Silver house had fresh yellow shutters and pots of geraniums on the porch. It was much like every other house on the street—well-kept for its age, not very big, but comfortable-looking. Tejeda straightened the front of his jacket and started up the short concrete walk to the front door.

The run from the shopping center had cleared his head, given him a chance to focus on what he wanted from Arty's mother. He was still deciding on the best way to get past the front door when it opened.

Behind the screen he could make out a round, squat silhouette. "Is that you, Mr. Tejeda?"

"How are you, Mrs. Silver?"

"I'm no better than you might expect, sir." Her

voice was soft, and with no trace of the hostility he had expected. "I don't think I should speak with you."

"Arty asked me to come."

"Are you sure?"

"Call him."

There was a long hesitation. He just hoped that after thinking things over, she wouldn't call his bluff. Because of the way Tejeda had left things at the jail, he had no idea what Arty might say to his mother. In the end, he heard her unlatch the screen hook.

"Come in, then." She held the screen open for him. "Don't want to waste one of Arty's calls—they only give him so many, you know. But if I don't like what you say, out you go."

"Fair enough." He took a good look at her as he squeezed past. Her dark hair was a mass of short coils, freshly permed for the start of the trial, he guessed. His overall impression was of roundness, from her pruned brush of hair to the full bosom that stretched against her shapeless housedress. She obviously wasn't working out with Jane Fonda, but she had taken some care with her appearance: her makeup was fresh, her thin browline carefully penciled in behind her eyeglasses. The lacquer on her nails was still fresh enough for him to smell.

Her house was clean. The front door opened directly into the small living room, and he could see the order of both this room and the dining alcove beyond. The furniture looked like vintage Montgomery Ward or Sears catalog, but it was in good repair. The wood surfaces shone and the gin bottle on the coffee table was nearly full.

Mrs. Silver went to a recliner in front of the television, where a soundless soap opera played out its latest tragedy. "Arty seem okay to you?"

"He seems a little nervous." Tejeda took a seat on

the end of the sofa. The end table beside him held a well-dusted collection of family mementos: a swimming trophy, a science-fair medal, a pair of tiny bronzed ballet shoes. He picked up a framed studio portrait and looked at the four well-scrubbed faces arranged in stair steps, from a toddler—the only girl—to a preteenager. The elfin slant to the eyes of the oldest child identified him as Arty. Tejeda set the portrait back under the lamp, haunted by the sameness of the expressions on the black-and-white faces; an ill-concealed anger behind the blank smiles.

Mrs. Silver was watching him, her mouth slightly open as if her chin had grown heavy.

"Handsome family," he said.

"They were. I always thought that when they grew up they wouldn't give us problems anymore."

"Did Arty give you problems?"

"Skinned knees and like that. No. Arty was my good one."

Tejeda raised his brows but didn't say anything.

"He still is my good one. He never did any of those things you say he did. He promised me."

"Maybe not, Mrs. Silver." He glanced at the four angry little faces beside him. "What kind of kid was Arty?"

"He was a very sweet little boy, always. Very cooperative. Tended to his studies, kept his room clean, obeyed his father. Sometimes when the other three were running around like wild Indians, I'd just go in and sit with Arty to get some peace and quiet. We gave him his own room so the little kids wouldn't bother him."

"He didn't get along with the others?"

"Oh, sure. They looked up to him. I just wish they'd been more like him."

Tejeda had to pause a minute. Even a mother

couldn't be that blind; this paragon she wanted the others to emulate was a mass murderer, no matter what he had promised.

In the media profiles, and according to his defense, Arty was like any valedictorian next door. Tejeda didn't remember anyone mentioning love, but Arty was portrayed as a nice, quiet man from a nice, quiet family. Like the rest of us.

Something was out of sync between the picture he was getting and the man he knew. He looked around the room again, hoping for some clue. How could a maniac like Arty come from such a place? There was order here, evidence of care and even pride. Obviously there wasn't a lot of money in the family—he knew Arty's father was an accounting clerk somewhere —but they seemed to make good use of what they had. The coffee-table leg showed a neat mend, there were some plaster patches on the walls, visible only because the paint didn't quite match, and even a closet door he could see had a careful repair job. Then he looked around again and started counting. Lots of careful repair jobs, he thought, a whole lot.

He heard a back door slam and noticed how Mrs. Silver was staring at the gin bottle.

"Why did Arty send you?" she asked.

"He wants you to stay away from the trial."

"No he doesn't." She smiled.

"Ma! Shut up!" The girl striding in from the kitchen was impossibly thin. With each angry step he was afraid she would break her pencil-thin legs. She had surprising strength, though, shoving aside chairs that were in her way. She stopped in front of Mrs. Silver and pointed an accusing finger at Tejeda. "You can't talk to him, Ma. Tell him to get the hell out."

"Now, Deborah." Mrs. Silver's voice was very calm. "Arty asked Mr. Tejeda to come see me."

"Who says?" Deborah tossed her head back and cleared some strings of dull brown hair from her face—she wasn't nearly as young as Tejeda had thought. "Did you call Axel?"

"No, dear."

"Ma, don't you ever *do* anything?"

"You interrupted Mr. Tejeda and I."

"It's not *Mr.* Tejeda, Ma, it's *Lieutenant*. Did your brain go dead or something? This is the guy who's trying to get Arty executed. Daddy says that *Lieutenant* Tejeda won't be happy until he destroys the rest of us too. He says they're even going to put Baby away again real soon."

"Who's Baby?" Tejeda asked. "And where are they going to put him?"

"My youngest son spent a little time in a group home." Mrs. Silver still smiled. "But he's fine now."

"Group home? He was committed to the county loony bin," Deborah screamed at her mother. Then she turned her wrath on Tejeda. "He was so talented and so sensitive and you guys ruined his life. I don't think you people are human. How would you feel if they said those awful things about your brother? Don't you care what you are doing to this family?"

"I don't have a brother," he said.

"Lucky for him," she seethed. She spun around and stumped off toward the telephone.

Mrs. Silver hadn't said anything for a long time.

"Where is your third son?" he asked.

"Haven't heard from him in a while." She got up and filled a juice glass about half-full from the bottle on the table. Without offering to share, she went back to her chair, to the seat cushion mashed into the shape of her body, and nursed the glass for a moment before she took a drink; straight and neat.

Through Deborah's entire tirade, Tejeda had watched

the two women with fascination. Mrs. Silver's placid expression had never changed, as if she were anesthetized. He expected her to be embarrassed, or outraged, or to join the attack. But she just sat there smiling dumbly, no more a part of this scene than she was of the silent soap opera running across her television screen.

Deborah offered him even more to think about. She was the loose wheel he had been looking for. To him she didn't seem physically healthy, she was so pale and emaciated. When he looked at her arms for the thick dark hair that gives away the bulimic and the anorectic, or for the needle marks of an addict, he found a homemade tattoo of a bleeding dagger inside her wrist. The drops of blood spelled "Dad."

No one had yet offered much of a psychological profile of Arty. The defense certainly wasn't offering him to county experts for probing. And because he wasn't pleading insanity, the prosecution hadn't gone to the expense of psychiatric opinion except beyond what was necessary to say that his personality at the time of arrest was consistent with what might be expected of a mass murderer.

Tejeda was beginning to see the crack, the line where two pictures that didn't quite match were spliced together. If you took the little pinched-face kids at his elbow out of their best clothes, let their hair blow a little, they wouldn't seem so ordinary. He thought about what that lineup would look like now: a mass murderer, a bulimic, a loony (to use Deborah's description of her committed brother), and a blank spot where one had gone missing.

When Arty was arrested, the neighbors had been interviewed. They had been very protective. The Silvers, they said, were good people. Tejeda looked again at the patched walls, the ten or more randomly placed melon-sized patches in the plaster, and wondered how fair it was to judge them after five years of hell. How had they been different before Arty's arrest?

Deborah slammed down the telephone. "Axel says keep your mouth shut."

Mrs. Silver took a gulp of her gin and shuddered. With unfocused eyes she looked up at Tejeda. "Did Arty really say that to you?"

"Yes." He stood to leave. "When the D.A. gives his opening statement Monday, it's going to be pretty graphic. I think Arty wants to spare you."

"If you're sure that's what he wants," she sighed, and emptied the rest of her gin down into the source of her pain.

23

Tejeda jogged along beside a red mini-van, using it for cover. Occasionally he would look through its windows, past the Mom's Taxi sticker, to keep tabs on the camera crew that was staking out the Rolls. He couldn't imagine whom they thought they were fooling, hunkered down among the sparse landscaping of a parking-lot planter with a mound of video equipment at their feet. Ordinarily he wouldn't bother to avoid them, but this time they wanted Theresa, the brokenhearted teenager who drove a Rolls-Royce. He couldn't let them follow him inside the store, where Theresa, he hoped, was still waiting.

The van's woman driver rolled down her window and smiled seductively at him. "Are we drag-racing?"

"Sure," he laughed. "Think you can keep up?"

"The question is, can you?"

"Maybe not."

The woman was attractive, funny. But not very good cover. He peeled off toward the freight entrance to the store.

She waved and tooted her horn twice. "I'll be at the sidewalk sale on Sunday."

He was still chuckling about her while he jogged down the truck ramp and into the loading bay. He passed two big rigs and a No Admittance sign, but no one stopped him until he was inside and halfway across the huge stockroom.

Even then, his presence wasn't challenged. An enormously overweight security guard glanced up from a clipboard. "You should wear your store I.D. down here."

Tejeda flashed his badge. "Where is the Juniors department?"

"Second floor."

"Point me to the freight elevator."

"What's the problem?" The guard seemed more scared than worried. "No one called me. I'm supposed to be notified if something's going down in the store."

"There's no problem. Yet. Where's the elevator?"

The guard showed him, but had him log in first. "No arrests in the store, okay?" the man pleaded as the doors closed on his face.

Tejeda came out in another stockroom, which gave him a chance to case the sales floor through a crack in the big double doors, making sure there were no straggling reporters before he ventured into the open.

"Excuse me." A young salesclerk, her arms loaded with bright pink sweaters, waited behind him to use the door.

He moved aside to let her pass. "Where's the Juniors department?"

The clerk looked him up and down, tossed her hair back, and batted her eyes at him. "Follow me."

He did, happily, watching her sway her narrow hips as she wended her way through the clothes racks. She was cute, and very young, and had him wondering again about his sudden appeal. He had been hit on twice in the last ten minutes. Not that he minded, it was just that he didn't expect it. He had watched girls literally fall over each other to get close to Richie. That he understood; he had always thought that Richie had extraordinary good looks and charm. But himself? He knew he could raise Kate's pulse, but that was different—that was love. So what was going on? He wondered whether maybe he had missed something. He was past forty and had a fresh scar on his face. Had he suddenly become the *in* type?

"Here we are," the salesclerk announced. "Juniors. My name is Starr. If there is *any* way I can help you, just call."

"Thanks," he said as she slunk away to help a woman customer. He was still puzzling over this new power of his when Starr's customer turned around, did a double-take, and gave him the same sort of overt appraisal. He found her stare especially bizarre, because the woman was Cassie.

As a reflex, he checked his fly. "Where's Theresa?"

"In the fitting room," Cassie said, selecting a pink sweater from the pair Starr held up for her. "She wears a size five and says her rear end is too big. Can you imagine?"

"Yeah, I've heard it before." He followed her around a rack of blue jeans. "How did you get here?"

"Theresa called me. She said she was frightened. You were awfully long getting back. She went out to check the car, and there were people all over it." She looked up at him through her lashes. "You really should drive something less conspicuous."

"Tell Theresa," he said. "Look, Cass, we need a ride home. Do you mind?"

"Not at all. Of course, I don't have a Rolls, or a Jag, or a Mercedes. But I can get you there." She pulled a pair of jeans off the rack, looked at the price tag, and shoved them back. "I need to know, however, where home is. Our house? Or *her* house?"

"If this is a problem, I can call Spud to come for us."

"It's no problem," she said sweetly. "But it is confusing. Our house looks great—the neighbors tell me you have a gardener and a cleaning lady come once a week. You took so little away with you, I could hardly tell you had moved out. It appears that you're planning to move right back in."

"Why are you looking at me like that?"

"Like what?"

"Like that."

She smiled. "You look great, Roger. Maybe a little tired, but I haven't seen you so fit for years. You're more relaxed, I think, the way you were when we first started going together."

He listened to her go on for a while, not stopping her as what she said became increasingly intimate. At first he was letting his emotional reflexes have some play, testing to see whether he had any residual feeling for Cassie lurking in the corners. He had, as he had expected.

She was playing the right chords, talking about the good old days when things between them had still been happy. Then he realized that she had to stretch back into the old, old days, to the time before she changed her mind about the course she thought their lives should take. Long before she had made a sharp right turn and asked her family not to follow.

She was saying how something had reminded her of a picnic they had had before Richie was born, and how she cherished the memory of that day—wildflowers in the meadow, just the two of them with no one else around. He remembered the day, and the hill of red ants under their blanket when they tried to make love, and the sudden rainstorm that had forced them into the car. As he listened, none of her stories seemed to recall the red ants. Or the kids.

He reached out and covered her hand. "The reason

the house is intact is that there was nothing there I wanted to take except Richie and Theresa. I think it's time to sell the place, Cassie. We could both use some money."

"But where will you live?"

"With Kate," he said. "I'm going to marry Kate."

He was still wondering where that revelation had come from and what Kate might say about it, when Theresa emerged from the dressing room with a pile of clothes draped over her arm.

"Oh, Dad! Good, you're back," she said, looking around, hesitating. "Is it safe to come out?"

"I think so. Did you find something?"

"Isn't this great?" she said, holding up pants, a shirt, and a sweater. "What do you think?"

"It's great," he agreed. "How much?"

She gave Cassie a quick and not very happy glance. "Ten dollars more than you said I could spend."

Cassie reached for the price tag on the sweater. "Theresa, these aren't even marked down."

"Are you paying for them, Cassie?" Tejeda asked.

"No. But Theresa can find something on the sale rack. She didn't look very carefully."

He put his arm around Theresa and kissed her cheek. "I trust Theresa to know what she needs. She's been on a clothes budget since she was fourteen, and she's done a damned good job of sticking to it. Without my help. Or yours."

"I didn't mean to start something, Daddy," Theresa whispered.

"This is between you and me, kid," he said. "You have the charge card. Go take care of your business."

Cassie's face was dark as she watched Theresa hand her purchases over to Starr; she was no longer bothering with sweet memories.

"What do you think about the house?" Tejeda asked.

"Would we split the proceeds fifty-fifty?"

"I think a four-way split would be more fair. Theresa and Richie both need college money. You seem to be supporting yourself."

"Roger, you sound so bitter."

"Bitter? No. Pissed, maybe. You can't walk in here and expect to start acting like Mom again. Not after the way you left."

"Won't you ever understand?"

"No." He looked across the racks of clothes and watched Theresa sign her charge slip. "Not ever."

Cassie leaned her back against the rack of jeans and sighed loudly. "You'll spoil her, giving her a Rolls-Royce to drive. Theresa isn't even sixteen."

"You're right, Cass. Tell you what. I have a stop to make and I don't want to burden you with it. Why don't we switch cars? You can drive the Rolls home—no one will bother you—and Theresa and I will take your bus."

"Me drive the Rolls?"

"Go ahead, live a little."

She seemed to loosen up as she thought about it. She gave him a sidelong glance. "My bus has a stick shift."

"Theresa learns fast," he said, but he hoped the old VW still had armrests for him to hang on to, and a good clutch. "Where did you park?"

"Behind the bookstore." She rummaged in her big bag for keys. "I'll ask again, does home mean our house or Kate's house?"

"Take your pick."

"Her house," Cassie said. "I want to talk to Richie."

"Chauffeur's cap is on the seat if you want it."

"Hell no." Cassie took out a brush and fluffed her

hair, then put on fresh lipstick. "Anyone mind if I take the long way?"

He shook his head. "Have a good time."

The old VW bus seemed to make Theresa nervous. But she concentrated hard, and by the time they had made one full circuit around the parking lot, she had coordinated her feet on the clutch and the accelerator well enough so that Tejeda didn't need to hold the dash to keep from hitting the windshield every time she shifted gears. Just the same, her first foray into traffic gave him white knuckles and damp armpits.

Pulling out after her third red light in a row, she managed to ease from first to second without a jolt.

"Nice job, sweetheart."

"Theresa," she said.

"I know your name."

"Sorry, just a reflex." She steeled herself for the shift into third gear. "Where are we going?"

"Silver's Meats, Third and Ocean."

"Oh, gross. Isn't that where . . . ?" With third gear there was a hiccup. "I'm sick of turkey, but we're not going to buy any meat *there*, are we?"

"No. I want a quick word with the owner."

"You want me to circle the block or park somewhere strange?"

"Just park out front." He chuckled. "No one is following us."

"Dad, I don't ever want to be a cop."

"I wasn't aware you had considered the idea."

"I hadn't." She remembered to put in the clutch when she braked for a stop sign. "I remember when you were looking for Arty Silver, when I was ten, and how all the kids at school were talking about the horrible things he did to those people he killed. They kept asking me if I had seen any of the bodies or if you told me anything gruesome. They thought I was like this expert on murder, and I didn't know as much as they did. You sent Richie and me to stay with Grandma after Arty left that head on our lawn. Grandma wouldn't even let us watch the news.

"Then last summer, when Kate's mother was killed and you got all involved with her, people kept asking me what her house was like, and what she was like. I didn't know. I had only met her like twice before she came and picked me up to move in with her, that night you went to the hospital."

"Theresa, what are you saying?"

"You never tell me anything, but somehow I always end up in the middle of your cases. I mean, I'm like this motherless child, and I never knew why she left me. Do me a favor."

"Sure."

"Tell me what's going on. Don't make me wait in the car anymore, or hide in somebody's house, or in a dressing room. God, I mean, it's my life."

"I'm sorry you felt left out. We were trying to protect you. Maybe we went too far," he said. "You may come in and meet Arty Silver's uncle. But if it starts to bother you, let me know."

Fortunately, the block in front of Silver's Meats was deserted—Theresa had lots of room to park next to the curb. There was a Closed sign on the front door of the store, but Tejeda knocked anyway. Lou Silver appeared from a back room, saw Tejeda, and hesitated for a moment before he came and unlocked the door.

"You have a problem?" Lou asked.

"Just need a quick word," Tejeda said. "Lou, this is my daughter, Theresa."

"Hi, kid. How'd a pretty thing like you get such a mug for a father."

She smiled shyly and shrugged.

Tejeda went to the door of the cutting room and flipped on the lights. Everything was spotless again. "Has the health department been in?"

"Not till Monday." Lou was at his elbow. "My wife and I talked it over last night. We decided not to reopen. At least, not at this location." He ran his hand up the smooth, pristine enamel of the doorjamb, caressing it. "I'm too old to start over. Maybe it's time to hang it up."

"Lou, I have a question for you."

"So what's new?" Lou turned to Theresa. "Your father always has a question. One more thing, he says, and no matter what you tell him, it makes him think of another question."

"Last night when Sergeant Green and I picked you up, you were sitting down to Thanksgiving dinner with your brother and his wife, right?"

"That's the question?"

"I saw your daughter and her husband. But where were your brother's children?"

"What?"

"Your brother has four children. Why weren't they with you at Thanksgiving?"

Lou stared at him. "Arty could hardly come, could he?"

"What about the other three? Over all the years I have known the Silver family, I don't remember ever meeting Arty's brothers and sister. Where were they yesterday?"

Lou scuffed his thumb up the stubble on his cheek and thought. "Deborah never comes to dinner—she won't eat in public. Gets that from her mother's side: all the Waters women have funny ideas about food."

"Where were the boys?"

"Aaron has gone off somewhere and Baby isn't speaking to his father."

"Why?"

"Baby thinks my brother hasn't done enough to help Arty. Baby worships Arty, always has. Sees him as some sort of, I don't know . . . protector, I guess."

"Protector from what? Is your brother a violent man?"

"No," Lou protested. "People all the time talking about violence, makes me tired. Bunch of wimps. I mean, our father used to knock us around, make us do what we were supposed to. Look at us, we grew up okay. Is my brother a violent man? I would say he is a strict disciplinarian. He had four noisy kids to keep in line, and he did a damned good job. He was just a disciplinarian."

Tejeda didn't bother mentioning how well this discipline seemed to have worked. What was the point? "I'd like to talk to Baby. Is he in town?"

"Yeah, but I don't have a number for him. I haven't seen much of him since he got out of the hospital."

"The mental hospital?"

Lou bristled. "He's okay. He kind of went over the deep end when Arty was arrested. But he's okay now."

"Does he have a name other than Baby?"

"A good name. Same as mine, Louis Michael Silver."

The front door closed, sending a draft into the cutting room.

"Hey, Lou? You here?" Heavy boots crossed the scrubbed linoleum in the outer shop. "You know you left the front door open?"

"Yeah," Lou called out. "In here."

Tejeda recognized the voice and looked around for the closest exit, in case Theresa needed one in a hurry.

"I think I got a line on a restaurant that will take two sides of beef . . ." Don Kelley saw Tejeda and made a similar check of the exits.

"Hello, Kelley," Tejeda said. "Missed you in San Quentin this morning."

Lou looked at Kelley and seemed confused. "You wasn't up at San Quentin this morning."

"That's what he just said," Kelley said. "I was here, helping you clean up."

"Willie missed you too."

"Yeah? Well, I couldn't help it. Lou needed me."

"How do you two know each other?" Tejeda asked.

Lou shook his head. "Questions, always questions."

"We go way back." Kelley patted Lou on the back. "Lou used to give us kids work in high school."

"You and Arty and Willie Tyler?" Tejeda asked.

"And Baby?" Theresa added.

"You know Baby?" Kelley asked her.

"No."

"Didn't think so." Kelley glanced at Tejeda. "New girlfriend? Kinda young."

"She is my daughter."

"Daughter, huh?" Kelley said, grinning obscenely. "Out doing a little family detective work?"

Tedeja moved in front of Theresa. "I need to talk to you, Kelley, about something Willie had to say this morning."

"Sure. Come into my office." He winked at Lou and walked off across the cutting room.

Tejeda squeezed Theresa's hand. "Get Lou to show you a telephone. Call Kate, tell her we'll be home shortly."

He touched the small of his back as he turned to follow Kelley, missing once again the weight of his service revolver. When he caught up to him, Kelley was sorting tools on a rack near the back door. His hands moved quickly, as if he knew where every mallet and bit belonged. The USDA Prime tattoo danced as his thick forearm flexed.

"What's the news from Willie?" he asked.

"He said he's innocent."

"Surprise, surprise." Kelley sneered. "They don't keep him busy enough up there. Too much time to think."

"Enough time to rethink taking the fall for someone else?"

"Is that what he told you?" Kelley slid a cutter disk into a slot. "Asshole. What else?"

"He thought he was taking the fall for you."

"Yeah?" Kelley put the tools down and faced Tejeda, arms folded easily across his chest. His smile was broad, but there was no glee behind it. "If I were you, I wouldn't pay too much attention to a guy who's sleeping down the hall from the gas chamber. Does things to his memory, if you know what I mean."

"I want to talk to Baby. Do you know where I can find him?"

"Leave Baby alone. I don't think he can take much more shit out of life. He was a good kid, always trying to fix things up, make everything right for people. What did it get him? A spell in the snake pit. You ever seen those state hospitals, man?"

"They could be worse."

"Not for Baby they couldn't."

"I still need to talk to him. Do you have his number?"

The corners of Kelley's smile slipped for an instant. "Sure," he said, "I have his number in my back pocket."

The move, when it came, was fast. Tejeda ducked from the slash of heavy arm that whipped up from below. Instinctively he blocked with his shoulder, but the black knob in Kelley's hand found its way inside and clipped him on the temple. The blow felt soft, a little black balloon. As he slid to the floor he had time to realize that the give was all in his skull. Oblivion, when it came, was a godsend.

24

He descended through a long black tube toward a cool blue light that grew slowly larger until it was so bright it dazzled him. He came out into the bedroom his wife had decorated in a frigid mood: ice-blue drapes, blue spread, hard blue chairs. He wanted to leave; so much blue made his head hurt.

Warm hands touched his face and went away too soon.

"I know you're in there."

He knew the voice and pulled himself up through the blue fog to find it again. He took a chance and opened one eye. Who he saw made it worth the risk.

"Welcome back," she said. He couldn't say her name, but she was clear in his mind. Where he was and why he hurt so much was another problem. He couldn't remember what he had done this time, but it was bad; even his hard-on hurt.

She put a straw to his lips and he drank. The water was cold but caused no pain. Encouraged by this, he moved his legs, his arms, and his hands and found everything functional. He reached for his head, but there was only a gauze wad stuffed with agony—it had to be ten feet wide.

"Do you know where you are?"

He couldn't shake his head, and when he tried to

speak, the growl he heard scared him. She gave him the straw again. He drank and closed his eyes.

"I know your head hurts, Roger, but please try to stay awake a little longer."

He cleared his throat. "Okay."

"It's Sunday morning. You're in the hospital. My name is Kate."

"What happened to Saturday? Where's my head?"

"You took a bump, but you're intact. Do you remember what happened?"

"Some." Just the flash of thick arm smashing something into his skull. But everything before that began sliding into focus. His head seemed to be condensing back to normal size, like Jell-O being poured into a mold. It still hurt like hell. "Theresa?"

"She's at home helping Richie pack for school. I'm very proud of her. When she found you out cold at Silver's she kept her head and took care of business, called the paramedics, me, and Eddie. In that order."

"I want to go home."

"Forget it. They can put wrist restraints on you here if necessary, hang on to you until you're ready."

"I need to talk to someone."

"I'm here."

"Someone named Baby."

"Eddie Green is looking for Baby."

He closed his eyes just for a minute, and started to fall back into the black tube.

"Roger." Her voice came through and yanked him back. "Don't go to sleep."

"I have to get up."

She smiled. "You can try."

He slid one leg over the side of the bed, braced himself on his elbows, and tried to raise his head from the pillow. It weighed far too much and he settled back down. The pain that shot through his head scared him awake.

"Kate, am I okay?"

"You need a shave." She leaned over him to straighten his sheets. "And a shower wouldn't hurt. Otherwise, you seem to be fine. You took a good blow, but Dr. Cassidy thinks there's no real damage—just some brain swelling."

He put his hand up again and explored the boundaries of the gauze bandage. "How big is my head?"

"No fatter than usual." She caressed his cheek and looked into his eyes. "You were lucky, Roger. But do yourself a favor and stay put for a while. Dr. Cassidy said you can't take any more blows."

"I think I'm going to cry," Kate said. "This is like the last day of summer camp, with everybody leaving."

"I wish you would come with us," Ricardo picked up the last of Lance's bags. "I don't like to leave you all alone."

"I'm hardly alone. Reece, Trinh, and one of the policemen are all here. Anyway, there isn't room in your car."

"That's true." The back of his station wagon was solid with luggage, surfboards, and books Lance and Richie had brought down for the weekend. Ever the organizer, Ricardo had arranged the gear in layers. The first tier would be unloaded at the airport with Lance, the second at Richie's apartment in Santa Barbara, the last when Ricardo and Linda returned to their own house later that night. Ricardo tucked in a stray sweater and closed the hatch. "I thought a little drive would give you a break."

"How much break do you think Kate would have wedged into that back seat?" Linda handed Theresa a tin of cookies and came over to kiss Kate good-bye.

She tugged on Ricardo's arm. "You should know she isn't going anywhere with Rigo in the hospital. Theresa, where are the boys?"

"They're coming."

Lance walked between Richie and Reece. They held his arms and seemed very chummy until she saw the frustration on their faces; Lance was balking.

"What's the problem?" she asked.

"Lance isn't ready to go," Reece said.

"What difference will a few hours make?" Lance whined. "I want to see the opening of Arty Silver's trial tomorrow. Why can't I stay for that? If you don't want me to stay here, I have some friends in town. Maybe Carl can get me an extension."

"Maybe you don't understand how close you came to going to jail, son." Ricardo wrapped his arm around Lance, more half-nelson than fatherly, and quick-walked him to the car. "You're going home *now*. When your plane lands in Billings at three, the local sheriff will be there to meet you. Anything goes wrong with that arrangement, and you're going to start seeing stripes before your eyes."

Richie dropped his duffel of clean laundry and hugged Kate against his hard chest. "Thank you. I'll miss you."

"I'll miss you too. Your dad said to tell you we'll drive up for a visit in a couple of weeks, with Jena. In the meantime, don't get another roommate."

He laughed, kissed her cheek, then slid into the back seat next to Lance.

"We should have Theresa home around nine," Linda said. "Have a nice, quiet afternoon."

Kate watched them go, waving, until Ricardo went out through the gates.

"What's so good about a quiet afternoon, huh, kid?" Reece said.

"I can't think of a thing. In spite of the circumstances, I liked having everyone around. This house was meant to be full of people."

"Have you noticed? Even the press has left us, gone on to the next twenty-four-hour wonder." He yawned. "Now what?"

"Change my clothes, take some things to Roger."

"*Roger*. I don't know what it is, but you say 'Roger' funny."

"It's not the way I say it, it's the name. 'Roger' is his cop name. 'Rigo' suits him better." She took Reece's hand as they walked back to the house. "What are your plans?"

"I'm taking Trinh and Lydia to a movie and to dinner."

"Which one is your date?"

"That's a dumb thing to ask. I thought Lydia was your best friend."

"So what? Doesn't obligate you in any way, does it? I couldn't help but notice you've spent more time with Trinh lately than with Lydia."

"Trinh's a nice kid."

"Trinh's a nice, smart, beautiful woman. And don't tell me you haven't noticed."

He nudged her with his shoulder. "Go change your clothes. Tell Roger we'll stop by to see him on our way home."

Kate showered and changed, packed a few necessities for Tejeda, stopped for a pint of rocky-road ice cream, and made it back to the hospital at about the time Lance's plane was scheduled for takeoff.

She found Eddie Green dealing a hand of gin rummy, using Tejeda's chest for a table.

"What did I get?" Tejeda asked; he was flat on his back with an arm across his forehead.

"Ten of clubs and hearts; two, four, and six of

spades; nine of diamonds; queen and ace of hearts; queen of clubs; seven of hearts."

"Dump the seven of hearts," Tejeda said.

"You draw nine of spades." Eddie fanned his own hand.

"Feeling better?" Kate asked.

Tejeda moved his arm to look at her. "When did the doctor say I can go home?"

"Can you sit up?"

"Sure." The cords in his neck stood out, his face muscles worked, but his head didn't leave the pillow. He relaxed. "I could do it if I wanted to. Did everyone get off okay?"

"Yes. Everyone says hello, take care, I love you, and so on."

He put his arm back over his eyes. "There it is again."

"What?"

"Love."

"That's sweet." She kissed him.

"Not that kind of love." Eddie discarded a king. "He means love and the mass murderer."

"I should have guessed," she said.

"No, *I* should have." Tejeda pulled his sheet higher and the cards spilled. "From the beginning, I knew something was missing, but I couldn't put my finger on it. I've been having so many memory problems that I thought it was something monumental. But it was just a subtle little thing that was right in front of me the whole time."

"Love?" she repeated.

"Love." The huge bruise under his bandage had seeped into his left eyebrow like a grape-juice stain. He looked sad and grumpy and boyishly vulnerable. And absolutely irresistible.

She held up the rocky road and a spoon. "Tell me about love."

And around spoonfuls of ice cream, he did.

"I always thought that Arty loved his victims," he said. "He loved them so much that he never wanted to give them up. He took pictures of them, he cut off little souvenirs. He wrapped their parts in pretty paper and wrote letters to the press about them."

She touched his cheek. "Do you have a fever?"

"No, I'm absolutely okay." He smiled. "*Love* was missing in the murders of Wally Morrow and Sean O'Shay. Someone has done a fair job of imitating the form of Arty's work, but not the substance."

"No fun?" she said.

"Exactly. It would take Arty a week to get a body ready for the freezer, not a few hours. What we have is a sham, a fraud, a forgery."

"But that doesn't make two boys any less dead," she said.

"True. Spud, you want some of this ice cream?"

"No, thanks."

"Arty had a compulsion to kill," he continued. "If he weren't in jail, he would still be cruising for victims and enjoying every minute of it. I think our imitator only kills because it's part of Arty's ritual. And if it's no fun for him, how long can he keep it up? He's headed for a dive off the edge of sanity."

The telephone bell served as jarring punctuation. Eddie picked it up. "Psych Ward here."

He listened for a moment. "Aw, shit. I'm real sorry. I should have taken care of him myself." He paused impatiently now and then, but there seemed to be simultaneous conversations over the wire. "You called the police? . . . No, that was the right thing. It's not your fault. . . . Tell her not to worry. . . . Any idea where he was headed? . . . No, don't rent a car. We'll come right up and get you."

Eddie put the receiver down and looked at Kate with a face as pale and sick as Tejeda's.

"Can't be that bad, Eddie," Kate said.

"Yes, it can. Roger, that was your father, calling from the airport. Somehow, when they were getting his luggage out of the car, Lance got hold of Ricardo's keys and drove off."

"Figures. Dumb little shit's determined to get himself hurt."

"He may come back to the house," Kate said. "Think I should go home and wait?"

"Don't go anywhere near him," Tejeda said. "Spud will get someone to watch the house."

"Kate, you talked to him a lot," Eddie said. "Where else would he go?"

"I don't know. Until his brother died he lived in Santa Angelica. He said he still knew some people."

Tejeda gripped her hand. "Help me up, Kate."

"Don't be ridiculous. Eddie, while you're at it, I want you to get someone to watch Roger, keep him in that bed. I'm going to the airport to pick up Linda and Ricardo."

"Yes, ma'am," Eddie laughed.

"I could ride along," Tejeda said.

"You could." She pinned his shoulders to the mattress and kissed him. "But I don't have a hearse. Promise me you'll stay put."

"On one condition."

"Name it."

"You bring me back a chocolate malt."

"It's a deal. I'll see you in a couple of hours."

Freeway traffic was light—the holiday outbound exodus hadn't reversed direction yet—but LAX was in gridlock. She managed to spot Ricardo, Linda, and Theresa among the mob waiting in front of the Western terminal. There were no curbside parking places, but she thought parking was redundant anyway, traffic moved so slowly. She simply waited for a standstill, got out beside her car, and flagged her riders down.

Unencumbered by luggage, which she assumed had gone away with Ricardo's station wagon, they easily wove their way across two clogged lanes. Theresa slid in beside Kate while Linda and Ricardo climbed into the back seat.

"How's Rigo?" Linda asked immediately.

"He's fine. Where's Richie?"

"He's on standby for a flight to Santa Barbara." Ricardo seemed shaken. "Kate, I'm so sorry about this."

"It isn't your fault, Ricardo. We should have arranged a police escort for Lance."

In the rearview mirror she saw him shake his head. "I have worked with young people for many, many years. When a boy is upset the way that one is, he needs someone who cares about him. Not police."

"Did he say anything?"

"The same things, over and over," Linda sighed. "If he had just a little more time he could find out what happened to his brother. But where can he look that our Rigo hasn't already been? I asked him."

"What did he say?"

"Rigo should stop looking around in the dark. Kate, if you could have seen his eyes when he drove away with our car. 'Oh, lonely death on lonely life! Oh, now I feel my topmost greatness lies in my topmost grief.' "

"What's that?" Ricardo asked. "Shakespeare?"

"*Moby Dick*. That's what Ahab said just before the whale killed him."

Kate turned to Theresa. "Would you call home? Maybe Lance has turned up."

Theresa punched the proper codes into the car phone, handed the receiver to Kate. "Reece wants to talk to you."

"Lance called here five minutes ago, asking for you," Reece said. "Sounded like 'Good-bye, cruel world' to me. Said to tell you how sorry he is for all the bother, but he hopes you'll understand."

"Did he tell you what he had in mind or where he was calling from?"

Most of what Reece said was lost as she drove through an underpass, but she got the gist of it: Lance had one more bomb to light and he wouldn't let anyone stop him.

"Reece," she said, "would you consider standing up your dates to go for a drive with me?"

"Where?"

"To look around in the daylight."

25

Kate had a stop to make before picking up Reece. She knew of only one connection Lance had made in town, Craig Hardy. It was a long shot, but Lance might have contacted the reporter.

When she entered the city room of the *Daily Angel* she wasn't expecting to find a scene from *Front Page*, but she was nonetheless disappointed: three metal desks in a littered storefront office. The place seemed to share a ventilation system with the takeout fish stand next door—it reeked of rancid cooking oil and brine.

Craig Hardy took one foot off his desk when she came in, but didn't bother to stand or clear enough space on his side chair for her to sit down.

"Would I sound clichéd if I asked if this was a case of the mountain coming to Mohammed?" He grinned.

"It would certainly be an overstatement."

"Paper's gone to bed twice now without the exclusive you promised. I don't suppose you've come to give it to me now, have you? I surmise from your humble posture that you have come seeking favors."

"Lance Lumsden is in trouble. I thought he might have contacted you for help."

"What if he had? Why would I tell you?"

"Look, Craig, you and I have been on opposite sides of events too often for you to expect to be on my Christmas-card list, but I think you're basically a decent guy. I'm appealing to your decency. Lance has gone off to look for a killer, all by himself. Just suppose he beats the odds and finds him."

"All by himself?" Hardy tapped the desk with a pencil, eyeing Kate with suspicion. The tap-tap-tap was like a metronome, keeping time as he weighed the possibilities back and forth. Finally he dropped the pencil. "I don't chase news stories for fun; this is how I pay the rent. A really good story might fly me out of this backwater, let me pay rent in, say, L.A. or New York. Before we talk about how I can help you, I want to hear what's in it for me."

"What do you want?"

"A big exclusive. Interviews with all the principals you've been shielding behind your palace gates."

"That can be arranged."

"I want signatures and all story rights." He pulled out a notepad and a Nikon. "And I want to come along."

"Come along where?"

"The kid did call me, maybe an hour, hour and a half ago. Said he was already in Montana, but I knew he was up to something. He wanted directions to the murder shack you and Lieutenant Tejeda found on the Marine base. But I couldn't help him—the Marines wouldn't let the press near the shack, said it was in a sensitive area. Lumsden said he would ask someone else, and he hung up."

"Who would he ask?"

"Didn't say." Hardy stood up and tucked an extra roll of film into his jeans pocket. "Ready?"

"You think I'm going to take you down to Camp Pendleton?"

"I know it." He grinned, shouldering his camera. "Because you know that's where the kid's headed."

Hardy set a fast pace out to her car. By the time

Kate slid in behind the wheel, he had already changed the radio station and readjusted his seat.

"We have to stop for my cousin, Reece," she said.

"Chaperon, huh?" He sniffed the leather upholstery and stroked the wood grain on the glove box. "He better be ready, 'cuz I don't think we should waste any time."

Reece was ready, and so were his dates; Lydia and Trinh insisted on coming along. Kate didn't know whether they had come for the adventure or to keep an eye on Reece, or on each other.

Kate mentally tried to cover every contingency. If Lance couldn't find anyone in town who would tell him where to find the shack, he might go back to Clyde's bar in Oceanside and try questioning the clientele. What if he ran into Don Kelley as she and Tejeda had? And what if Don Kelley took him to the shack?

Over the steady hum of her tires on the asphalt she heard the tap-tap-tap of Hardy's fingers. He was an observer, taking mental notes for his big story. She felt this must be something like sitting beside a body snatcher; he was searching for some essence of each of them, some bit of their souls to use as background in his article. She thought about warning the others that if they gave him enough material, they might end up as featured players in a book.

Going south against traffic, they made good time. All the way down, Kate worried that there might be Marine patrols around the shack. The sudden notoriety had been an embarrassment to the Marines and they had gone to some lengths to keep the press away, as Hardy had told her. Surely they had done something to close off the access road as well.

She had a sudden sick feeling; if Lance had managed to find the shack, even without Don Kelley, what might he do if someone tried to stop him? Especially if that someone was carrying an M-16.

The immigration check station came up on her left, gates on the northbound lanes. Kate took the first off-ramp she came to, circled under the freeway, and joined the crunch of holiday traffic headed north. After they had themselves cleared the check station, she began watching for the access road she and Tejeda had taken Wednesday night.

By daylight everything looked very different; even her perspective of relative distances seemed warped. But she recognized the access road by the bent and BB-shot No Trespassing sign. She passed the dirt turn-off, staying on the freeway for another mile, trying to judge distance by time rather than a territory covered. She remembered thinking while struggling through the sagebrush with Tejeda that it might have been easier to get to the shack by scrambling down the freeway embankment than approaching from the access road. And her car sailing along through the dust would certainly be a flag to any patrols.

There were no significant landmarks; all the scrub looked essentially the same from the freeway. When she judged they were nearly abreast of the collapsed bunker, she pulled onto the emergency shoulder and got out to look.

Hardy followed. "You lost?"

"Not yet." There was a glint of something shiny through the overgrowth less than a quarter of a mile ahead, possibly the tin roof of the shack. They drove on, Kate trying to watch both the side of the road and her rearview mirror; she didn't need to be stopped by the highway patrol.

When she stopped a second time, she could see a corner of the shack roof and the collapsed mound of the abandoned bunker beyond it.

"That it?" Hardy asked.

"Yes." She summoned the others to come.

"What about the car?" Reece said.

"Lock it up," she said. "We passed enough break-downs along the shoulder that I doubt anyone will notice."

"Not notice a jade-green Jaguar?" he said. But he locked the car and joined the others down the steep gravel-covered embankment.

They were all very quiet, aware of being somewhere they were very much not supposed to be. Kate noticed Trinh especially. She was as swift and quiet as a Saturday-matinee Indian, and as well-rehearsed. Kate found this hidden skill to be oddly poignant; Trinh had grown up in a war zone. Keeping out of sight of the Marines might even hold some nostalgia for her.

At the bottom of the embankment they stopped to regroup and catch their breath and decide how to cross the next obstacle.

Lydia clung to Kate's elbow while she dumped gravel from her shoe. "Going up will be a whole lot trickier. Had you thought about that?"

"No," Kate laughed. "We'll probably go out in a paddy wagon."

"Comforting thought." Lydia slipped her shoe back on and followed Reece to the next obstacle—three rusty strands of barbed wire strung between a snaggle-tooth line of wooden posts.

Reece, ever the gallant picnicker, was trying to spread the strands for the others to slip through. But Trinh tested a couple of fenceposts, selected one, manipu-lated it back and forth a few times, then laid it on the ground.

Lydia walked beside Kate as they picked their way across the flattened barbed wire. She was watching

Trinh and Reece help each other through the dry weeds.

"Lydia," Kate said, trying to think of something comforting yet not untruthful, "they're good friends."

"Forget it." Lydia walked on with her. "Doesn't bother me to see Reece and Trinh together."

"I think he just feels very paternal toward her."

"Paternal?" Lydia held back a branch of sage for Kate. "They put fathers who feel that way in jail. But trust me, Kate, it's okay. Reece and I have been going together for a long time. I know that he's probably the nicest man I have ever met. He's smart, he's considerate, he looks cute even when he doesn't shave. But he's just not for me. He's a rich kid and, college professor or not, I'm strictly working-class. And ne'er the twain shall meet."

"Now you sound like Roger."

"Roger?" They ducked together through a stand of eucalyptus. "No way. Both of his parents are college graduates, schoolteachers like you, for Chrissake. They gave him music, literature, taught him which fork to use. My father works on the docks, my mom slings chili. I love them dearly, but they don't know Mozart from Mantovani. Tell Roger he's full of it."

"I already have. Now you give Reece some credit. None of that matters to him."

"I know. But, Kate, I think it matters to me. Even though Trinh comes from another culture, she has more in common with him than I do. She was certainly no peasant farmer. She has polish, and I don't. And I don't think I want it. I like whistling at basketball games and scratching when I itch."

Lydia caught her pant leg on a bush and Kate stooped down to help unsnag it.

"Do you feel uncomfortable whistling and scratching around me?" Kate asked.

"Never. But that's different. We're friends, not lovers."

"That's it, isn't it? You've found someone else."

"Maybe."

"I'm happy for you, but I'll miss our old foursome."

"No need." Lydia kicked her leg free, ripping her cuff in the process. She had blushed a furious red, but she was smiling broadly as she gave Kate a hand up. "I've been seeing Eddie Green."

The others had reached the edge of the clearing behind the shack and waited for Kate and Lydia to catch up. They all stood in silence for a moment in the last of the sage cover, looking for signs of Lance or anyone else. If someone was there, he was being very quiet; the only sounds were crickets in the weeds, occasional birds, and the background rush of the freeway.

Craig Hardy moved into the clearing first, and they all followed, moving in sets: Trinh and Reece, Kate and Lydia, with Hardy as a solo.

The clearing seemed larger by daylight, and the shack smaller. Kate saw evidence of the police search that Vic Spago and Eddie Green had led on Thanksgiving morning. The adobe-hard ground was scuffed everywhere with dusty footprints, and there were shallow trenches dug in regular rows, like corduroy, across the exposed area. Heavy-treaded vehicles had been driven up to the front door of the shed, and away again.

Kate followed Hardy around to the front and stopped beside two holes that were deeper, rounder, and cruder than the trenches. Hardy shot about half a roll on the holes, the police padlock and seal on the sagging door of the shed, the tin roofing Kate had tossed aside during her earlier visit.

"It's too quiet," Reece said, edging up beside her. "The place feels haunted."

"I don't think this is a good time to start believing in ghosts, because if anyplace is haunted, this one is."

"Should we look inside?"

"The door's locked, the window's boarded up."

"How big a head start did Lance have?" Reece asked.

"At the most, two hours." She could hear an occasional truck pass by on the access road, but she couldn't see anything beyond the chaparral until low hills rose in the distance. At night the sky full of stars and the lights of the freeway had made her feel vulnerable to exposure here. But by day she could see how isolated the spot was, how perfect for keeping illicit secrets.

Lydia came and looked into the holes. She shuddered.

"Lie down in the bigger one, Lydia," Reece said. "Let's see if there's room enough for a body."

"Fuck you," she laughed, and turned to Kate. "Lance isn't here. Any point in waiting around?"

"Maybe he'll show," Kate said. "There are some chairs inside if anyone wants to break the lock."

"I'm not going inside." Lydia sat down on the front stoop. "Isn't that where they found all the blood?"

Hardy had backed toward the weeds to get a full frontal shot of the shack. Kate turned in a full circle— she had lost track of Trinh. As Kate turned to ask Reece what had happened to her, he seemed to notice her absence as well.

"Trinh?" he called softly, dashing around to the side of the shack. And then, more loudly, "Trinh!"

Kate had started in the opposite direction, when the command came.

"Freeze!" An enormous uniformed Marine crashed into the clearing and grabbed Hardy by the scruff of the neck. He trained his M-16 in an arc, showing each person he or she was within easy range. "This ain't no public picnic ground, people. You are trespassing on restricted U.S. government property."

Reece raised his hands theatrically, but he seemed fairly calm. "Sorry, we didn't see any signs. We were just out walking, taking some pictures for the folks back home."

"Walking from where to where?" The Marine snickered. His skin was very fair and deeply burned. Even his scalp, visible under his fine white-blond crew cut, looked sore. Burs clung to his camouflage fatigues all the way to his shoulders. "How about we all walk back out to the road and take a little ride to see the CO?"

"Kate, do we have time for that?" Lydia asked. "When is the general expecting us for tea?"

"The general is out on maneuvers," the Marine said. "Let's cut the talk and get a move on."

He steered Hardy around by the neck and waved with his rifle for the others to follow.

Hardy wriggled under his hand. "Hey, man, you're hurting me."

"Move."

There was no sound, only the flash of Trinh's size-two body sailing through the air. She landed on the Marine's back and locked his throat in the crook of her arm. Even though her feet didn't reach the ground, the chop she gave the top of his head was sufficient to drop him. She pushed herself away as he fell and landed on her knees beside him, a brick-size rock poised over his head in case her first blow hadn't cooled him.

Lydia leaned close to Kate. "That should give Reece something to think about."

Reece took Trinh's small hand in his and helped her to her feet as if she were a delicate flower.

"Good shot." He held her close. "Where did you come from?"

"All Marine use Zest soap," Trinh answered shyly. "I smell him coming, I think maybe I should make preparation."

Kate went over to the Marine and bent over him. His pulse was strong and regular, the pupils of both eyes dilated to the same size. Hardy was beside her, clicking his camera shutter in her ear.

"Now what?" Kate said. "I don't think he's going to stay out very long. And I don't want to be here when he comes to."

Hardy aimed the camera at her face. "What about Lance?"

"Hell, I don't know. Maybe if we put Junior here inside the shack and restrain his movement, we can wait a little longer."

"I don't believe it," Lydia laughed. "The very refined Professor Kate Byrd wants to tie up a Marine. What next?"

"Lydia, Hardy, grab his arms." Reece had already lifted the Marine's feet. "The door's padlocked, Kate. Go see if you and Trinh can hairpin it or something."

Kate ran beside Trinh. "Think you can coldcock a lock the way you coldcocked that big lummox?"

"A lummox is a Marine?"

"Not always." Kate knelt in front of the police padlock and gave it a trial pull; it fell away along a neatly sawed line. Trinh's almond-shaped eyes grew round. "I didn't do that. It's broken."

She got to her feet and gently pushed the door open, half-expecting some animal to run past her again. Trinh was pressed behind her, peering around cautiously from the side. Trinh seemed frightened, but after what Kate had seen outside, she could never again imagine Trinh being afraid of anything.

When the door was open about halfway, it stopped against something with a metallic thunk. Gripping Trinh by the hand, Kate eased inside, letting her eyes adjust to the dimness.

The big redwood log was gone from the near corner, but she had known it would be; Vic Spago had carted it back to his lab. She pushed the door further open so they could fit through together. As she pushed, the blockage gave a little but felt solid. Pulling Trinh up so their arms were linked, she peered around the edge of the door.

When she saw what was stopping the door she wasn't surprised because it seemed somehow fitting, if that was the word. But she felt sick, just the same.

Lance lay sprawled on his back with his feet away from her, his head by the door. As she moved further in to kneel beside him, the door again hit the business end of a garden shovel so new that its $13.99 Sears price sticker was unsoiled. The only evidence of use on the shovel's shiny tempered-steel end was a spill of red where it had cleaved his skull.

26

" 'Nobody knows the trouble I've seen.' "
"Shut up, Reece," Kate groused. "Your cheerfulness is getting awfully goddamn tiresome."

"Think the others got out yet?"

"Don't ask me that again, either." She drank the last of the tepid coffee in her cup, but it only made the sourness in her stomach worse. "What time is it?"

He looked at his wrist. "Don't know. They took my watch when they booked us."

"We're not booked," she said. "We're being held for questioning."

"So why did that amazon in uniform take my watch?"

"Maybe she liked it." Kate picked some more at the burs in her socks. If she'd had it to do over, she decided, she would have asked Trinh or Hardy to run back through the thicket with her to call the authorities, and left Reece behind with Lance's corpse, the comatose Marine, and his M-16.

Better yet, she would have opted for Lydia, who could be foul-mouthed and infuriatingly pushy when she wasn't getting her way. Kate had learned to ignore her bluster, but Lydia could make the uninitiated snap to attention when she bellowed. And that's what they needed now, Kate thought, a good show of unbridled aggression. All that politeness and cooperation had gotten them so far was a tongue-lashing from some local sheriff and an interminable stay in a stuffy inter-rogation room at the Oceanside police headquarters.

The worst part of this ordeal was not knowing what was happening to the others. None of them had been willing to leave Lance alone or to desert the Marine. So they had split up, some staying, some going for help. It had seemed like a sensible plan at the time. The Marine was far too heavy for them to carry out, but he was moaning strangely and they couldn't leave him. For all they knew, Lance's killer was still in the brush nearby.

Logic said help had to be summoned in a hurry. But now she thought it had been stupid to split up. Within ten minutes of leaving the shack, she and Reece had called the authorities from her car phone, everyone from the military police to the paramedics. Maybe they should have gone back to the others then instead of waiting on the freeway for help to show up. In every Saturday-matinee thriller she could remember, when the good guys split up it meant doom for one of them. She had survived; what did that portend for the others?

She slouched down in her hard chair and sucked at a splinter in her finger.

"Hey, Kate, I think I can remember all the words to 'Swing Low, Sweet Chariot.' "

"I'm warning you, Reece, don't get started again."

"Helps keep my mind off Lance. What was he trying to dig up outside the shack, anyway?"

"His brother. But Lance didn't dig up anything—there wasn't a mark on his shovel."

"Except where it—"

"Don't say it." The bile she had to swallow had nothing to do with the three cups of inky coffee she had drunk to kill time. Lance's face, frozen in wide-eyed surprise, kept flashing in front of her like a slide in a stuck projector. Thinking about the force that had been used to embed the dull-edged shovel into his skull made her scalp itch.

"Poor Lance," she sighed.

"He was a good kid." Reece stood up and stretched. "If he weren't dead, though, I'd be madder than hell at him for getting us into this mess. Did you have time to call a lawyer?"

"Whom would I call, Carl? I left a message on Eddie Green's machine. Why didn't we let him handle Lance in the first place?"

Reece smiled. "Because we're so fucking nice we wanted to save the little bastard from being arrested for skipping out at the airport in a stolen vehicle. I'm tired of nice, Kate. I think it's time to rattle our cups on the bars."

She handed him her empty Styrofoam cup. "You first."

"Figuratively speaking."

"Right." She went to the door and tried the knob. When it turned, she was surprised. They had been questioned, bawled out, then given a pot of coffee and told to stay put. Their questioners had been so threatening that she had assumed something more dire was in the offing, and that she and Reece were locked in until the time came to lower the boom. She had had enough time to think, to work out a variety of guilt assignments and forgive herself for a few infractions along the way. Now she felt calmer and less contrite than she had been when she was brought in, her defenses shored up a bit as the numbness of shock wore off.

She combed her fingers through her hair, smoothed the front of her soiled jacket, and stepped out into the corridor.

The clock on the wall had stopped, but the pervasive aroma of greasy fast food helped her set the time—maybe six, six-thirty. There were voices coming from the squad room down the hall, some shuffling of stiff papers, and a good deal of hearty laughter of the sort offered in acknowledgment of jokes that are more raunchy than they are funny. She quailed for a moment, wondering whether she and Reece figured somehow in that discussion.

She looked back at Reece. "How do you feel about making a run for it?"

"They took my wallet, your keys. How far do you think we could get?"

"To Rio, if necessary. I have contacts."

"If you don't mind, I'd like to stop on the way out and ask the amazon to give my watch back."

"You won't need a watch in Rio."

"I want my watch."

"Wait here, then." Kate walked into the squad room and stood in the middle of things with what she hoped passed for assertiveness until someone noticed her.

The sergeant who had grilled her earlier looked up from his Big Mac. "Ladies' room is down the hall, on the right."

"We want to go home."

"Don't we all?" He grinned, showing a string of lettuce caught in his teeth. "Just hang on a little longer."

"Where are my friends?"

"Last I heard, they were having dinner with the Marines."

"Can the Marines hold civilians?"

"Around here, the Marines can damn well do anything they want. Why don't you go back inside? Won't be much longer."

"Right." She picked up the telephone on the nearest desk and punched in her MCI credit-card number

and then her home phone number. When there was no
answer, she called Lydia's condo and left a message on
her machine, telling her where she was. She left a
second message on Eddie Green's machine before calling the Santa Angelica Police Department and asking
them to page Eddie. Finally she tried Vic Spago. If
anyone in Santa Angelica knew what was going on,
Vic did. Though she was feeling desperate for some
definite answers, she also needed to hear a familiar,
friendly, living voice. But Vic was not at home and he
wasn't in his office and the woman who answered his
line could only take a message. At least it was a
two-way conversation. Kate sighed as she hung up.

No one had challenged her use of the phone. "Any
word on the Marine who was injured?"

"He's okay." The sergeant looked up from his dinner, eyeing her coldly. "Says a cougar must have jumped
him. I never saw a cougar yet, though, that carried a
blackjack. Maybe he'll remember better when he wakes
up tomorrow."

"Where's my car?"

"Out front," the sergeant said around some fries.

"May I have the keys?"

"You're a real pain in the ass, you know that?" The
lettuce between his teeth had worked partway out and
hung over his lip like a limp fang. It was very distract-
ing. "We could book you on a variety of charges, from
abandoning a vehicle on an interstate highway to de-
struction of federal property—cost you some money to
fix that fence. So don't push it. Why don't you just go
back down the hall and wait quietly like a good girl?"

She weighed adding assault on a police officer to the
charges. Instead, she leaned toward him and whispered confidentially, "You have something green stuck
in your teeth."

"Shit." His face turned red and he slam-dunked the

remains of his burger into the trash. She could see his tongue working furiously behind his lips. Then he abandoned all those years of his mother's training and picked out the chunk of lettuce with his thumbnail.

While he was thus engaged, Kate sat down on the corner of his desk and crossed her arms.

"Look," she said, "I know I overstepped myself. None of us would be in this mess if I had thought somewhere along the way to call the authorities. We have no excuse to offer other than pure intentions, and I know what that's worth. But why don't you just talk to me? It's not going to hurt you to tell me what you know about the others."

"You think so?" He wasted some time shuffling papers on his desk before he seemed to come to a decision. He looked up at her over his glasses. "You ever hear of a cop named Tejeda? Lieutenant Roger Tejeda?"

"Yes, I've heard of him. I understand he's very famous and very handsome."

"We worked a big case together a few years ago." He was bragging, the way people over in Orange County brag when they say they knew John Wayne, as if they had touched folklore. "I had a call from Roger Tejeda himself tonight, asking me to give you special treatment."

"What special treatment? Thumbscrews and cattle prods?"

"You weren't treated like that."

"You're right. I'm sorry. Too much coffee makes me cranky."

"I'm holding you in protective custody until Lieutenant Tejeda sends for you."

"He's not coming himself, is he? He's in the hospital."

"Yeah, he told me." The sergeant leaned back and grinned. "Sounds like a cougar attacked him too."

"Right." She smiled, but she was beginning to feel sick. Roger was the worst patient she had ever attended; he hated to be in bed. She hoped that his head hurt badly enough to keep him from coming to fetch her personally.

The sergeant answered a call on his desk phone, then got to his feet. "You've been sprung. Someone's waiting for you out front."

"Tell me it's not Tejeda."

"Desk watch didn't say. You want to go get your friend?"

Kate found Reece lying on the table in the interrogation room, ankles crossed, arms folded over his chest, and snoring softly. Must have forgotten about rattling the bars, she decided as she shook him awake.

"Time to go," she said.

"Where?" He yawned.

"The big house. Get your shoes."

Reece followed her and the sergeant toward the front desk, tucking in his shirt and combing his hair along the way. By the time they reached the end of the corridor, he looked completely fresh, as if he had never scrambled down a gravel-covered bank and back up again, discovering a dead man in between.

She almost stopped the sergeant from opening the door: she wanted very much to see Tejeda, but not here.

But it was Eddie Green who was waiting in the reception area, looking like a beleaguered scoutmaster after a long outing. His charges, Lydia, Trinh, and Craig Hardy, were a grubby-looking lot, their soiled clothes full of burs.

Kate gave up trying to answer the questions hurled at her, and grabbed Lydia by the arm. "Where have you been?"

"We had dinner in the officers' mess. They think we're heroes for saving one of their own."

"Saving him from what?" Kate asked.

"When that big Marine Trinh sedated came around, he thought he'd been hit by a truck or half a dozen guys, at least. Things were just a bit unclear in his mind, and we didn't do much to clarify the situation."

"I'm not hearing any of this," Eddie said. "What happens on federal land is the feds' problem."

Trinh giggled behind her hand. "That is not what you told the military police when you come for us."

"I'll fix things with them tomorrow." Eddie sighed. "Now, can we please go home?"

"Wait a sec." Craig Hardy was reloading his camera with film he had taken from a K-Mart bag; somehow he must have persuaded Eddie to make a stop on the way.

When Hardy aimed his camera at her, Kate turned it aside. "I don't want to have my picture taken in the police station," she said. "I'm sure you understand."

He offered Kate a sly, crooked smile. "I have had the best day of my life. I only got one shot of the military police, but I think it's a good one. I'm thinking now of an in-depth series to run during the Silver trial. What do you think?"

"I want to go home."

There seemed to be general agreement that home was a good idea. They split up again, Kate riding with Eddie while Reece drove the others in her Jaguar.

Kate sank into the front seat next to Eddie and kicked off her shoes. "Where's Lance?"

"Vic Spago came and got him." He glanced at her. "Kate, how did you know where to find Lance?"

"He told Ricardo and Linda he had friends in town, but the only person outside of our household I knew he had talked with was Craig Hardy. So I called Craig and got lucky."

"Whether that was luck or not depends on your viewpoint, doesn't it? Why did you go looking for Lance without telling me?"

"I thought that if we could locate Lance right away and get him on a plane to Montana, he wouldn't be in too much trouble. Ricardo wouldn't press charges if he got his car back intact. Besides, I really didn't think we would find him. Looking for Lance was something to do; I'm so sick of sitting back, waiting for shit to happen."

"Hope it was worth it," Eddie sighed.

"Okay, I'm sorry. Have you found Ricardo's car?"

"Not yet."

"Learn anything new?"

"Besides never tell a civilian about the case I'm working on?"

"Right. Besides that."

"The holes at the shack were interesting. Something— actually, two things—had been buried and dug up within the last twenty-four hours; there was no rainwater in the holes."

"Are we talking about body parts?"

"According to Vic, the size and shape of the holes, the patterns of compaction in the dirt at the bottom of the holes, and la-di-da like that, are compatible with a couple of missing body parts we have been trying to locate."

"One big, one small?" she asked. "Like the head of Sean O'Shay and the body of Wally Morrow?"

"Consistent with that, yes."

"Jesus, Eddie, what's going on?"

"Roger thinks it's cleanup time. Arty's trial starts tomorrow morning. Our perpetrator needs to complete his program by then, let us know what the point of all this has been."

"Something has to happen tonight?"

"Roger thinks so."

"Where's Theresa?"

"Ricardo and Linda are back at your house with her, and I've doubled the watch there. Richie arrived safely in Santa Barbara and he's staying with friends for a few days. My only problem is Cassie—she's alone and vulnerable but simply will not cooperate. She'd be better off if she went back to New Mexico."

Kate shook her head. Cassie hadn't finished her own program yet, whatever it was. Kate had the feeling Cassie was waiting for something, like a vulture waiting to pick the bones clean after the feast. But whose bones?

"Want to stop for some dinner?" Eddie asked.

"No, thanks. I couldn't eat. But I'd like to say good night to Roger."

They reached the hospital near the end of visiting hours. People with plants and books and a variety of goodies strolled the polished corridors like holiday browsers, walking people in fuzzy robes solicitously or sitting with them among a welter of wrapping paper, ribbons, and boxes. Enough of them walked around looking shell-shocked that the disarray of Kate's clothes seemed to go unnoticed.

Tejeda's closed door was guarded by a uniformed officer with a semiautomatic revolver on his hip.

"How's it going, Mick?" Eddie asked.

"All's quiet. The lieutenant's asleep."

"I won't wake him." Kate pushed the door open and went in alone. There was only a night-light on beside Tejeda's bed. His slow, even breathing told her he was asleep. She took his hand and leaned over him, taking inventory. The big gauze wad that had wrapped his head had been replaced with a smaller bandage that covered only the four stitches in his scalp. There was a lot of bruising, but in the soft light it blended with the shadows and didn't seem so alarming.

He hardly stirred when she kissed his warm lips. Quickly she scrawled a note, telling him she would drop by in the morning and giving him an IOU for something especially delicious in the bedroom when he got home. She folded the note and propped it against his water pitcher. Then she fussed with his sheet, kissed him again, and reluctantly left him alone for the night.

27

"Did you sleep?" Ricardo poured himself a glass of juice.

"Off and on," Kate said. "Kept hearing footsteps in the hall."

"But all was quiet. Nothing happened last night."

"You sound disappointed."

"Of course not." His voice boomed through the kitchen. "Maybe Rigo had a vision when he bumped his head, and he dreamed up all this danger."

She patted his hand. "Maybe he just likes having you around."

"I hope so," he laughed. "You still driving me to school?"

"Yes. Do you have time to stop and see Roger on the way?"

"If we leave now." He went to the door and called, "Theresa! The express to school is leaving." He gathered his bulging briefcase and the two sack lunches he had packed. "What time is your first class?"

"Lydia is covering my classes today. I'm going to the Arty Silver trial with Eddie."

"I would like to go myself, but there is so much to do at school, getting ready for the Christmas programs." He opened the door again. "Theresa!"

"I'm here." Theresa swept in, breathless, fussing

278

with the bottom of her new sweater. "Kate, what's wrong with this?"

"Let me see." Kate bunched the sweater up, then pulled it back down exactly as Theresa had had it. "How's that?"

"Good. Thanks." She scooped up an armload of books and finished her grandfather's juice. "Can I drive?"

"Okay with you, Ricardo?" Kate asked.

"I have already survived two teenage drivers. She can't be any worse than her father." He dropped a lunch on top of Theresa's books and followed her out the back toward the garage. "Besides, if I die today, I have already had a lovely, full life. I prayed to my maker last night, in case Rigo was right and we were all killed in our beds. So I am ready, Theresa, my darling. Drive on."

Theresa rolled her eyes at Kate. "See where Daddy gets it?"

"Yes, I do," Kate laughed. "And I love it. I suppose you won't mind driving the Rolls? Reece still has my Jag."

"If I don't hear anything about my station wagon soon," Ricardo said, "I'll have to see about renting a car. I was sure they would have found it by now—Richie needs the textbooks he left in the back."

Kate touched his arm. "Why would you rent a car when there are normally three in this garage?"

"You would trust me with one of your cars?"

"It's only fair. You trust me with your son and granddaughter."

"How many tubas you think I can fit in a Rolls?"

"Plenty. Have you ever seen the trunk?" she asked, taking Theresa's books so that Theresa would have both hands to open the heavy garage door.

The middle door, behind which the Rolls was parked,

was the toughest. First Theresa pulled the door open wide enough to get behind, then wedged herself in and pushed. This took so much effort that she had the door halfway open before she bothered to glance inside.

She stopped dead, staring. "Grandpa, look."

Kate ran to her, arriving at her side an instant before Ricardo. She looked where Theresa pointed and almost laughed, until she realized how impossible this situation was; Ricardo's blue station wagon was parked in the space usually taken by the Jaguar.

"How did it get here?" Ricardo asked.

"Good question," Kate said. "Don't go in there, Theresa."

"Okay. Should I go get the policeman from the house?"

"Please," Kate said. "Ask him to call Eddie Green."

Ricardo was peering through the hatch-back window. "Everything is here. Even Lance's bags. Help me unload the back and you won't have to bother driving us this morning."

"Ricardo, Rigo would tell us not to touch the car in case there are fingerprints. We don't know when the car was put here—before or after Lance was killed."

She knelt down on the threshold and looked under the cars for anything that didn't belong there. The man who came to wash the cars every week also swept the garage floor and put away any tools that might have been left about.

The car man had come on Friday. It had rained off and on during that day and drizzled some more on Saturday. Under the Rolls she found dried mud, and on the left, under the station wagon, a number of muddy treads that matched the absent Jag. She looked at the mud flaps behind Ricardo's rear wheels; the mud was the same pale yellow-brown she had kicked off her shoes the night before while waiting for the

Oceanside police to meet her on the freeway. It was a long way from the dark, oily color of city dirt.

"Ricardo, there's nothing we can do here," she said, picking up Theresa's books. "I want to go see Roger."

"What's the matter, honey?"

"Look there, beside your car. What do you see?"

"Grease spot," he said.

"Grease spot *beside* the car?"

"What do you think it is?"

"I'm not sure I want to know. Here comes the policeman. If he'll let us take the Rolls out, I want to go. Now."

Tejeda waited in a rocking chair beside his hospital bed with his small bag packed and ready beside his feet. His bruises had turned from livid purple to dull blue-gray. But the color in his cheeks was good, his dark eyes were bright. Seeing him look so healthy, Kate wished she had already dropped off Ricardo and Theresa. His two nights in the hospital had been the first time she had slept without Tejeda since he had moved in. It wasn't the footsteps of the policeman in the hall that had kept her awake, it was the empty place in the bed beside her.

Kate bent over him for a kiss. "Where do you think you're going?"

"Home. I have an IOU to collect, remember?"

She kissed him again, letting her tongue slide between his lips. "The house is too empty without you."

"You look fine, son. But don't push yourself this time." Ricardo tested the springs on the bed. "Did you hear? Theresa found my car."

"Theresa did?" Tejeda looked up at his daughter, who was waiting impatiently just inside the room. "Where did you find it?"

"If you're coming with us now, can I tell you on the way to school? I'm going to be so late for my biology lab."

Tejeda refused the wheelchair and walked out holding Kate's hand. His one concession was letting his father carry his bag. He had left behind a cart mounded with flowers and potted plants which a nurse said would be distributed wherever they would be appreciated.

Theresa drove, with Ricardo beside her to apply imaginary brakes, leaving Kate and Tejeda to snuggle in the back seat.

Though he insisted that he was just fine, Kate noticed that the short walk to the parking lot had left him a bit pale. He rested his head against her shoulder and scarcely moved during the fifteen-minute ride to Santa Angelica High School. It felt wonderful to have him in her arms, but he was so quiet Kate began to worry; Tejeda was never one to sit still for very long.

With occasional amendments from Theresa, Ricardo recounted the discovery of his car in Kate's garage. Tejeda just listened, offering no comments and asking for no clarifications except to say they shouldn't have moved the Rolls. It was enough of a response that Kate began to relax.

"Where are you getting out, Theresa?" Ricardo asked.

"North campus, by the science building."

She found a spot in a loading zone and pulled the Rolls to the curb. " 'Bye, everybody," she said, sliding out with her armful of books. "Dad, stay in bed." Then she looked at Kate and blushed furiously. "You know what I mean."

Ricardo moved around to the driver's seat and gave Theresa's back a quick "Shave and a Haircut" with the horn. Theresa ignored him but a dozen students stopped to applaud.

Ricardo waved to them, laughing. "They can do that because I'm not their grandfather. Poor Theresa has the double burden of having both her grandparents on the faculty. She does a good job of avoiding us, like her father and aunt did before her. Except, of course, when she forgets her lunch money or her life falls apart before three o'clock."

"How's Mom?" Tejeda asked.

"Fine. She's taking today off to talk to Cassie about the facts of life." Ricardo pulled into a faculty lot and parked in a space with his name on it.

"Rigo," he said, "I want to show Kate my band room."

"The Ricardo Tejeda Museum, you mean?"

"Only take a minute. You can wait in the car."

Tejeda roused himself. "I'm coming in. I could turn old and gray during one of your minutes."

"Suit yourself," Ricardo laughed. He took Kate by the arm as they walked. "Did Rigo ever play the saxophone for you?"

"No."

"He was a decent musician in high school. If it hadn't been for football, he might have been damned good." He led them into his office, a long, narrow enclosure with a glass front that overlooked the cavernous band room. "What instruments do you play, Kate?"

"The piano, badly."

"I don't suppose you went to high school here?"

"No. My mother sent me to boarding school."

"I've been at this school since 1952." He showed her a wall lined with framed group photographs of kids holding their musical instruments. "Virtually every kid in town has passed through my classes, music appreciation if not band or orchestra. I see them around all the time. Usually I can't remember their names, but I rarely forget their instruments."

"Phew," Tejeda breathed. "Dad, did you leave a tuna sandwich in your desk over the weekend?"

"Damn kids. I keep telling them to dump their lunches outside." Ricardo was throwing his office windows open, when he stopped and pressed his face against the glass and peered into the dark band room. "Hey, who's in here? Early practices are Tuesdays and Thursdays. Rigo, hit the switch there by the door, will you?"

Fluorescent overheads blinked on, showing the crescent of band risers, chairs, music stands. There was a boy sitting in the third tier and to the right of the conductor's podium. He wore clean jeans and a print shirt; his hair was neatly combed. Kate couldn't see his face because he was sitting with his arms draped over a music stand, his chin resting on his chest. His pose seemed natural for a youngster, very loose. But he didn't move when Ricardo called out to him again.

"Maybe he's sick," Ricardo said.

Tejeda caught his arm. "Stay here, Dad. Kate, you know who to call."

Kate just missed Eddie Green and Vic Spago at the house, Trinh told her. They had left less than five minutes earlier, following the truck towing Ricardo's car. Kate called headquarters and had them paged.

She watched Tejeda make three circuits around the boy, studying him from a wide, respectful distance, as if he were examining an unusual sculpture in a museum. The boy was dead; the smell made that clear. But there was something oddly beautiful about the tableau in the band room. She saw symmetry and grace and sadness in the way the body was arranged; this was an imitation of life. She saw the boy in a posture of profound grief.

Tejeda had to get down on one knee to see the boy's face. He looked. Slowly he moved away and sat down on a riser. He glanced once more at the boy, then dropped his head into his hands.

The stench in the band room was overpowering, but Kate inured herself and went to Tejeda. His honey-colored skin had faded to an unhealthy yellow, as if he had no more blood than the boy beside him. When he raised his head, she saw tears in his eyes.

"I can't remember his name," he whispered. "I can't call his parents until I know his name."

"Do you want me to look at him?" Kate asked.

"If you can."

She held her breath and bent over to see the face. Close up, he wasn't nearly as clean as he had seemed at first. His skin was puffy and colorless, with dirt ground into the creases. The muscles of his jaws had knotted, skewing his features to one side. But she still recognized him.

As she stood up, gagging, she saw the line of industrial staples inside his collar, attaching the head to the body.

She reached for Tejeda's hand. "Sean O'Shay," she said.

"Oh, God."

"Is he attached to Wally Morrow?"

"Probably."

"This is what you were waiting for, the final act?"

He shook his head. "I expected something very different; maybe I've been wrong all along. Come away. There's nothing we can do for him."

The putrid smell wasn't as noxious in Ricardo's office, but it seemed to cling to her hair and clothes until she felt contaminated. From the other room, she had noticed Ricardo's back and thought that he didn't have the stomach to look at the corpse. But he seemed to be very busily searching for someone or something among the band and orchestra photographs on the wall.

"Dad?" Tejeda said.

"I think I'm getting close," Ricardo said.

Kate tried to see what he was looking for. On the whole, the photographs looked very much the same, standard eight-by-ten black-and-white glossies in thin walnut frames. But as she looked at them individually, she found a capsule history of high-school kids for the last thirty-seven years.

The styles they wore changed from one year to the next, the shapes of collars and styles of barbering pinpointing the passage of time with as much exactitude as the dates on the frames. Ricardo had started his search in long hair and love beads and segued into designer jeans and gold neck chains.

He took one picture off the wall and held it up to the scene in the band room. It apparently didn't have what he wanted, and he moved on to the next semester.

"Had a kid come in and test for the orchestra," he said as he searched among the tiny faces. "Wanted to play flute, I think. But his family didn't have money, or wouldn't spend money on an instrument rental. So I loaned him what was available—a trombone. Not a bad horn, as I recall."

He pointed to a boy sitting in the same seat in the trombone section that Sean O'Shay now occupied. The boy's face was small, capped with short dark hair. There were so many people in the eight-by-ten picture that each face gave only an impression of features. Ricardo looked at it closely, then moved on again.

"His father was either a music lover or hater," he continued. "Either way, he apparently took violent offense at the sound his son produced with that trombone, because he threw it against a wall with enough force to bend the slide. Or so I was told."

Throughout this search, Sean O'Shay sat in mute pantomime of the boys in the trombone sections on the wall.

"The kid offered to work off the repair costs. So I told him the only way he could do this was by coming in early or staying after school to practice. I got the horn fixed and for a while I would see him in that chair, making the most god-awful noise while he learned to play the trombone. He had a good ear, and he was getting to be a pretty fair player. But he quit coming. Had to work after school or something. I'd pass him in the halls and he would promise me he was coming back. Always said he wanted to make things right. But he never came back.

"Ah, here he is." He held up the picture from the fall of 1976 and pointed to a tiny young face behind an enormous trombone, sitting in the third tier back, to the right of the conductor's podium. "I think they called him the Kid or something."

Tejeda took the picture and tried to find some message in it. After a while he looked at Kate. "It wasn't Kid."

She nodded. "Baby?"

"That's it." Tejeda went to a bookcase and pulled out the 1976 school yearbook. He started with the freshmen and worked his way up to the junior class before he found the name he wanted, Louis Michael Silver. Kate looked over his arm while he counted, fourth name in the list, fourth little black-and-white portrait in the row.

Kate took the book from him and studied the face closely. Louis Michael Silver was dark, with hairless cheeks and a shy, vulnerable smile; aptly named Baby. The eyes were the giveaway.

"I saw him at your house the other day," Ricardo said. "I remembered his instrument, but the name still doesn't ring a bell."

She handed him the book. "He calls himself Mike Rios now."

28

Kate unlocked the car door for Tejeda.
"Where do you think Mike is now?"

"Where he's always been, hiding in Carl's house."

"But why?"

"To fix things."

"I know that. That's his job," she said, pulling into traffic. "But why did he do all those unspeakable things to us?"

"Just as I said, to fix things. What motivated Lance Lumsden, the Morrows, and all of the Silver Threads to pull some damned bizarre stunts? Their lives have been turned upside down by a monster and they can't put things right again until the monster fries.

"Mike has the same problem, except to him, I am the monster. I took his brother from him, and his whole family came apart, just like Lance's. We'll probably never know what originally happened within the Silver family history to spawn Arty's madness, but believe me, they're a sad group now.

"Think about what we've heard about Baby. His big brother, Arty, protected him. Arty's friends watched over him."

Kate said, "He told me that his brother had promised to put him through college, but something happened to him."

"Sure," Tejeda said. "I caught him."

"Mike has so much talent, everyone has said so—
your dad, Carl. I've seen it. But something always
seemed to get in his way."

"One way or another, it was always Arty."

She parked the Rolls in front of her house. "What
are you going to do?"

"I need to pick up something. Will you watch the
front of Carl's house and yell if Mike comes out?"

"Sure."

Running made his head hurt, pulled his stitches.
The pain wasn't so bad that he would slow down; time
was of the essence. His watch said eight-thirty-five and
charges were scheduled to be read against Arty Silver
at ten-thirty.

Mike had thrown him a curve this morning. He saw
the return of the bodies as an offering of appeasement,
a gesture of closure. Arty had always withheld some
part of his victims' remains as a way to maintain control over the emotions of the survivors; that control
was a large part of his pleasure. But Mike had not
only given up the remains of Sean and Wally but also
handed over clues to his own identity. Tejeda remembered Ricardo asking Mike if he had ever played trombone; Mike had to know it wouldn't take too much
digging to come up with his name. Maybe it was a test,
to see whether he had left any impact on a man he
apparently respected.

Even if Mike was ready to give up, Tejeda wanted a
little weight behind his belt.

He found his mother at the kitchen table grading
papers, while the uniformed policeman assigned to
watch over the house loaded breakfast dishes into the
dishwasher. It was a very cozy scene, and it slowed
him down a little. She might just as well have been in
her own sunny breakfast room as here in Kate's
industrial-size kitchen, she seemed so settled in.

"Rigo, dear." She smiled and lifted her face for a kiss. "What a surprise. How are you feeling?"

"Fine." He opened the bread box where his snub-nose .38 was stashed. It felt awkward, heavy in his hand. "Where's Trinh?"

"Reece took her to her class. Cooking, I believe she said it was. She told me what they were preparing, but it didn't sound familiar."

"It won't look familiar when she makes it, either." He caught the eye of the officer. "I'm going in next door, and I want to go in alone. But I'd sure appreciate a little backup."

"Rigo?" Linda said with the same tone of voice she used to use the instant before he jumped out of a tree or dived into the wild surf at the jetty. "Have you thought through what you are about to do?"

"I love you, Mom." He kissed the top of her white head on his way out.

Kate was leaning against the Rolls's hood, watching Carl's house. There was a crew of workmen putting in new window frames along the front.

"Mike's inside," she said, her expression puzzled. "Working in the dining room."

"Thanks." He motioned the uniform to come closer. "There's scaffolding over the back, so if he comes out in a hurry, it's going to be from the front."

Mike was, as Kate had said, in the dining room. He seemed absorbed in his work, putting up the moldings he had cast from the impressions taken at Kate's on Friday. His concentration was unnerving because it made him seem so at peace. For a moment Tejeda wondered if he had taken a bigger shot to the head than he thought, and bollixed up the facts of the case.

But Mike's entire scenario played out in front of him like a good documentary film, each frame clear, each leading smoothly to the next.

Who would have more inside information about Arty Silver than his younger brother? And maybe he'd had some help from Arty, maybe some from Don Kelley. He had condensed Arty's eight-year killing spree into two victims, hitting the high points like a *Reader's Digest* novel; a framework short on substance.

Tejeda ran it down: A Marine lured from Clyde's, beheaded at the shack, his head then gift-wrapped and left for Tejeda to find. A second boy somehow lured from the beach—certainly Sean had seen Mike around the grounds, he wouldn't have his guard up—and left in Lou's meat freezer for Tejeda to find. How much thought went into the selection of victims, he couldn't guess. Maybe none, which made the loss even harder for families to accept; like the O'Shays, everyone wanted a *reason*, even if it was insane.

Mike, in and out of the grounds all the time, certainly had access to the beach and the house. And as a workman, a degree of invisibility.

Tejeda watched Mike work, impressed by his precision and skill. The moldings were nearly flawless reproductions. Looking at the lengths beside him on the floor, Tejeda could see and feel the difference from the originals. But when they were installed along the ceiling, ten feet up, they were indistinguishable from Kate's.

Talented, vulnerable Baby, he thought, always left to patch things up, from holes his father bashed in the walls to the chaos his brother had made of so many lives. What had this detour into horror done to his soul?

"The moldings look great, Mike," Tejeda said. "You must have put in a lot of hours over the weekend."

"I'm almost finished," he said. "Have to be somewhere at ten-thirty and I want to get this done first."

"Take your time, Mike. You don't have anywhere else to go."

Mike made a noise somewhere between a cough and a sob. But he picked up the next three-foot length and fitted it into place without a pause.

"You want to talk?" Tejeda asked.

"No. I want to finish this."

"Have you finished the other job, the one you were doing for Arty?"

"I can't." He brought his arms down and rubbed his shoulders. All vestiges of his former cockiness had vanished. "I really tried, but I couldn't do it all."

"What about Lance?"

"He kept getting in the way, you know? I had this definite plan of things to do, and he kept getting in the middle of it. He drove up yesterday afternoon, saying he had to find the shack. So I took him down. Tell your father I'll pay him back for the gas."

"No sweat. I take it you don't like interruptions."

"I think you should finish what you start." Still holding his hammer, he turned to look at Tejeda. His eyes were like shiny licorice disks stuck on his flat white face. "I didn't know the conductor was your father. I never put the names together."

"That makes a difference to you?"

"He was nice to me once." He shrugged. "I never met people like you. You really like each other, don't you?"

"We like you too, Mike."

"Maybe if you had met me before. But it's too late now."

"You're a nice kid. How did you get talked into murder?"

"Do you love your son?"

"Very much."

"Would you kill someone to save his life?"

"Not the way you did."

"I guess we do things a little differently in our family. We protect each other."

"Mike, you know I have to take you in."

He looked at the stretch of ceiling that still had no molding. "I can finish in half an hour."

Tejeda leaned against the door frame and crossed his arms. "I'll wait."

Mike turned back to his work.

"I talked to William Tyler the other day," Tejeda said. "He says he never killed anybody. What do you think?"

"He didn't. I helped this other guy do it, to help Arty. They just let Willie take the fall. He was so much in love with this other guy, he would have done anything for him."

"This other guy wouldn't be Don Kelley, would he?"

"I won't say."

"If it was Don Kelley, I think he tried to set you up. He sent me down to the Marine base where you killed Wally Morrow."

"Don did?" His hammer stopped. "Why would he do that?"

Tejeda shrugged. "Get you in, get Arty out."

"Arty wouldn't let him do that."

"Are you sure?"

Tejeda felt the air stir behind him; then a thick arm vised his neck in its crook while another slipped the revolver from the small of his back. Out of the corner of his eye he could see the blue tattoo—USDA Prime—and the extended barrel of his own gun.

"You motherfucker, Baby." Pricks of Don Kelley's cold spit landed on Tejeda's ear, and he braced himself because the end of his revolver was nearly as close. "I been waiting to hear you had finished your task. But here you are spilling your guts. You were supposed to do one more. Today, before Arty goes up."

"No more." Mike looked into the barrel of the gun and raised his hammer in a useless defensive move. "I'm through, Don. I fixed the others up the best I could and gave them back. Didn't I, Lieutenant? They looked real nice. Don, tell Arty, no more."

Tejeda saw the muscles tighten on Kelley's trigger finger. He didn't have much slack to maneuver in, but he got his head forward a few inches, then rammed it back into Kelley's face. He wasn't sure whether the explosion was the gun going off or his stitches exploding. The arm was gone and he sat on the floor, deafened, with lights dancing around his head like cartoon stars.

When he could focus his eyes again, Kate's face was in front of his. Her lips were moving, but he couldn't hear anything she said. There was a big blue-gray blob of brains on her arm. He touched his head to make sure they weren't his. Then he saw the mess all over the freshly sanded floor and up the walls. Don Kelley lay behind him, with his head popped like a firecracker in a cantaloupe.

The uniformed backup officer still held his .38 Magnum poised in the firing position, his face bloodless.

"Thanks," Tejeda said. His own voice sounded incredibly loud, but the ringing in his ears was settling down. "Where's Mike?"

Kate pointed. Mike had fallen off his ladder and lay in a heap on the floor. Not ready to trust his own height yet, Tejeda crawled to him and rolled him over.

Mike's eyes were fixed, as dead-looking as Sean O'Shay's. There was no blood, no visible hole. Not even a bump on his head. Mike's pulse was as quick as a bird's, his breath hot and shallow, as if he couldn't expand his chest.

"Is he hurt?" Kate asked, taking Mike's hand and rubbing it. A flicker of light crossed his face; then his lids closed. "What's wrong with him?"

"He'll be okay. Stay with him. Talk to him. He just got an overload of stuff he didn't want to know."

"You saved his life."

Tejeda shook his head. "I only postponed his death."

A group of workers in grubby coveralls had come in to gawk. Over their heads a camera appeared, its flash dazzling him for a moment. Then Craig Hardy stepped away from the crowd.

Tejeda got to his feet, testing his equilibrium before he walked as far as the door.

"How'd you get in here, Hardy?"

"I thought since you were in the hospital, Kate might want someone to go to the trial with. What happened?"

"I'll tell you on the way."

Tejeda took a rag from a carpenter's pocket and wiped Don Kelley's brains off Kate's sleeve.

"What is that?" she asked.

"Don't ask." He took her hand. "Feel up to going to the trial?"

"You're asking me? If you can make it, I certainly can."

"I've got us an escort through the press mob at the courthouse."

"Who?"

He grabbed Hardy's arm. "Why, the press, of course."

29

The courtroom was eerily quiet in spite of the enormous crowd. Tejeda found two seats near the jury box and sat down to wait for Kate to get in through the civilian crowd backed up behind the metal detector at the door.

Like all policemen, Tejeda had spent a lot of time in court. It was rarely as much fun or as orderly as Perry Mason. There were frequent delays and recesses for flu epidemics, judges' vacations, and jurors who gave birth. Even when the court sat through an entire day, most of it was pretty boring—the telling of facts in no particular order. Still, the beginning of a trial was usually interesting.

Tejeda watched the official cast gather behind the bar. The court clerk came in with an armload of papers, deep in conversation with the court reporter, who carried an Avon catalog. They both wore new-looking outfits, maybe in case they appeared in a shot on the six o'clock news, or, more likely, because they wouldn't have much time to shop until the trial was over.

Hymie Osawa came in from the judge's chambers wheeling a two-drawer filing cabinet. He parked this behind the prosecution table and began laying his notes, handwritten on yellow legal pads, in ranks in front of his chair. He cased the house, waved to familiar faces, gave Channel 5 a good profile.

The Silver Threads families must have come early, Tejeda thought, and saved prime seats for each other. They sat in a block at the front, the first row less than six feet from the defendant's chair. All of them had passed through the metal detector, but the bailiff seemed to be keeping a watchful eye on their ranks anyway.

There was a good deal of weeping, sharing of tissue packs, hugging among the victims' families. A cluster to the side stood and locked arms to form a circle. Tejeda could hear their whispered prayers over the whir of video cameras; this was prime time drama. Real emotion as opposed to the celluloid variety. As such, it had a higher market value.

He recognized a good number of faces among the families. At some point in the investigation, either he or Eddie had interviewed most of them. Talking to parents was always the hardest part of his job.

He had been spotted coming in, and a few of the more brazen reporters pushed cameras or notebooks in his face. What did he think about it all? No comment. No comment later, either. No, he wouldn't be testifying. He didn't bother to tell them that Hymie Osawa was nervous about his faulty memory and would rely on Eddie Green unless he got desperate.

Kate had managed to get through the crowd and locate him. She sighed as she sat down.

"It's over now, isn't it?" she said.

"Except for the shouting, and that will take about a year in court."

"I was watching the people outside. You know what I think this trial opening is?"

"What?"

"It's a mass funeral. These people have come to lay their children to rest and to get on with their lives." There was a catch in her voice. "If only Lance could have waited."

"Do you want to stay?" he asked.

"Not particularly. There is so much sadness."

He took her hand and looked for the path of least resistance to get out through the mob. In the elevator down, they were alone. He wrapped his arms around her and held her close.

She slid her hand into his. "You told me once that this was all about family. But I didn't understand that until I saw them all together in there, trying to patch up the holes in their families the way poor Mike patched up holes in the walls. Keeping emotional drafts out."

They went out into the hazy morning sunshine, holding hands.

"Do you ever think about being a parent?" he asked.

"Sometimes."

"How do you feel about you and me having a baby?"

"Right now?"

"I thought maybe we would be traditional and wait nine months."

"The way things are between Richie and Jena, you may have children that aren't much older than your grandchildren."

"Think how much fun Christmas would be."

"What brought this on?"

"It's been in the back of my mind for a while. Did you notice when Theresa got out of the car this morning, she didn't even kiss me good-bye? I'm not ready for that. I like kissing sticky kid faces."

"You didn't just think this up because you're bored staying home?"

"Bored?" He laughed. "When have we had time to be bored?"

"Maybe you'll feel differently when you go back to work."

"I'm taking your advice. I'm retiring. Thought maybe

I would stay home, maybe do the Wambaugh thing and try a book, play with the kids and the little woman."

"Is this a proposal?"

"Consider it a proposition."

She kissed him, hard, on the lips. "Proposition accepted."